The

Heron Catchers

The

Heron Catchers

a novel by
David Joiner

Stone Bridge Press · *Berkeley, California*

Published by
Stone Bridge Press
P. O. Box 8208, Berkeley, CA 94707
sbp@stonebridge.com • www.stonebridge.com

Book design and layout by Peter Goodman.

Front-cover photo by Shreyasi Gupta, pexels.com. Map on page 8 by John Sockolov using base image from OpenStreetMap.

A draft version of Chapter 1 of this book first appeared on www.writersinkyoto.com.

Text © 2023 David Joiner.

First printing 2023.

p-ISBN 978-1-61172-081-5
e-ISBN 978-1-61172-962-7

*For Garry and Jeff, who've helped make
this long writerly journey worthwhile*

The

Heron Catchers

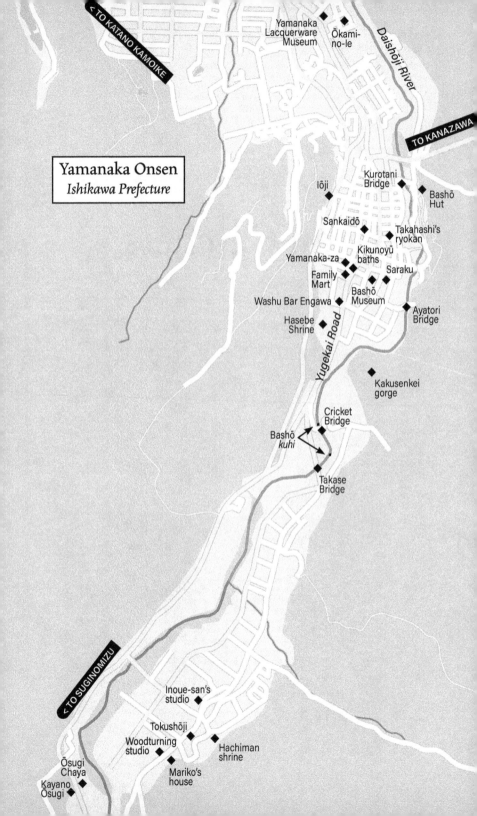

Yamanaka Onsen
Ishikawa Prefecture

TO KATANO KAMOIKE >

Daishōji River

TO KANAZAWA

Yamanaka Lacquerware Museum

Ōkami-no-Ie

Kurotani Bridge

Iōji

Bashō Hut

Sankaidō

Takahashi's ryokan

Kikunoyū baths

Yamanaka-za

Saraku

Family Mart

Bashō Museum

Washu Bar Engawa

Ayatori Bridge

Hasebe Shrine

Yugekai Road

Kakusenkei gorge

Cricket Bridge

Bashō *kuhi*

Takase Bridge

< TO SUGINOMIZU

Inoue-san's studio

Tokushōji

Woodturning studio

Hachiman shrine

Ōsugi Chaya

Mariko's house

Kayano Ōsugi

1

Sedge stumbled up Mayumizaka slope into Kenrokuen garden, yawning loudly enough almost to hasten the full blossoming of its cherry trees. For the last two weeks, since permanently closing the ceramics shop that he and his wife Nozomi had run, Sedge had started each day increasingly late, sometimes even past lunchtime. He was grateful for a reason to wake up early today, though it had been a trial to get here.

Taking his ticket and a map from the attendant at Kenrokuen's entrance booth, he was keen to walk off more of his anxiety. In fifteen minutes he would meet the wife of the man Nozomi had run away with.

The woman's name was Mariko. She'd asked him to meet her on the west side of Kasumigaike pond, with its view toward Mt. Utatsu. She had included directions on where to sit and described what she would be wearing. Sedge's brother-in-law, Takahashi, at whose ryokan inn Mariko worked in the hot spring town of Yamanaka Onsen, had forwarded him her email.

Sedge hadn't expected her invitation. After all, nine months had passed since their spouses had disappeared. But he had welcomed her suggestion that they "compare notes" about what had happened and try to help each other through this difficult time. He hadn't bothered himself with her situation—had hardly even considered it—but it made sense that she'd be struggling, too. He wasn't hopeful that talking to her would change anything, however.

The tourist crowds at Kanazawa's famous landscape garden were small that morning, and the mild, late-March weather was perfect for strolling. He hadn't visited Kenrokuen since last May, when he and Nozomi had come to see the garden's celebrated irises. Afterward they had wandered to Kanazawa Castle Park to birdwatch, a tradition they'd started after moving to the city.

He stood on a short wooden bridge over a stream winding away from Kasumagaike pond, admiring a newly blossoming cherry tree, and pines here and there recently freed from their protective winter *yukitsuri* ropes, when a snapping of branches made him spin around. To his astonishment, a wild boar burst from a bush, colliding with a heron upstream and sending a cloud of feathers into the air.

Unaffected by the collision, the boar charged into an open space before rushing toward the opposite end of the garden. The tourists there swept themselves into a tight, terrified circle and watched the animal dash past them. After several attempts, it clambered over a low wall.

Sedge edged toward the heron. It lay sprawled in the shallow water, long and grayish white. The current swept into it, billowing its plumage, and where the stream soaked its body it appeared half-melted. Before he reached it, the heron stood unsteadily and shook itself dry.

He noted the gray body and wings; the black nuchal markings; the dark crests on either side of its crown, like long painted eyebrows; and the drooping black topknot—an Asian gray heron.

One wing hung awkwardly against its body, no doubt broken.

A college-aged gardener in a light blue uniform, who had been sweeping fallen leaves into a burlap sack, stood before Sedge staring at the heron. Sedge tugged the man's arm to get his attention.

"Can't you call in the bird's injury to a supervisor?" Sedge asked him.

The gardener's eyes widened at his Japanese. He dug in a

pocket for his phone and did what Sedge suggested. After hanging up, he shyly nodded his thanks.

"Hand me your bag," Sedge told him as he took off his own jacket.

"What did you say?"

Sedge repeated himself more forcefully.

"What do you want it for?"

"To catch the heron with. It'll hurt itself more if it tries to fly."

"You want to put it in this sack?"

"No, I want to wrap its body with it."

The gardener looked at the jacket in Sedge's hand. "Can't you use that?"

"That's to drape over its head. If it can't see, it won't be as frightened. Your bag would catch on its beak."

Looking around for help but finding none, the gardener shook the leaves from his burlap sack and reluctantly handed it to Sedge. Behind them, a crowd of people had gathered.

"Maybe we should wait for someone to come with a net," the gardener said. "I'm not keen on getting injured."

"A net would make things worse," Sedge said. "A heron's beak is like a weapon. And because it's probably scared, it may lash out. What we have is better protection."

The gardener grudgingly followed Sedge.

They reached the stream at the same time a middle-aged man from the crowd crouched before the heron to videotape it with his phone. He was much closer to it than Sedge would have been.

Sedge told the gardener where to place himself and what to do. The young man, finding his voice, barked at the man with the cell phone to back away.

The heron had been squawking since it regained its footing, and it now shook its long beak at them and released what could only be described as a warning cry.

Sedge moved slowly toward the bird, shielding himself from it with his jacket and the gardener's burlap sack pinched together. He jumped behind it before it could turn completely to face him. The burlap sack fell to the ground as he draped his jacket over the bird's head. He had covered its eyes, but its beak peeked out.

"I need the sack," he yelled at the gardener.

He ran over to hand it to Sedge.

"You do it." He looked down at the bird as it squirmed beneath his hands. "Wrap it around its body. Gently so as not to aggravate its broken wing, but firmly enough to immobilize it."

The gardener kneeled beside him and wrapped the burlap sack around the bird, encircling its thin body. Beneath the light pressure he applied, the heron resisted. Its strength seemed to jolt him, and he lost his balance. The sack fell to the ground again, and the bird took advantage of its freedom to raise its one good wing and try to escape.

The man with the phone continued to videotape, and he came closer again only for the heron, which somehow sensed his presence, to stab at him with its beak. The bird aimed well, striking his thigh. The man fell to the ground and, shrieking in pain, rolled to where the heron couldn't strike him a second time.

Sedge used one hand to help the gardener wrap the sack around the heron again. And though it thrashed beneath the young man's arms, it soon stopped struggling.

"Now what?" the gardener said.

Slightly unsure of himself, Sedge said, "We wait for the people you called to arrive."

Two groundskeepers finally approached them, while two others set up a barrier around the bird with ropes and metal poles. Because the heron had stopped resisting, it was a simple task to transfer it to these men.

"Thank you for what you did," one of the groundskeepers

told Sedge, ignoring the gardener. "We're sorry to have put you to the trouble. Are you hurt?"

Sedge assured him that he was fine. The groundskeeper apologized once more, this time about the boar, which he said had made its way into the garden several times in the last few months, though always after hours. This was the first time it had been in the garden when it was open to tourists.

He walked away, coming back a moment later holding Sedge's jacket. He asked Sedge for his name and phone number, saying that the garden might need to contact him later about what had happened. When Sedge spoke his name, a woman broke off from the gathered crowd, a hand over her mouth as if surprised by something.

"You're Sedge?" she asked. When he nodded at her, she laughed in disbelief. "I'm Mariko."

She appeared to be in her early thirties. Her face—the overlarge eyes and slightly aquiline nose, the dimples that emerged in her cheeks when she spoke, and the messy bob that swept her forehead—was somehow different from what he had imagined. But what had he imagined? Until now, when he thought of her, the face that came to mind was her husband's.

The groundskeeper led him past the barrier they had erected. Mariko came up to him there.

"Sorry," Sedge said. "We were supposed to meet at the pond, not here."

She laughed again and said, "Are you all right?"

"As far as I know."

They walked toward a refreshment stand. He ordered coffees and brought them to a bench under a cherry tree, whose pink blossoms were on the verge of escaping from their buds. In front of them, the pond's black surface rippled where a family of spotbill ducks swam by.

"Thank you," she said, pulling her coffee closer. "You know, I've also helped rescue herons before. There are many of them in Yamanaka Onsen. And many bad drivers, too, unfortunately."

He looked at her incredulously. "You should have come forward to help me. I hardly knew what I was doing."

"I'm sure I would have only got in the way."

"Anyway, I'm glad it didn't end worse."

She glanced at her watch. "We have a lot to talk about, but I'm afraid I only have thirty minutes."

"Do you have to get back to the ryokan already?"

"No," she said. "I have to prepare for an exhibition."

"You're an artist, too?"

"It's Kōichi's exhibition."

Sedge started at hearing her husband's name.

"Will he be there?" he said, confused.

She shook her head. "It will make things easier on me in the long run if I represent him."

"But he left you. Why are you still helping him?"

"His son and I could use the money. But this will be the last time."

"Is he not required to support you?"

She smiled embarrassedly. "We haven't divorced."

Sedge didn't know why this surprised him. He and Nozomi hadn't yet, either. A divorce was still too much to deal with. Once she disappeared, nobody she knew had been able to communicate with her. If she had left Japan and couldn't be reached, he was unsure if the Japanese courts could legally issue a divorce. Similarly, he felt paralyzed about the money she had taken, leaving him with much less than he'd need to hire a lawyer.

"Why didn't you want to meet like this at the ryokan?" he said. "I'll be moving there in another week. Takahashi suggested it."

"He told me. But I didn't know how awkward this would be, and I didn't want either of us to have to endure that at the ryokan, where my colleagues often gossip. Also, my preparation for the exhibition was a perfect excuse to meet you here."

He appreciated her considerateness. It was unlikely that Nozomi would have given their circumstances so much thought.

"The exhibition's over there," she said. She pointed back toward Mayumizaka Gate, where Sedge had seen posters for an exhibition of *kutaniyaki*, the same local porcelain ware that he and Nozomi had sold in their shop. It was known for its colorful overglazes and named for the village where it had originated over three hundred sixty years ago. One of the garden's teahouses, Shigure-tei, was holding the exhibition. "It doesn't start until tomorrow. But the exhibiting artists have to attend a meeting today before arranging their work."

"What did you want us to talk about?"

She looked toward the lake. "There's no rule about what we discuss. I much prefer to know who you are than talk about our spouses' infidelities."

Sedge doubted that they could discuss what they'd come here for in only half an hour. Before he could suggest meeting again when she had more time, she went on.

"But I hate thinking that what they did—their selfishness— continues to drag us in their wake. I'm even worse off than I was when they ran away together." She turned to him again. "Did it shock you when she left?"

"Of course. I had no idea they'd been having an affair. Maybe I was too wrapped up in work to notice anything but that she'd grown distant."

"Yuki confided in me about the money she took. That must have been a shock, too."

Sedge nodded, mildly taken aback that Takahashi's wife had shared this. "She arranged for me to leave town on business, then withdrew most of what we had. She took everything from my personal account but left a bit in the one for our shop. I guess she thought she was being kind." He tried to laugh.

"You could get the police involved, you know. Maybe that would help you find her. And Kōichi."

"Takahashi made me promise not to involve the police. Anyway, I don't care that much about the money. I would have given it to her if she'd asked."

Mariko turned thoughtful for a moment. "How did your divorce lawyers deal with her if no one knew where she was?"

"We're not divorced, either."

"I see." Mariko leaned back, her arms locked straight behind her, and stared into the crisscrossing branches overhead. "We've met before, you know. You look different now, though. Your hair, maybe, or it could be that you're not wearing your work clothes."

"Did we? I'm afraid I don't remember."

"Kōichi and I came to your shop once."

On her phone, she showed him her husband's photo. The face he hadn't wanted to see stared up at him. It was a handsome face, if somewhat blocky like a boxer's, and a bit aged and worn. He had to be nearly Nozomi's age, since they'd been in high school at the same time—that much Sedge knew about him. But it was the very opposite sort of face he would have expected her to fall for.

"In his public photos," she said, "he looks younger. Most people don't recognize him in person. He preferred it that way. Do you remember him?"

Takahashi had apologized once for his role in Nozomi's affair.

He had introduced her to Kōichi. Because Kōichi was a well-known ceramicist, and the husband of one of his workers, Takahashi thought Nozomi and Sedge might sell his work at their shop. They had agreed to, but Kōichi never followed through with the arrangement.

"Yes, I remember." He had entered their shop two-and-a-half years ago. He was highly esteemed by Kutani-ware artists and dealers. Though neither loud nor brash, he acted remarkably confident, and Sedge had failed in his attempts to engage him. He tried to recall Kōichi's interaction that day with Nozomi, but nothing came to mind. Only that Kōichi had gravitated to her, talking to her for longer than their customers ever did. Because he was an artist, this wasn't strange. "I don't recall you coming in with him."

"His presence usually overshadowed mine."

Wanting to know who she was and hoping she might shine a light on why Nozomi was gone—and what he might yet do about it—he let her continue.

"He left me with his son, you know. His real mother doesn't want him, and he doesn't want to go back to her anyway. She lives in Osaka with another man. Her son's no longer welcome in their flat or in the ramen shop they run. After Kōichi left us, I sent him to Fukui to live with his grandparents. I just couldn't deal with what had happened and with him, too. But now he's back with me."

"You mean you've recovered enough by now?"

She smiled faintly. "I don't know about that. But it's not the first time this has happened. I've built up a sort of endurance for it, I suppose."

Takahashi had told Sedge about these previous times. "It must be traumatic for your stepson."

"I'm sure it is. Like I said, it's not the first time his father has run off. But this time it's different. This time we know he doesn't mean to come back."

Sedge couldn't tell who she blamed for the affair. Perhaps intentionally, she hadn't said anything about Nozomi.

"Have you had any news about your husband?"

She shook her head. "I wasn't expecting to. Have you heard anything about your wife?"

"Nothing. I thought one of us would have by now." He set his coffee down on the bench between them. "Why did you want to meet me?"

"How can I say this politely?"

Sedge attempted a smile. "You can be impolite with me."

"I wanted to see if there was something wrong with you. Something that explained why your wife left you for a man like Kōichi. But all of it makes even less sense now. Why would she throw away someone like you?"

He could have told her about the arguments he and Nozomi had, the distance between them over their last few months together, and the problems they faced with their shop, but he didn't see how it would help. He had a feeling Mariko wanted to know about the intimacies they shared, that she guessed this had been the driving force behind Nozomi leaving, but he wouldn't volunteer it. His answer would have disappointed her, anyway.

"Maybe she left because there's nothing wrong with you. There was so much wrong with Kōichi that she must have found that quality more attractive." She looked at Sedge questioningly. "Maybe she had a lot wrong with her, too."

"Sometimes I thought so. She became despondent about things in the end."

"Despondent how?"

"I'm not sure how to explain. I think she was suffering from a kind of depression. But she also didn't want to get better and seemed satisfied being that way. I never understood it." That he could state this so plainly surprised him.

"And that's how it was in the end? With your wife, I mean."

"It was like it always was between us, I suppose. Maybe a little strained at times, but isn't that normal? I never guessed she had a lover."

Mariko looked down as if contemplating her coffee, which, like Sedge, she hadn't touched. "What would you do if she came back to you? Would you give her another chance?"

Sedge shook his head.

"I don't feel sorry for her," Mariko said. When he didn't reply she smiled half-apologetically. She looked at her watch and slowly stood up, giving him the impression that she didn't want to leave. "What will you do with your shop?"

Sedge stood, too, and shrugged. "It's closed now. I couldn't keep it going."

"You don't make ceramics yourself?"

"No."

She nodded a long time, a far-off look on her face. "I have to go. I'm sorry I had so little time today."

They bowed to each other.

"I'll be moving to the ryokan soon," Sedge reminded her.

"Then I suppose we'll see each other there sometimes. By the way, what will you do in Yamanaka Onsen? Can't you find work here in the city?"

"I can't afford to stay." To cover up his embarrassment he added quickly, "Takahashi promised to introduce me to some ceramics shops near the ryokan. Hopefully one or two will take me on."

Not wanting to make her late for the exhibition meeting he said, "Maybe we can talk again soon. I'm sure one of us will hear something."

"Please let me know if you do." She bowed again and walked away.

A moment later he called out to her. "You said you'd captured herons before."

She turned around. "Every now and then I find myself in a position to. Usually a car has hit them and I have to bring them to a rehabilitation center. But I've never helped one that was assaulted by a boar. I wish they were more grateful. You should see my scars."

Knowing how dangerous a heron could be, Sedge found it difficult to respond.

"They aren't particularly disfiguring," she added, "but I'd rather not suffer those injuries again. I guess that's why I didn't try to help you earlier."

After she left, a breeze lifted through the trees and a cherry blossom fell on the bench where she had sat. In another week the cherries would reach full bloom. He wanted to see them here before moving to Yamanaka Onsen, but he knew this was unlikely.

As he stood to walk home, he felt that summer had eclipsed spring, that the seasons had advanced by some unnatural calamity. And that he was woefully unprepared for the days ahead.

2

April arrived. Sedge vacated his apartment in Korinbō, Kanazawa's small but bustling shopping district, and boarded a bus headed south to Yamanaka Onsen. He carried a single suitcase and a backpack. An hour later the bus dropped him off at his destination, beside Kikunoyū baths, which were fed by a one-thousand-three-hundred-year-old hot spring. Having entered the baths on previous visits to Yamanaka Onsen, he knew about the spring's origin—in around AD 700 a Buddhist monk named Gyōki had followed an injured heron here and watched it heal after bathing in the curative waters.

He glanced around to see if Takahashi had come to greet him. Not spotting him at the bus stop, and aware that his arrival probably wasn't as momentous to him as it was to himself, he decided to wait for a few minutes in case his brother-in-law was only running late. He crossed in front of the men's baths and into the open space of Yamanaka-za, a plaza used equally by tourists and residents. Even in the early afternoon, local people approached the baths on foot and by bike. They were easily distinguished from tourists, who congregated in the outdoor foot bath nearby or stood beneath a clock tower that opened hourly to reveal automated figurines performing "Seicho Yamanaka Bushi," a classic song from the town's celebrated geisha days.

Sedge soon gave up on Takahashi and started toward the ryokan.

He hadn't traveled here since New Year's Day last year, when he and Nozomi visited after a traditional *osechi* meal with her parents in Kanazawa. It had been cold and snowy, and though they had suffered the inclement weather to climb to Iōji temple behind Yamanaka-za, they had returned to Kanazawa before nightfall. Running a shop six days a week was unconducive to travel, even to places only an hour away. When they did go out, it was either to birdwatch somewhere new or to see Nozomi's parents on the eastern edge of the city.

One could be forgiven for thinking that, aside from some modern conveniences, Yamanaka Onsen had changed little since the Edo period ended a century-and-a-half ago. This was part of the town's charm, and the old wooden architecture, traditional sake and crafts shops, narrow back roads filled with ryokan and small eateries, and the shrine-ringed, forested mountains in whose shadow all of it sat added to that atmosphere. To Sedge, time here moved at half the pace it did in Kanazawa.

On the back streets leading to the ryokan, wooden sandals clattered distantly. A woman in a light green kimono hurried in his direction. A moment later she called his name. It was Yuki, waving as she ran toward him. Her enthusiastic greeting lifted his spirits.

When she reached him, she bowed and smiled, breathing too heavily to say anything but "Konnichiwa!" She tried to take his suitcase but he declined her help. She made a cursory attempt to fix her hair, a few strands of which had fallen over her face. Her cheeks pink and full, she had filled out slightly since they'd last met. The extra weight was becoming.

"Thank you for coming to meet me," Sedge said.

After catching her breath she said, "At the last minute Taka-hashi told me you were arriving. He was too busy to go to the bus stop himself. He told me to hurry to meet you. I guessed which way you'd come and luckily saw you halfway. I'm sorry I'm late." She bowed again.

"You shouldn't have gone to the trouble. I'm not worth worrying about."

"Don't say that. You're our special guest now."

As they started walking Sedge said, "If I seem awkward, it's because I don't know how to repay your kindness."

"Are you doing all right?" she asked with a tone of concern.

Rather than bog her down with the truth, he smiled and said, "I'm fine. Thanks to you and Takahashi."

They passed through the ryokan's front gate and walked down a traditional welcome mat, woven from stitched rush, twenty or thirty feet long. A doorman reached for Sedge's suitcase and led him inside.

The lobby staff greeted and bowed to them. He glanced around for Mariko but saw no sign of her.

When someone set on the counter a form for him to fill in, Yuki explained that he was a personal guest and she'd take care of the form later. She asked if her husband was available but was told he was still in a meeting.

"In that case, I'll show our guest to his room. By the way, this is Mr. Sedge. We've invited him to stay for a while, so please make him feel welcome."

As Sedge and Yuki walked down the corridors to his room, he noted the familiar interior as well as the old historical objects, Ko-Kutani and Kutani-ware pieces, and black-and-white photos of Yamanaka Onsen displayed against the walls. The ryokan was well-kept, but in places showed its age.

His suitcase and backpack were already in the room waiting for him. Stepping up from the *genkan* entranceway, he took in the small tatami room in front, where a low tea table sat but would be replaced at night with a futon to sleep on. Behind it was an even smaller room whose tall, wide window half-jutted into a forest. He was pleased to have his own shower and toilet, a small refrigerator, a thermos and teacups, and a water pitcher and glasses. It was perhaps one-fifth the size of his former apartment, but it was more than big enough.

"Does the room meet your expectations?"

"It's perfect, thank you."

She pointed to the large window opposite them. "You'll be able to see many birds from here. It was one reason we gave you this room."

He could hardly believe they'd chosen a room for him because of this, but he appreciated it and was flattered they'd remembered.

"You're sure I can stay for three or four months? I hope it goes without saying that I want to be on my own again much sooner."

She shooed away his question. "You can stay as long as you need to. Please, don't mention it again."

"Thank you."

"By the way, unless you plan to eat outside our inn, we'll have your breakfast and dinner delivered to your room every day. When you decide what time you'd like your meals, please let us know. Sometimes, of course, my husband and I may want us to eat together. You're still family to us, you know."

Sedge hadn't expected her to say anything so kind. Or to *be* so kind, after Takahashi had let it slip once that she thought it would be troublesome to let him stay at the ryokan for several months. Trying to compose himself, he bowed and thanked her again.

She smiled and said, "I'm sure you'd like to unpack and relax, and maybe go to the baths downstairs."

After she left him, he did what she suggested—all while humming and talking to himself, in his habitual attempt to ward off loneliness.

ᨓ ᨓ ᨓ

Perched above the Daishōji River, the ryokan sat on the edge of Kakusenkei gorge, an area famed for its natural beauty. Sedge had read Matsuo Bashō's *The Narrow Road to the Deep North*, so he knew that centuries ago the haiku master had passed from Kanazawa south into Kaga and stayed in Yamanaka Onsen. Bashō had strolled along the Daishōji River, somewhere below the window of his room, writing poems about the exceptional water of the town's hot springs, whose scent he compared to chrysanthemums and which he suggested would bring longevity. All over town were old stone *kuhi* monuments celebrating his visit and the haiku he wrote during his stay.

Late that afternoon, Sedge wandered downstairs in his inn-issued *yukata* robe, carrying a bag containing a small and large towel. For an hour he shuttled between the indoor and outdoor baths, which offered views of the forest and river. A light rain fell, and a chill wind blew through the trees, sweeping the steam off the surface of hot water.

After soaking in the baths, he returned to the lobby. In the empty tea lounge there, he took a table by the window. As he wiped sweat from his face with the drier of his two wet towels, a movement in the treetops pulled his eyes upward. Balanced atop an enormous pine tree was a gray heron, its long head and neck tucked into its shoulders while the rain battered it. On the bus that morning, once past Kanazawa's suburbs, the landscape had opened to forests and farmland. The farmland soon became almost exclusively rice fields, which, now that it was early April, farmers were tilling and laying with straw to prepare for seed rice before inundating them. In another few weeks, rice shoots would poke out of the sky-mirroring plots. Herons and cranes had appeared in a great many of the rice fields as the bus drove along.

From behind his shoulder a woman's voice startled him. "Excuse me. Would you like something to drink?"

For a moment he worried she would scare the heron away, but he quickly realized his foolishness. He turned around. Dressed in the kimono of the ryokan, Mariko stood holding an empty tray. He hadn't expected to see her so soon, yet here she was.

"Oh!" she said. "With your hair wet I didn't recognize you. Did you check in today?"

"Two or three hours ago. I didn't know you worked in the lounge."

"Takahashi transferred me here yesterday from my normal guestroom duty."

The phone near the bar rang and she hurried to answer it. She came back to his table smiling even more broadly than when she'd recognized him.

"Have you seen the heron on top of the tree?" he asked.

She looked through the window. "It comes whenever it storms."

"Only then?"

"For some reason it seems to enjoy being beaten by the wind and rain."

"A form of masochism?"

Mariko laughed. "It must have a reason to suffer like that, don't you think?"

"I wonder if it's suffering. With all the typhoons in Japan, it must have experienced worse weather." Sedge squinted at it. "It appears to be a male."

She looked back at the heron. "How can you tell?"

"See the sticks in its beak? Surely they're to build a nest. But it's the females that build them; the male only brings what she needs."

Peering again at the treetops she smiled. "How interesting. You seem to know a lot about birds."

"Birdwatching's a hobby of mine. Even so, I'm not sure how much I actually know."

"I should apologize. Here we are talking, and I still don't

know if you'd like something to drink." She nodded to the menu on his table.

"I'm just here to relax after my bath."

"That's perfectly all right. Please come whenever you'd like."

A silence fell between them. Sedge worried it might compel her to leave. "What other wildlife do you see here? And have you lived in these parts a long time?"

"All my life. Aside from birds, I've seen boars, a few deer, an occasional mountain goat. Some stoats and a lot of *tanuki*, too. And every few years bears wander from the mountains to the edge of town, though I've never seen one." Her smile flickered and she said, "It hasn't been long since we met in Kenrokuen, but have you heard anything new?"

He knew she was referring to their spouses. "No. And I'm not expecting to. Not unless it's about a divorce. Have you?"

"No."

They both turned as Takahashi entered the lounge.

"You two look like you're enjoying each other's company," he said. Coming up to Sedge, he patted his shoulder. Nodding to the opposite end of the lounge he added, "The bar is over there."

"It's too early for me."

"It's okay. Yuki and I want you to feel at home here, so do whatever you'd like." He glanced between Sedge and Mariko. "I'm afraid our small garden here is nothing like Kenrokuen."

"No place is," Sedge said. "But your garden is lovely."

Takahashi smiled at Mariko. "I'm glad you're working here now. From the front desk I can look up anytime and see you. You're a more pleasant sight than old Ms. Yoshino. I don't know how many times I used to catch her napping in a chair."

Mariko laughed uncomfortably. "She must not have had any customers."

"She's very kind, isn't she?" Takahashi said to Sedge. Looking between them once more, he turned back to Mariko and said, "Those glasses on the counter have been there since last night, haven't they?"

"I was just about to put them away."

Mariko bowed and departed for the bar, where she started organizing the glasses in a rack above her.

Turning to Sedge Takahashi said, "If you'd like a beer or glass of sake, it's on me."

"I was about to go back to my room, actually."

"Another time, then. I'll stop by your room later if you'll be there." He gestured for Sedge to leave before him.

Mariko didn't look up from her work for him to say goodbye. As he walked to the exit, he glanced again out the window. The rain and wind had grown stronger, and the heron had flown away.

Shortly before six p.m., Takahashi came to his room carrying a bottle of Shishinosato sake, which Sedge knew was brewed in town. Sedge didn't understand why he'd brought it. He and Yuki had done so much for him already. The more they gave him, the more his obligation toward them increased, and the more helpless he was to return their kindnesses.

Takahashi surveyed the room. "That's what I thought. You have nothing worth drinking sake out of. It's good I came prepared."

"For someone who used to run a shop specializing in that sort of thing, I'm embarrassed not to have one or two."

"You didn't bring any with you?"

"What I didn't sell is in storage. I should have known I'd be drinking sometimes."

From a pocket in his kimono jacket Takahashi withdrew a small wooden box. Inside were two Kutani-ware cups. "These were made by a Yamanaka Onsen craftsman," he said, and Sedge knew he meant a ceramicist who had shaped and fired the cups prior to painting them in the *aote* style he recognized. Sedge recalled unpleasantly that Mariko's husband was such a craftsman.

"Do you always carry sake cups with you?" he joked.

Takahashi smiled. "Don't tell Yuki, but I borrowed these from the display down the hall." He held the green bottle out to Sedge. The kanji on front, a calligraphic streak of electric blue on a white paper label, was 旬. Pronounced *shun*, it meant that the sake, or the rice it was made from, was in season. The bottle had been chilled.

"Don't expect me to bring sake every night." Takahashi blew into each cup, ridding them of any dust they held. He set them on the table by the window and sat in a chair. Sedge followed him into the room and poured for them.

"I noticed you went to the baths this afternoon."

"What with the rain, and it being my first day here, I thought I'd take things slowly."

Takahashi lifted his cup and waited for Sedge to do the same.

After they drank, Sedge noticed the small paintings of cranes on the cups' sides, and he admired them even more.

"Is the room adequate?" Takahashi said. "Yuki and I worry it's too small. Especially after living in such a large apartment. It must seem extraordinarily quiet to you, too. Like a temple or something."

"Remember, it's only me now. And I brought next to nothing."

Takahashi frowned and shook his head. "Anyway, let's not discuss depressing things. Actually, I wanted to talk to you about teaching English. Have you given it any thought?"

One of two conditions to staying here was for Sedge to teach English. At first he had resented that Takahashi and Yuki would insist on any condition at all, but he quickly realized he wasn't in a position to bargain. The second condition was that Sedge not approach the police about the money Nozomi had stolen.

Because local newspapers reported these sorts of stories, Takahashi and Yuki feared it would bring bad publicity to the ryokan,
which was old and well known, and disgrace both of their families. They felt bad for Sedge but didn't want him to tell anyone
what had happened.

"A little. But I don't have much to go by yet. I'd like to know
how many classes you want me to teach and on what days of the
week. Also, how many students in each lesson and what their pro-
ficiency levels are. If you have materials you want them to study
from, I'll want to see them beforehand, too. And what is the classroom like?"

Takahashi turned to the forest outside the window, listening
to the questions. He refilled their cups, murmuring to himself, "I
see, I see. I wonder if this will be difficult."

He explained that Sedge could teach what he liked, but the
goal was to help the staff learn and properly use greetings, advise
about local tourism, and respond to questions about the ryokan
and its services. He wanted Sedge to teach one or two classes five
days a week. Most of the staff had only rudimentary English skills.
Sedge would need to take roll and submit a weekly attendance
report. He had no teaching materials on hand, but tomorrow he
would show Sedge the meeting room that would be available as a
classroom. He wanted classes to start next Monday.

"I'll start designing a class tonight."

Takahashi waved the suggestion away. "Tomorrow or the
day after is fine. Remember, you're not our employee. But I do
ask that you earn some of what we give you here. It's not even for
Yuki and me that I want this. It's for you. If you don't have a normal work routine, and no responsibilities, it will take longer to get
your life back together. And the people working here will respect
you more, which is no less important."

Sedge agreed with what Takahashi said. "By the way, have
you heard anything from Nozomi?"

"Nothing at all."

They settled into more casual conversation and soon finished half the bottle of sake.

There was a quiet knock on the door. Imagining someone burdened with a tray or a wheeled cart, Sedge hurried to open it. In the entrance was an old woman in the kimono of the ryokan. She had pushed a wheeled cart to his door, and its top and bottom tiers held more food than he'd expected. Takahashi helped bring Sedge's dinner inside. When Sedge tried to do the same, Takahashi said, "Please, sit down. I insist you behave like a guest."

Takahashi and the woman filled the table where Sedge was sitting with small dishes and bowls. It might not have been what the other guests were eating, but it was still a feast.

"I don't need to eat like this every night, I hope you realize," Sedge said, embarrassed.

"It's the least we can do."

After the old woman wheeled her cart into the hallway, Takahashi told Sedge to call the front desk when he was finished and they would send someone to take his dinner away. "Then you should go for a walk or to the baths again. While you're away the staff will lay out your futon."

"I can easily do that myself."

"I know you can. But I want the staff to treat all our guests the same. If they think of you as less important, you might become uncomfortable. Enjoy your dinner. I'll leave the rest of the sake for you."

Takahashi took the cup he had been drinking from and returned it to the box inside his kimono jacket. As he closed the sliding doors to the genkan, he wished Sedge goodnight.

3

For Sedge, not knowing his teaching responsibilities meant having time to explore his surroundings more than he had on previous visits. Although he could easily reach hiking trails through the woods and along the Daishōji River, he hadn't yet found a decent birding spot. He glimpsed birds on his walks, but not a concentration of them like he'd seen along the Sai and Asano rivers in Kanazawa. The heron he'd spotted from the tea lounge hadn't returned, though once at night he'd awakened to a low hooting. A Japanese scops owl had stood on the balcony railing, gazing into his room.

On Sedge's third evening at the ryokan, Takahashi approached him in the tea lounge. No one was working there now. A sign atop the bar counter told guests to contact the front desk for service.

"I'm afraid life must be boring for you here," Takahashi said, glancing at the lighted pond beyond the window.

Sedge shook his head. "It's a good change of pace."

Smiling at this, Takahashi sat across from him. "Yuki and I want to make sure you're ready to start teaching. As I said before, we'd like you to begin Monday, after the dining room closes. You would start at eight-thirty and finish at ten p.m. It's a bit late, but it's the only time the majority of our staff is available. Maybe later we'll arrange a few morning and afternoon classes, too."

Sedge welcomed the classes as something to do and as a social outlet for himself—and because he didn't want to be viewed as a freeloader.

"That's fine. I've been ready to teach since I came here."

"Good. How are you doing, by the way? Is this arrangement working out so far?"

"I'm hanging in there. And yes, the arrangement couldn't be better. Though I've run into obstacles looking for work." He paused, embarrassed to ask for more help. "I've been meaning to ask if any of your friends in town have mentioned wanting me to help in their shops, even part-time. It doesn't have to be ceramics."

"Yuki and I frequently ask around. But at the moment no one has any need. You'd hardly earn anything, either, which might become frustrating. But I'm sure your luck will change." Takahashi knitted his brow as if preparing to say something difficult. "The other day when Yuki and I were talking about you, she asked if it had taken you seven weeks to recover from the worst of the hurt Nozomi caused. I told her I didn't know and asked her why. She's been studying Buddhism lately, and something she came across explained that this was how long the initial mourning period in Buddhism lasts. She also heard that modern psychology says one needs fifty days to accept the loss of a loved one. Of course, she knows you haven't fully recovered. Sometimes people in your situation never do."

Sedge was surprised by Takahashi and Yuki's references to death. When he answered, he couldn't keep his disapproval from entering his voice. "Seven weeks? As you said, it's been nine months since she left."

"I shouldn't have told you what Yuki asked. It was a stupid question."

"Anyway, I hope I'm over the worst of it. It took me well over fifty days to get there, though."

"It was just so unlike her to run away. There must have been a strong trigger for her leaving how she did."

His tone conveyed that he could hardly believe Sedge didn't

know the reason himself, that he must be hiding something from everyone. Sedge said nothing.

"She became someone else," Takahashi went on. "Like a member of a cult."

"Cults normally have more than two members. I already looked into that."

"But how else could she have done this?" He glanced at his watch and stood up. "It's late. Why don't you come by in the morning and I'll show you where you'll teach?"

"Sure. Thanks."

"One last thing. Yuki said we should keep you here for as long as possible in case Nozomi comes back."

"What do you mean?"

"When you agreed to move here, you said you might take her back if she could make you forgive her. If there were compelling reasons."

"Did I?"

"Yes. You don't remember?"

He supposed he might have said such a thing. But it was foolish to think there had a been a good reason for her to throw away their marriage and business and run away with Mariko's husband. "I used to think all kinds of things about Nozomi. Now, I can't imagine that scenario."

"But it's one reason Yuki and I stepped in to help you. Of course, we don't want to raise false hopes." When Sedge didn't reply, Takahashi added: "Give it a little more time. The money she took can always be paid back." He waved goodnight and walked away.

In the window overlooking the ryokan's dark pond and garden, Takahashi's reflection receded. And though he left Sedge alone in the tea lounge, their conversation about Nozomi didn't disappear with him. Sedge could hardly believe he'd promised to take Nozomi back if she returned, or that Takahashi, at this point in her absence, would hold him to it. Before he'd moved to the ryokan it still seemed possible that she'd come back, but after leaving Kanazawa, maintaining that hope felt absurd.

One place he suspected she and Kōichi might have run away to was Hegurajima, an island off the coast of Wajima, nearly two hours north of Kanazawa. The Noto Peninsula's remoteness had always appealed to her. Also, Kōichi could make a living in Wajima, even as a ceramicist in a town famous for its lacquerware.

Hegurajima was one of Sedge and Nozomi's favorite places in Japan, full of rare birds stopping over on their migrations from China, Russia, and Southeast Asia. They had most recently visited last year, as the island's spring migration was winding down. With summer bird species settling in, they had been excited to spot Oriental cuckoos, dollarbirds, streaked shearwaters, Kamchatka leaf warblers, and even a few red-necked phalaropes. Nozomi had told him afterward that the trip was one of the highlights of their travels together. A few weeks later she left him.

His phone still contained photos of the trip, not only of the island's birdlife, but also of the ninety-minute ferry ride from Wajima Port, during which birds flocked overhead and dolphins raced alongside them. There were photos, too, of Shinto shrines overlooking the island; of female *ama* divers, old women mostly, hauling abalone to the surface of the sea; of other *ama* pushing their abalone carts into what passed for a town, while still others returned to the sea to toss back the part of their catches too young to have reproduced; of the small inn where they stayed in simple tatami-floored rooms, the sound of the ocean at night strange but exciting to them.

As he searched through the photos, a conversation they'd had beside a small shrine on the island's Lake of the Living God came back to him. In addition to discussing the death of her first boyfriend, she had suggested for the first time—though it hardly seemed that she'd only just thought of it—that Sedge had never suffered.

She had complained of a headache that day, and her criticisms had been mounting since breakfast. Sedge found her attitude unwarranted and encouraged her to try harder to enjoy their trip.

"I am enjoying it," she said. A wind blew her long hair over her face, obscuring her still-youthful features, and her shoulders appeared narrower where she held herself tightly like she was cold.

"In that case, what exactly is upsetting you?"

She looked at him irritably, hesitating before speaking. "You're one of the most stable people I know," she said, making him recall a story she'd told at breakfast about a college friend who'd lost his business and marriage after gambling away all their money. "Certain people or situations might annoy you, but you never lose your cool. You just sail along and the waters beneath you never swell. You've never even grieved before. You've never experienced real suffering."

"Are you saying you want me to?"

"I'm sorry if it sounds bad. But I wish you had suffered in the past. Your life now . . . you'd feel deeper about everything."

"I feel like I've been lucky not to have suffered greatly until now. And I don't think that's prevented me from experiencing my life deeply."

She frowned and looked away. "Sometimes I think I've had a bad effect on you."

Unsure if she was continuing their conversation or changing the subject, he waited for her to go on.

"I realized recently that I make people behave in ways they shouldn't. Because of things I say or do. It's always been like that."

Was this another way of criticizing him? If so, he didn't know what she might be referring to. "What people are you talking about?"

They were standing beside a short wall of piled rocks surrounding the shrine, facing the placid water that birds occasionally skimmed. He turned sideways to see her. "The most obvious example is Tetsuya. My first boyfriend. The one who killed himself."

She almost never raised the subject, and he never did, either, in order to protect her from that time in her life. He knew little about the suicide, only that Tetsuya had taken his life after she'd cheated on him. "You can't blame yourself for what he did."

"But I hurt him. I saw other guys behind his back, some of whom were his friends, and rejected him in the worst possible way. He learned about it a week before he jumped off the rocks at Tōjinbō."

"That wasn't your fault," Sedge said quickly. "It's unfortunate, but people are unfaithful all the time. Hardly anyone takes their life as a result, no matter how much pain it causes them. And you were only fifteen. Do you really think what you did was unexpected? I'm sure that fifteen-year-olds do that kind of thing all the time."

"Maybe it's silly to expect anyone to be faithful at that age, but he still took his life because of me. You've never had to live with that knowledge gnawing away at you all your life."

"Nozomi . . ."

Her eyes turned glassy. "You always support me, Sedge. But I wish you'd help me face my guilt more."

"How am I supposed do that?"

"I don't know. Maybe by dropping me into the fire for once instead of holding me safely above it. It might hurt me, but if it burned away the guilt I feel, in the end it'd be worth it."

He'd moved closer to her, worried by what she was saying. "You didn't push him off those rocks. And the guilt you've felt all these years is worse than anything you might have done to him. Maybe he was wired to jump. If he hadn't done it then, something later in life probably would have triggered it. Couldn't it be as simple as that?"

She moved away from him. "I only know that my selfishness made him do that."

"It was a fifteen-year-old's selfishness, if it was even that."

She turned from him toward the water. "For you it was only a fifteen-year-old's selfishness. But for me that doesn't diminish the significance of what happened."

Sedge wasn't sure why he asked the next question, but it caught them both by surprise. "If you could go back in time, would you do things differently?"

She didn't answer right away. "I don't think I'd choose differently, except to do whatever I could to help him through his pain. But maybe every person is born to bear a certain burden, and that's mine. Maybe my life is wired to be exactly like this. And this is who I am."

"Are you saying you could do the same thing to me? Now, when you're twenty years older and we're married?"

"If I was simply wired that way . . ."

She stepped toward the lake, stones crunching beneath her feet.

He winced at her answer. "So it doesn't matter if I'm more critical with you or not. Isn't it better to be how I am? Even if that means wanting to support you?"

"I only know the situation we're in. And for some reason I find it inadequate."

Off to the side, a mass of tall grasses and reeds exploded with the chatter of twenty or thirty birds.

"Does it worry you hearing yourself talk like this?" he said.

"It worries you, doesn't it?"

"Of course."

"I'm sure it will pass," she said after another long moment. "After all, I haven't always had these thoughts. I feel better having told you, though."

She tossed into the water a twig she'd been turning between her fingers. Returning to where Sedge stood, she pressed herself into him. He held her, gazing beyond the lake. The color of the sea blended perfectly with the sky, creating the illusion that the horizon had plunged and the world was tilting downward.

That moment, he realized now, was when she began to put distance between them, though she had already started her affair with Kōichi. If so, and if she had really felt responsible for Tetsuya's death, wouldn't she have worried just as much over him? And if not, was he to infer that Tetsuya had meant more to her than he ever had?

The memories hit him with increasing clarity. Even now, he could remember the smell of the sea in her hair where he'd pressed his lips, and the softness of her cheeks when he'd touched her and turned her to meet his eyes. His disappointment that day returned, too, along with the troubling sense that she'd been preparing to make him suffer in a way he never had before.

In the pond behind the tea lounge window, what looked like a red-and-white Kutani-ware decanter floated through the water. As his eyes adjusted to the distance, what he'd momentarily mistaken for a piece of *akae-kinrande* was in fact an orange-and-white carp. Every day, no doubt, it swam slowly, almost aimlessly, in the same pointless circle. It soon disappeared beneath a footbridge, carrying on its back a lily pad it had flitted under.

4

The next day it rained. Sedge spent the morning and afternoon in the tea lounge, reviewing his lesson plan. For his first class he would emphasize introductions. The lesson only required polishing, but he stayed in the lounge for nearly four hours.

The heron had returned to the pine tree out the window, and his attention kept drifting to it. Had he not had more to do, he would have stayed even longer. The heron perched there bravely again in the wind and rain.

That night Mariko and a coworker wheeled his dinner to his room. She smiled broadly at him and asked if they could bring anything else. She held out a small menu on which appeared a choice of coffee, green tea, orange juice, or beer, and a paper cup of either vanilla or red bean ice cream.

He ordered a beer and red bean ice cream. After Mariko and her coworker conferred with each other, her coworker left to get them.

"I hear you'll be our English teacher," she said after an awkward silence passed.

"For a while, anyway."

She looked around the room, her eyes lingering on the decorative objects in the *tokonoma* alcove.

"Will you come to my classes," he said, "or do you already speak English? You never told me, and I didn't think to ask."

Her face reddened slightly. "I don't know English at all. And I'd like to come to your classes, but I need to be home on my free evenings to take care of my stepson."

"What's his name? And how old is he?"

"His name is Riku. He just turned sixteen."

"He should be fine if you leave him at home for a short time. I thought he was probably younger."

"If I don't come back when he expects, he often causes trouble. But I'll see what I can do."

He assumed she lived far away, and that the distance deterred her from attending his class. "Is your house far?"

"It's in Sugatani-machi. On foot it takes twenty minutes to reach."

The name didn't mean anything to Sedge. "Why don't you bring him to my class? I don't mind teaching a teenager. It might even be interesting for him."

"He has no interest in foreign languages, unfortunately. And I don't think Takahashi and Yuki would approve of it. Also, he has things he likes to do at home and hates having his routine disrupted, if you know what I mean."

She gave another short, embarrassed laugh as her colleague returned with Sedge's beer and ice cream.

"Good luck with your English class," she said, exiting his room with the other woman. "People here are eager to learn from you."

He wanted to continue their conversation, but he knew he couldn't while she was working. He turned back to the trees outside his window and began eating the meal she'd brought him. He hurried to finish it before his ice cream melted.

🌿 🌿 🌿

The next evening before his first class, Mariko again wheeled his dinner to his door, this time by herself. As she entered his room Takahashi came in behind her. He was carrying another bottle of sake.

"It's nothing to thank me for," he said. "I've never figured out why, but guests sometimes leave behind unopened bottles of sake. If later they decline our offer to ship them, I give them to the staff. I only take for myself what's too good to give away." He handed Sedge the unopened bottle. "Don't worry, this isn't bad at all."

"I'm sure your staff are more deserving of it."

"You're about to teach your first English class here. I'd say you deserve it more than anyone."

"But I have to teach in two and a half hours."

"A little will loosen you up. Besides, if I say it's okay, there's nothing to worry about."

Mariko shuttled between her cart outside and the table where Sedge and Takahashi sat talking. She made no sound except for the whispering of her *tabi* socks as she shuffled across the floors and kneeled at the table to serve Sedge. Takahashi turned his gaze to her. He watched her attentively, stroking his chin. Sedge waited for him to acknowledge the strangeness of her being in his room, both of them victims of the same infidelity. But Takahashi, his gaze turned unashamedly indelicate, never did. His rather lewd attention to her embarrassed him.

Nozomi had told Sedge about Takahashi's past philandering. Apparently, Yuki knew nothing about it, which was surprising since his trysts had always involved their staff, none of whom remained working for them. For a while he convinced Nozomi that he'd changed. But a year ago he'd admitted two new affairs. When Sedge suggested he risked a lot with his entanglements she said, "I'd take in a heartbeat how my brother is now over how reckless he used to be. Besides, his affairs are infrequent, and he's discreet about them." Sedge was staggered that she was so forgiving. Or cared so little about what Takahashi did.

Takahashi had come to check Sedge's lesson plan, but he only glanced at it. "I'm sure it will go well," he said, handing it back.

"At least have a drink with me," Sedge said.

They had nothing to drink out of, which prompted Takahashi to produce sake cups from his kimono again.

When Mariko reached the *genkan*, Takahashi called out to her. "Is that everything?"

"Yes, sir."

"In that case, you can go home now. Thank you for filling in for Tsubata-san again."

She bowed, her eyes on their cups, before shutting the door behind her. Sedge was sorry to learn she wouldn't come to his class after all.

Takahashi leaned back and gave a contented sigh. "I've had to ask her to stay late for a few nights because another staff member is ill. I don't think Mariko was happy about it, but she's not one to put up a fuss."

"How long has she been working here?"

"She's been with us a long time. She's one of our better employees, one of our more reliable ones. Since getting married, though, she's had a hard time. Yuki and I have been doing what we can to help her."

"A hard time because of her husband?"

Takahashi half-sneered. "He's what people here call *warui me*—a bad sprout. She now raises his son, who seems to have inherited his disposition. Some people say the boy is worse, though he's young enough he may turn out okay. He's lucky Mariko's so devoted to him."

This was the first time Sedge had been told of the man's character.

"What else did her husband do besides run off with other women?"

"Yuki follows these things more than me. I only know he went with a lot of women, and once nearly gambled away all they had.

He sometimes created excitement in town with the trouble he got into. What Nozomi saw in him is beyond me. Yuki disliked him personally, but she said his ruggedness pleased many women. Combined with his artistic ability, which he was fully confident of, she thought he stood out from other men."

It was hard to imagine Nozomi running off with such a man, but he was surprised that Mariko had been with him for much longer, such was the gentleness and kindness he saw in her. Hearing that he'd gambled away most of his and Mariko's savings, Sedge nearly gave up on the possibility that he'd see his own money again.

"His exploits were so well known you might almost call him a local celebrity. From a distance people found him entertaining, I guess. I admit that, when he wanted to be, he could be charming."

"But that's not the sort of person Nozomi was drawn to. If anything, just the opposite."

"He wasn't showy or bigmouthed. He was quiet, like Nozomi. Introspective and philosophical, too, apparently. But he had his moments. It was how he won over Mariko." Takahashi finished his cup and stood up. "You know, you're a celebrity around here, too. But that's probably not surprising considering the circumstances."

Sedge asked Takahashi what he and Yuki had told their staff about his circumstances.

"I haven't said a word. As for Yuki, you'd need to ask her. She's closer to the female staff than I am. You should realize, though, that people know Mariko's husband left her again. And not because she told them, but because Yamanaka Onsen is small and you can't keep people from knowing certain things."

When Takahashi stepped down into the *genkan* Sedge said, "Do they know it was Nozomi who ran off with Mariko's husband?"

"Not that I'm aware of." Takahashi opened the door and looked back into the room. "But you've stayed here several times with her. Some staff may put two and two together now that you're here alone."

※ ※ ※

Twelve staff members attended Sedge's first class. Although their knowledge of English varied, none possessed more than a basic command of the language. They were shy about using what they knew. Most of the time they insisted on using Japanese to answer anything he asked them in English. At one point, Takahashi and Yuki came to observe the lesson from the back of the room. After a few minutes Takahashi left, and Yuki soon followed him, giving Sedge a thumbs-up on her way out.

The students had seen Sedge every day for more than a week and wanted to know what he was doing there. He knew there were rumors, and he said he would answer honestly any question they asked in proper English. No one could manage it, though perhaps their reticence that day was only due to good manners.

On their second meeting, when again they wanted to know more about him, he explained in Japanese why he was there. No one asked follow-up questions, and from then teaching became easier.

One afternoon, Mariko approached him in the tea lounge. He was searching online for job opportunities, but also watching birds on the pond and in the garden beyond the window. She had replaced another worker after lunch.

"I'm sorry I haven't been to your class. My coworkers tell me how helpful it is, and I'm envious they get to learn from you."

"Are you still tied up every evening?"

"Yes, unfortunately."

"That's too bad."

She looked around, clearly worried that others might overhear. No staff was within earshot, though Takahashi, who'd been coming and going all afternoon, occasionally turned toward them and watched. After an awkward moment she said, "It may be rude of me to ask, but would you consider teaching me outside of work?"

"Outside of work?"

"I have to return home as soon as my afternoon shift ends. The only way I could study with you is in the evening at my home. The problem is that Riku is usually there."

It would be easier to teach her here, he knew. There would also be less risk of gossip. Wouldn't people think it strange if the two of them—whose spouses had run off together—sometimes spent the evening in her house? Yet he also understood her desire to study where she could look after her stepson.

His concern about gossip was for her, not himself. Though he no longer reeled from the hurt Nozomi had inflicted on him, there was little chance of his becoming romantically involved again for a long time. He also hoped to decide on a plan to move forward soon, one that took him back to Kanazawa or to a much larger city like Kyoto, where he could start anew.

"Why don't you suggest a study schedule and I'll decide how I want to proceed."

She nodded. "I told Riku that you have an affinity for birds. He does, too. I thought you might be able to talk to him about them."

"I'd be happy to. What else does he like?"

"I don't know if he likes it, but he gets in a lot of fights." After laughing to herself she apologized. "It's just that he came home yesterday with a bloody nose and black eye. And the new school year is still young. I'm sorry, I only joked about it because it's on my mind."

Sedge shook his head to show he wasn't offended. "Is he bullied?"

"Some students at his school pick on him, but they're learning to back off. I'm afraid he doesn't have any close friends."

Sedge hesitated before asking, "Does he miss his father?"

"Never. If his father tried to get in touch with him now, he'd have nothing to do with him. Kōichi used to punish him for any number of things, but as soon as Riku turned the tables on him and gave him a dusting up, he left us. I think he was planning to for a long time."

Sedge hardly knew what to say. "What about his grandfather?"

"In general, my stepson doesn't trust men." She laughed at the uncertainty in his face. "You have nothing to worry about. He'll probably spend most of his time in our kura, which we no longer use as a storehouse. He's converting it into a livable space for himself. In any case, all he needs is for people to be nice to him, to treat him with a little respect. That may be overly simplistic, but he responds well to people like that."

"I don't want to make promises I can't keep, but I'll try to come over sometime. We can work out the details later."

"Thank you. Please take as much time as you need."

Four guests had entered the lounge and were sitting around a table. Sedge nodded in their direction before Takahashi noticed and scolded Mariko. Startled to see them waiting for her, she hurried away.

When she disappeared behind the kitchen door with the guests' orders, Sedge returned to his room. What had made him hesitate at her suggestion that he teach her at her home? Had it really been because of what she told him about her stepson? Although he wasn't eager to meet the son of the man who'd run off with Nozomi, Sedge hadn't been able to tell Mariko no. He didn't know what it was, but he found her intriguing.

5

Two weeks later, in the small office behind the front desk, Takahashi asked Sedge how many staff members attended his classes. He was paying them for the time they studied after work, and he wanted to make sure that everyone who attended earned this extra wage. Over the fifteen or so classes he'd taught, Sedge was aware of only two students with single absences.

Yuki stepped into the office as Sedge gave the students' names.

"Good, that's good," Takahashi said. "Those two have a lot going on. Since they live farther away than the others, it's okay if they don't attend every class."

Takahashi scanned the list again. He mentioned a handful of employees he hadn't asked to attend class, most of whom only worked part-time. The only consistently absent full-time worker was Mariko.

"We'd like her to study, too," Yuki said, "but she says she hasn't found a way to manage it."

"I spoke to her about it once and she said she wanted to learn," Sedge said. He decided not to tell them about her request that he teach her at her home. "It sounds like her hands are full with her stepson when she's not working."

"Well, it's not the end of world if she can't study, but I thought it would be useful to her. When I mentioned the classes in a staff meeting before you arrived, she was one of the most supportive of the idea. It's too bad for her."

"Her situation sounds complicated."

The comment elicited more of her story from Yuki.

According to her, when Kōichi was still around, certain domestic incidents compelled her to leave home for several days. With nowhere to go, Yuki and Takahashi let her stay at the ryokan—in the same room where Sedge now stayed, in fact. But her absence from home endangered Riku, who at that time was too young to defend himself against Kōichi. All he could do was try to appease his father by stringing together a thousand origami cranes, which for a time made Kōichi go easy on him. At Mariko's urging, Yuki and Takahashi reluctantly took the boy in, too, treating them as they now treated Sedge—providing a room, meals, and access to the ryokan's laundry facilities for free. But Riku had been a problem. He had inherited Kōichi's unpredictable outbursts, and when they'd confronted Mariko about this, saying they couldn't abide such behavior around their guests and staff, the two of them moved back home.

Mariko lived in a village on the way to Wagatani Reservoir. Yuki had heard that her parents had bequeathed their house to her before they died—her mother from cancer nearly ten years ago, her father from a heart attack shortly after that. Whereas her father had been a woodturner all his life, her mother had worked as a *geigi* in Awara Onsen, in Fukui Prefecture—she was apparently renowned for her dances and ability to play the *koto*—after training in Asakusa as a geisha. She retired in her late twenties to marry, then worked again as a kimono-maker in Yamanaka Onsen. Yuki and Takahashi had dropped by Mariko's house a few times, most recently two years ago on their annual New Year's visits to the homes of their long-term workers. Mariko had told Yuki that local men occasionally dropped by to check on her in Kōichi's absences; it was hard to convince them that she wasn't interested in their companionship and to make them leave, and their unwanted presence set off her stepson. He took his frustrations out on the kura, and she had to box up and move the valuable things she normally stored there because she feared he'd break them. She had a flowerbed and small vegetable garden, too, and when Yuki came by once she learned that the boy had trampled much of what Mariko was growing. Although Mariko didn't live far away, Yuki hadn't visited her home in a long time. Other acquaintances had stopped going there as well. Yuki hoped for Mariko's sake that the boy would move out when he turned eighteen. Mariko had told her, however, that she was trying to persuade a local woodturner to allow Riku to apprentice part-time with him. Yuki couldn't imagine the arrangement would succeed, but if the boy didn't go off to college, he was likely to remain in her house for the foreseeable future.

When Yuki finished speaking, Sedge took a deep breath and said what he'd kept to himself before. He wanted to help Mariko now if he could. "I don't know how serious she was, but she suggested I come to her house to teach her. I wonder if it's not a good idea."

Takahashi shook his head. "I wouldn't recommend it. She's a nice person, and one can't help feeling sorry for her, but why potentially endanger yourself?"

"I imagine you're making too much of it. The boy's only sixteen."

Takahashi raised his eyebrows at this. Glancing at his wife he said, "Yuki and I promised each other never to go there again if we could avoid it."

"I've told Mariko that I'll only go back if her husband and stepson are no longer living there," Yuki declared.

"I see," Sedge said, surprised at the strength of Yuki's pronouncement. "Where exactly does she live?"

"Haven't we convinced you to stay away?" Takahashi's voice held a note of anger.

"It doesn't matter if we tell him," Yuki said gently to

Takahashi. "After all, he could ask anyone working here, or even Mariko herself." Turning to Sedge she explained, "She lives a few doors down from Tokushōji temple. Directly across from the prefectural woodturning workshop."

"Be careful what you commit to," Takahashi said to Sedge. "Maybe staying in Yamanaka Onsen temporarily makes you feel like nothing you do really matters. But for everyone else here, this is where they'll live the rest of their lives. This is where they'll die."

"I don't plan to make trouble for anyone."

"I know you don't. But people talk. Especially in small towns where the outside rarely intrudes."

Sedge understood that he wasn't to make life any more difficult for Mariko. But surely she knew the risks better than he. Why would she have invited him to teach her at her house if she hadn't thought these things through?

He appreciated Yuki and Takahashi's candor, in any case. Nozomi was no longer around as an informal teacher or liaison, and increasingly Sedge found himself lost and questioning everything that fell into his path. Where his in-laws were concerned, he wished he could trust them unquestioningly. If Nozomi were here, he was sure she would tell her brother and sister-in-law not to worry.

6

On Saturday morning, Sedge borrowed a bicycle from the ryokan and rode in the direction of Kayano-machi. He wanted to see Kayano Ōsugi, one of four sacred cryptomeria trees on the grounds of Kayano Sugawara Shrine. Yamanaka Onsen had several two-thousand-year-old *ōsugi* trees; there was another in Daishōji, but this was the oldest of them, dating back over two thousand three hundred years. Some people revered the ancient trees as survivors of a prehistoric forest, while others thought that Jōmon-period relics excavated on a nearby hill suggested the trees had been planted as offerings to Shinto gods. For all the significance Kayano Ōsugi had, on previous visits Sedge had found the site empty of other people, which was one reason he wanted to visit it again.

When he arrived at Kayano Sugawara Shrine he was relieved. Though only a twenty-minute trip from the ryokan, at some point his front bicycle tire had punctured and he'd been thumping along uncomfortably for the last half-kilometer. As he'd expected, there was no sign of a bicycle store or repair shop in this village. He dismounted and gave the flat tire a cursory look.

He hadn't eaten all his breakfast, and now, at midmorning, he felt hungry. He regretted not stopping at the roadside station he had passed ten minutes ago and buying something. But then he saw the small shop across the street with "Ōsugi Chaya" engraved on a wooden signboard above its entrance and pushed his bicycle there. The shop specialized in mugwort rice dumplings. It was a local landmark, and he had heard somewhere that it had been in business for eight hundred years.

Buying two sticks of green *kusa* or "grass" *dango*, he ate them on a bench outside the shop while gazing at the shrine opposite him. A grayish white streak entered his vision from the edge of the shop's roof—with its wings outstretched, a heron descended to the long wooden bridge extending from the *torii* entrance to the shrine. Standing up as he continued to eat, Sedge watched it cautiously proceed across the bridge to just before the steps to the shrine. Again it flapped its ungainly wings, this time lifting to the tiled roof. From there it peered at its surroundings, its head turning slowly toward a bamboo stand on a hill to the side.

As Sedge stood there, the middle-aged woman running the shop came outside, trailed by a younger man. Dressed in the baggy *tobi* pants of a carpenter, as if he'd just been pulled away from work, he walked straight toward Sedge's bicycle and squatted to check its tires.

"After you asked me about a bicycle shop, I went to get my son," the woman said. "I told him about your flat tire and he came out to fix it. I don't know what he can do, but since he maintains all the bicycles in our family I thought he might have a look."

"Thank you," Sedge called to the young man, who didn't react to his words. "I'm sorry to put you to the trouble."

"It's no trouble," the woman answered. "He was in the back of the shop reading manga, not doing anything important."

Sedge noticed her glance at the naked stick in his hand. "The *dango* was delicious. I've never had mugwort dumplings before."

As she bowed to thank him, the phone rang inside her shop and she hurried away to answer it, leaving Sedge and her son outside. Her son had opened a small box of tools and begun removing the front tire. Not wanting to hover over him, Sedge decided to cross the street and approach the heron on the roof of the shrine.

"Why do you speak Japanese?" the young man said as Sedge started to leave.

Sedge turned back to him. "I've lived in Japan a long time."

"In that case, you've probably married a Japanese woman."

"There are more of them in Japan than from anywhere else." He'd said it as a joke but didn't know if it had come across that way.

There was a long silence, then the young man asked Sedge what had brought him to Yamanaka Onsen.

"I'm staying here for a while. I used to live in Kanazawa."

"Yamanaka's good," he said. "But there's not a lot to do."

"Maybe that makes it better than other places. There's enough for me in its beauty."

The young man glanced at him, half-smiling. "What's beautiful about it?"

"Lots of things," Sedge said. He nodded to the shrine. "The ancient trees across the street. Also, there's a heron on the roof of the shrine. One doesn't see that every day. At least I don't."

The young man left to get a bucket of water. When he returned, he ran the tire tube through it, searching for bubbles escaping from the puncture.

"Do you mind if I go across the street?" Sedge said.

"Not at all."

Sedge crossed the road to the *torii*. Bowing before walking through it, he thought the heron, if it understood human ways, would think he'd honored not the gods of the shrine with his bow but itself.

Halfway toward the shrine hall, Sedge came to the ancient cryptomeria climbing into the sky. The Kayano Ōsugi was said to be 180 feet tall, its girth so wide that seven people could wrap their arms around it together before their fingers touched. Sedge gazed into the massive branches high above him. Reaching over the railing of the bridge, he patted the cool damp bark of the tree while glancing at its sacred *shimenawa* rope slightly overhead before continuing slowly forward. He didn't want to scare away the heron.

The heron stood directly on the middle tile above the long hanging rope that worshipers shook to get the gods' attention. The heron seemed to be watching Sedge—like the god on duty that day, deciding what to do about this strange-looking foreigner. They watched each other for a minute. Then, as if bored by Sedge's presence, the heron bent slightly before pushing itself into the air. It rose to the tops of a cryptomeria and disappeared in its enormous green canopy.

Sedge climbed the steps to the shrine, tossed a few small coins into the offertory box, then rattled the bell on its rope and made a quick prayer for the welfare of Yamanaka Onsen. Glancing across the street and seeing the young man still working on his bicycle, Sedge squatted on the mossy steps and watched sparrows chase each other around the pebbles on either side of the shrine path. Down the street, crows cawed distantly to each other.

"How was the shrine?" the young man said when Sedge returned. He had patched a hole he'd found and was already replacing the tire on its frame.

"Magnificent. By the way, do herons nest on top of the ōsugi?"

"Not that I know of. I don't think they'd be allowed to."

"You mean the people who take care of the shrine would disapprove? Or the gods enshrined there wouldn't allow it?"

The young man laughed. "The people who take care of it. Who knows? Maybe the heron you saw was a god."

"I thought the same thing," Sedge said. He watched the young man check the tightness of the tire in its frame, then stand and pat the bicycle seat as if to tell Sedge he could now go wherever he liked. "May I pay you for the repair? You saved me from having to push the bicycle back to town."

The young man shook his head. "You did enough buying my

mother's *kusa dango*." He dumped the dirty water in the bucket onto the grass beside his mother's shop and without another word walked inside.

The young man's mother was peering at Sedge through the shop's glass door. He collected his bicycle and, waving to the woman, pedaled slowly back toward the ryokan. He stopped a moment later in the middle of the road to see if he could spot the heron atop the ancient cryptomeria. All he could see, however, was the canopy's mass of leaves that floated cloud-like in the sky.

7

Sedge's alarm failed to go off on Sunday morning. He woke up confused and in a panic at someone knocking on his door. Only when he opened it did he remember having requested an early breakfast. It was seven a.m. He had agreed to go to Kanazawa with Takahashi at eight.

Since they planned to visit Takahashi's mother, they spent the beginning of the hour-long ride talking about his parents' health. Takahashi's seventy-year-old mother lived in a semi-rural community behind Mt. Utatsu, but her husband, six years older, had recently entered a care home. Last year he'd suffered a stroke and was struggling with dementia. Nozomi had been particularly close to her parents, especially her father. Because of his declining condition it was even harder to believe she had run off. Takahashi once told Sedge that she was closer than he to his parents, though he tried to visit them every month. Yuki, who rarely accompanied Takahashi to see them, often sent *wagashi* sweets from Sankaidō, an old Yamanaka Onsen confectionery his parents were fond of.

Sedge and Takahashi had always talked easily, without ever quite having an easy friendship, and since Nozomi disappeared Takahashi had not only helped Sedge in unexpected ways but also spent more time with him. At the ryokan he frequently came to Sedge's room in the evening, sipping sake while Sedge ate. Sedge sometimes thought Takahashi's kindness was motivated by the fear that Sedge would break his promise about Nozomi, disgracing his family and business. But at other times he felt that Takahashi, if he weren't simply keeping tabs on him, had his own social needs that this arrangement satisfied. In any case, he had become a confidant since Nozomi left Sedge—or left them both, as Takahashi sometimes reminded him.

As they drove along the highway, two herons descended into a field from overhead. They had glided by only fifteen or twenty feet above their car.

Takahashi said, "I heard your last English lesson covered birds."

"That's right."

"Why exactly?"

"Haven't you seen all the birdlife around the ryokan? I've spotted a dozen bird species just through my window. Anyway, that was only for fun. And it was about animals in general, not just birds. Your guests are sure to notice the animal life, so I thought it might be useful."

"Maybe you should take me birding one day. It might awaken in me a latent passion."

"You probably have no idea what a great bird habitat the ryokan is."

"Come to think of it, Nozomi once told me something similar."

It occurred to Sedge that Nozomi would inevitably arise again in conversation when he met his mother-in-law, and he wondered where it might lead. He hadn't seen either of her parents since she disappeared.

"Did you tell your mother I'm coming with you?"

"Of course. I'm not sure how much time the three of us will have together, though. She wants to be at the care home to speak with my father's nurse before having lunch with him."

Sedge decided to ask a question that had long bothered him: "Do your parents blame me for what happened?"

"With Nozomi?" He paused to think about it. "My father doesn't always remember what happened, and my mother's confused, too, but for different reasons. She can't understand why Nozomi ran off and wants to find a reason to forgive her. Anyway, you know what they're like."

At her house they found her packing clothes, toiletries, and food for her husband. Until he had entered the care home, she had dyed her short hair black. But her hair had reverted to its natural gray, Sedge noticed. She still looked younger than her age, and there were times when Nozomi emerged in the angle of her face, in various expressions passing through it, and in certain movements of her eyes and mouth. Realizing he was staring, he retreated from his close focus on her.

She had set out tea and cookies in anticipation of their arrival.

"Why did you prepare refreshments for four people?" Takahashi said, looking at her strangely. She had put placemats, napkins, and cups and saucers out for one more person than was there.

She glanced at Sedge, her mouth open either in surprise or to explain. But she only shrugged and removed the fourth setting. Had she been thinking of her husband, who normally would have joined them? Or had she imagined that Nozomi would be here as well?

Sedge hadn't visited her home since morning on New Year's Day last year, a month before his father-in-law moved out. The house struck him as unusually clean, with its knick-knacks arranged in the windowsills and on the low shelves along the room's perimeter, and with the tatami floor free of his father-in-law's things. On a long shelf across from them, family photos were aligned. A few of Nozomi when she was a child had been added since his previous visit: praying at a crowded shrine during a summer festival; wading to her knees in a sea the color of fire, turned halfway to what remained of the setting sun; bent down on the edge of a marsh, peering into the distance. And there was one he had never seen, taken at a small river: Nozomi clinging to Takahashi's back as he waded through the shallow water, laughter contorting their faces. Takahashi couldn't have been more than ten years old in the photo, Nozomi no more than five.

Takahashi and his mother spoke about the care home, Yuki, and the ryokan. Sedge didn't want to interrupt them, but during lulls he tried to join the conversation. At one point he asked his mother-in-law if she planned to visit Yamanaka Onsen soon.

"No, I don't. Visiting Otōsan every day keeps me too busy."

"You visit him every day?"

She nodded. "He couldn't get by if I didn't."

She set down her tea and looked at him, and he read in her eyes an invitation to continue speaking. "Does he ever come home?"

"He hasn't yet. I wonder if he wants to. It might be difficult to return to the care home if he came back for a visit. Are you planning to see him today?"

Takahashi broke into the conversation. "Not today. I'm not sure if Otōsan would recognize Sedge. And if he did, he might not remember that Nozomi has disappeared. I thought it would be better not to risk upsetting him."

She turned back to Sedge and said, "Have you heard from her?"

He took a deep breath and shook his head. "I expect you and Takahashi will hear from her before me. If I ever hear from her again."

The ticking of a clock filled the room.

"Do you think she's all right?"

Again Takahashi answered for Sedge. "What would she need all that money for if she didn't plan to spoil herself?"

"I wonder what happened?" she said, not taking her eyes off Sedge. "Weren't you a good husband to her?"

Sedge withered at her words. "I was very good to her. Better than she was to me, ultimately."

She blinked once and turned away.

"I'd just like to know she's all right. Safe and happy, wherever she is. Is it true she took your money?"

"I'd like to know she's all right, too," Sedge said, ignoring her question.

"Let's not talk about her," Takahashi said. Awkwardly he added, "Did I tell you that Sedge is teaching English to the staff at our ryokan? By all accounts, he's done an excellent job so far."

As his mother reached for her teacup, her hand started to shake and tea spilled onto the floor. Takahashi found a box of tissues, and without mentioning what had happened he mopped up the spilled tea. He changed the subject again, asking what she needed to do before visiting the care home.

Ten minutes later, after Sedge had washed their teacups and plates, and after Takahashi had made a phone call, they led Sedge's mother-in-law to the car.

When they drove past the care home, Takahashi's mother spoke in alarm. "Where are you going? Otōsan is back there."

"I'm dropping Sedge off closer to the city. We'll turn around at Higashi-chaya."

Takahashi's mother glanced to the back seat where Sedge was sitting, then turned to Takahashi. In a low voice that wasn't low enough to keep Sedge from overhearing she said, "Why hasn't he divorced her yet?"

"We've talked about this before, Mother. There's no need to bring it up again now."

"But I don't understand. Must we still treat him as part of the family? Nozomi's leaving means they're finished, doesn't it?"

Takahashi sighed. When his mother tried to speak again, he silenced her.

"I can walk from here," Sedge said. They were a few blocks from Higashi-chaya.

When he stepped out of the car, he returned Takahashi's parting nod and watched them drive away. A group of tourists bumped into him, and he started walking in the direction of Korinbō.

⚜ ⚜ ⚜

The side of the road below Kenrokuen was aflame with red azaleas. Above him a walking bridge crossed the road, and to his right Ishikawa Gate loomed, followed by tiers of long stone walls. They were fronted by cherry trees that, for the first time since moving to the city, he'd not bothered to see this spring. Tourists and students on bicycles drifted past as he gazed toward Kanazawa Castle.

After passing Imori Moat and Ishigaki Corridor, he crossed over to Fourth High School Memorial Park. The only thing between him and his old apartment was the Daiwa department store, and after cutting through it and making his way across Hyakumangoku Street, he saw that nothing had changed in the city block where he once lived.

The building custodian, one of two who always worked there, emerged from the lobby onto the sidewalk and began sweeping up leaves and dust. He didn't recognize Sedge immediately, but when Sedge blocked his way he looked up and smiled with a brightness and warmth Sedge had rarely witnessed in him before.

"It's been a long time," the custodian said.

"It has been, yes. How are things here?"

"Not so different from when you and your wife were tenants. How are you both?"

Sedge had never told him about Nozomi's disappearance. He

was amazed the custodian hadn't guessed what had happened. Perhaps he assumed she'd only gone away to work or had left to care for her parents. "We're both fine."

"Where did you move to?"

"Kaga," Sedge said, which wasn't a lie; Yamanaka Onsen was part of Kaga City.

"There are nice *onsen* around there."

Sedge nodded and smiled back. "Since I'm in Kanazawa again, I thought I'd stop by to ask if my wife or I had received any mail or packages after we left."

"Nothing has come for either of you."

"Also, Nozomi thought she left a pair of earrings when we moved out. I suppose she hasn't come back to inquire about them?"

"Not while I've been working."

"I see. So you haven't seen or heard from her?"

The custodian looked at Sedge without replying. Sedge knew it was an odd question, but the custodian would probably think the oddness came from Sedge's foreignness, fluent though he was in Japanese. "Not once," he finally said. "This is the first I've seen either of you since you left."

Sedge removed an old business card he still kept in his wallet. Pointing to the mobile phone number there he said, "On the off-chance you need to get in touch with either of us, please call me."

The custodian took Sedge's card and inspected it. "Of course. Thank you."

"You may have Nozomi's number, but she often forgets to return people's calls. Please contact me if there's anything for either of us."

The custodian nodded.

"I miss Kanazawa," Sedge told him. "But my dream is to live here again one day. Please take good care of these apartments."

An hour later, on the train to Kaga Onsen, Sedge wondered how long Nozomi's parents would remain his in-laws. Had she finally begun divorce proceedings? Was she expecting him to? Or did she think she could come back to him whenever she wanted, and their marriage would be unchanged? No one he knew was in contact with her or could tell him where she was. That she hadn't notified him of her intention to divorce him felt like a secret promise that she would come back one day.

As the train left the station and eventually met farmland, Nozomi faded in his mind the way Kanazawa faded into the increasingly rural landscape. And in her place, Mariko appeared. They were to have their first English class tonight, but the trip had drained him, and all he wanted to do was return to the ryokan. She had given him her phone number if for any reason he needed to cancel. He took out his phone and sent a message asking to reschedule their class for next weekend.

"Of course," she wrote back immediately. "I'm sorry to cause you so much trouble."

He lay his head on his seat-back and closed his eyes.

8

Rain poured down the following Sunday as Sedge trudged up
Yugekai Road. After passing Kagari Kisshōtei, the last ryokan on
the main drag, he veered left down a steep path to Kōrogi-machi.
He could hardly see where he was going. Crossing the wooden
"Cricket Bridge," he didn't stop to watch the river roar by beneath
the dense branches of trees below. He glanced at the stone *kuhi* at
the end of the bridge and remembered the engraved Bashō verse
flowing down its flat surface that Nozomi once taught him.

> By the night's fishing fire
> a bullhead in the waves
> choked with tears

He hurried by it, Nozomi unwelcome on the edges of the
memory.

On the other side he ascended a flagstone path to a back road,
which turned and led past an eel restaurant and a cafe, an old
samurai house, and another moss-covered *kuhi*, nearly black with
rain, with a Bashō haiku flowing down it, too. Despite holding a
large umbrella, by the time he reached Mariko's house his shoes,
socks, and the bottom third of his pants were soaked.

Lit from inside, her house cast stripes of light at his feet
through the vertical *kōshi* slats on its first-floor windows. Perhaps two hundred meters ahead, the road entered a forest; the
half-dozen houses before it were quiet and dark and, aside from
numerous potted plants in front of them, might have been unin-
habited. He rang Mariko's doorbell.

A shadow appeared and grew more distinct as it neared the door's clouded glass. The door slid open and Mariko stood there, a strange sight dressed in a light sweater and thin pleated skirt rather than the ryokan's kimono. She stared at him open-mouthed—either astonished that he had come, or that he was half-drenched from the rain.

"Hello . . ."

His English jarred her from whatever vision had frozen her in the doorway. She ushered him inside, sliding the door open further for him to enter. She shook out his umbrella and leaned it against the front wall.

"My feet are soaking wet," he told her before peeling off his shoes and socks at the wooden step leading up from the *genkan*. "Do you have a towel I can dry them off with?"

"Of course. Just a moment." She removed her own footwear and walked quickly into her house.

The *genkan* was freshly swept, and a heavy wooden cabinet lined the wall to his right. Atop it was an empty vase, two ceramic guardian lions, and an iron incense burner, all of which wore the sheen of antiques. On the wall above them hung a square board with two lacquered Noh masks—a horned devil and a white-faced hag. Behind the wall was a bathroom, with a wooden stairs across from it; straight ahead was a tatami room; to the left of that were two similar rooms, but larger. To the immediate left was a room with its sliding doors pulled shut, and beyond that a kitchen. Nearly every room was lighted, which lent the house a cheerful atmosphere despite the rain. He saw no sign of the stepson, and no indication of Mariko's husband's former presence.

Mariko hurried back with two small towels, one for his feet and one for the sweat beading his face.

"Is it just you here?" he said after a bit of small talk about the weather.

"Riku's in the kura behind the house. But he'll come in soon. He has homework still to do."

Sedge glanced toward the back of the house but couldn't see outside.

"Does he study English at school?"

She laughed. "English is required at every Japanese school. But that doesn't mean he speaks it. Don't let this offend you, but he detests the subject. To be fair, though, he detests all his school subjects. He's tried to quit going many times."

Sedge gave her back both towels. "He has no interests academically?"

"I wouldn't call it an academic interest exactly, but he's keen on local history, and also the woodturning, lacquerware, and pottery local craftsmen make. And like I told you, he's keen on birds."

"Has he always been?"

"Since moving here, I guess. He and I have helped injured sparrows and crows we've come across. One day maybe you'll see the birdhouses he's made and hung outside the kura. Unfortunately, because he's always coming and going, and making so much noise inside, birds don't want to live in them."

Sedge followed her into the front room where a dining table stood. The sliding *fusuma* doors between the connected rooms and wooden-floored veranda had been removed, making the area more open, and the tatami flooring was in places worn and discolored. The *fusuma* that remained, both before the Buddhist altar at the back of the second room and that separated the first tatami room from the one beside the stairs, had large holes in them, as if someone had kicked or punched them. As he sat at the table he spotted holes in the plaster wall of the second room's inset alcove, too. Two were sloppily replastered, but two had been left untouched, suggesting they were more recent.

"Does he birdwatch?" he said, his eyes returning to the

veranda, at the end of which a roll-curtain had been raised. Beyond the window was a shin-high, mossy stone wall—the edge of a long, waterlogged flowerbed—but with it dark outside and bright inside, the reflection of the house's interior made it difficult to see anything else.

"Not really. But he's learned to recognize the birds he sees around here. For years he's had a thing for *senbazuru*—making and stringing together a thousand origami cranes. In fact, when he was eight or nine years old, he made his first *senbazuru* and with a teacher's help sent them to schoolchildren in Fukushima. That was before I'd met Kōichi."

Sedge remembered Takahashi telling him about the one thousand origami cranes the boy had made and given to his father. He wondered if what Takahashi told him referred to this incident instead. There was a world of difference between doing such a thing to lift the spirits of disadvantaged kids and wanting to appease an angry father.

"He knows you're coming tonight. He was curious about your name. He looked it up in his dictionary and saw that the kanji for your name in Japanese is the same first kanji in the name of our village."

"I didn't know that."

She disappeared into the kitchen. "Can you drink *mugi-cha?*"

"Of course. Thank you."

He approached the Buddhist altar, its exterior lacquered black and easily as tall as himself. It stood open and gleamed inside with gold leaf. His gaze fell on the altar's votive objects, the ornate religious carvings along its top and sides, and two small hanging scrolls in back, one with a painting of the Buddha and the other of a kneeling, heavily robed priest. The Buddhist names of several deceased ancestors were written on small wooden mortuary tablets to one side.

Sedge had lifted his eyes to the transom overhead, where wooden carvings of winged bodhisattvas flew among clouds— two of which were missing—when Mariko returned carrying a small lacquered tray.

"Is this altar yours or your husband's?" he asked.

"Mine," she said softly. "Actually, it belongs to my brother in Kyoto. But because I inherited our parents' house when they died, and the altar has been here as long as I remember, I agreed to take care of it."

"I didn't know you have a brother."

"He hasn't come back for five years. He and Kōichi don't get along."

She set their barley tea on the table as he eyed a wall-hanging in the *tokonoma*.

"Normally the altar's closed," she said, looking at Sedge across the room. "I light incense there every morning, but I'm not as diligent as I should be about changing the offerings. Riku used to help me, even though he's not direct family. But he doesn't anymore."

"It's beautiful. Your entire house is a work of art."

She laughed. "If it's art, it wouldn't fetch a high price. In the mountains and countryside, houses like this are a dime a dozen."

The naturalness of being here with her, the unpretentiousness of the atmosphere inside her home, made him think he could spend the next hour just chatting with her. But he remembered why he was here and said, "Shall we get started?"

He began organizing the lesson. He had expected to be struck by her husband's presence—and by association, with Nozomi's—but there were no obvious signs of it: no photos of him, no certificates of achievement framed on the walls, none of his Kutani-ware on display.

He spoke to her in English using simple grammatical structures and vocabulary. He changed the speed with which he spoke, too, but it quickly became evident that her English abilities ranked among the worst in his ryokan classes. Yet she was more attentive than those students, more intent on learning.

Half an hour into the lesson the front door slammed open and shut, rattling the glass in its pane. Sedge's back was to the *genkan*, and though Mariko ignored the interruption, he turned to see the boy he'd heard much about. He stood atop the *genkan* step, his chin tilted down as his eyes shifted between Sedge and his stepmother. He was around Sedge's height, with a wrestler's strong wiry build, and his dusky skin indicated time spent in the sun. His face was round, his jawbone thick, and his hair was short against his scalp, which was marked with a few pink scars. When he wiped the rain from his face, Sedge noticed his hands were cut and bruised. So strongly did he resemble the photo Mariko had shown him of her husband, for a moment Sedge apprehended that they were finally in each other's presence again.

"Hello," Sedge said.

"Hello," the boy murmured back.

Mariko waved him into the room. He came over, not stomping but walking with a forcefulness that shook the floor.

"This is my teacher, Sedge-sensei," she said.

The boy's face relaxed and he smiled. "Suga," he said.

Mariko asked Sedge if he minded the boy using the Japanese word for his name.

"Not at all," he answered. To the boy he said: "I was told your name's Riku. What does it mean?"

When Riku didn't answer, Mariko explained: "The first kanji means 'overcome.' The second means 'sky.' Together they don't necessarily mean anything. His parents just liked the sound of it."

She told Riku to dry himself off. "You're dripping on the tatami."

Riku left the room to find a towel. Again, the floor shook under his footsteps.

Sedge continued his lesson. With ten minutes remaining, Riku returned, dressed in pajamas old Japanese men often wear, and poured himself a glass of water in the kitchen. After gulping it down, he marched into the room beneath the stairs and flipped on the TV there. Sedge noticed with annoyance its volume rise. A minute later Riku called out to ask when Mariko would help him with his math. When she ignored him, Sedge saw in this an effective way to deal with her stepson.

They continued their practice conversation. Riku returned to their room and placed himself behind Mariko, leaning into her and groaning like he was bored. Sedge again noticed the facial resemblance between Riku and his father and stopped teaching. Rather than make eye contact with Riku, and inadvertently encourage his disruptive behavior, Sedge instead studied Mariko, waiting for her to admonish the boy.

"English is difficult for me," she said, still leaning forward under Riku's weight. She attempted to ignore him again; a moment later Riku laughed, then abruptly turned serious and lifted himself off her thin shoulders.

"It's good if it's difficult," Sedge said. "It should feel like a challenge, but not hopeless."

"You're too old to learn anything," Riku said, stifling a laugh.

"Don't say that," Sedge retorted. "It's not true, anyway. How do you think I learned Japanese?"

Mariko smiled hesitantly. "He's only a boy, you know."

"He shouldn't interrupt us while we're studying."

Mariko sighed and looked at Riku without saying anything. "You didn't mean anything by it, did you?"

Riku was staring at Sedge the way he did when he first entered the house. The boy smacked the end of their table with the palm of his hand and walked quickly to the *genkan*.

"Rik-kun!" Mariko called out as he kicked his feet into his shoes and stalked outside, slamming the door again. Through the veranda window, Sedge watched him cross the stone path toward the kura. He wasn't sorry to see him go.

He rose to turn off the TV. When he returned, it was time to end their lesson. Rather than sit down again, he pushed his chair under the table.

"I thought the lesson went well. Unfortunately, there were too many interruptions."

"I'm sorry about Riku. He's not a bad kid. It's because you're new to him, and we rarely have anyone come inside our home. I could see he was eager to impress you."

"Is that what he was doing?" Sedge let her keep the textbook he'd brought. "When you have time, maybe you can study this on your own."

When he looked at her he saw that his manner had hurt her.

"Next time," she promised, "Riku won't bother us."

Sedge couldn't bring himself to apologize. He had no experience admonishing a boy Riku's age and wished Mariko had done it herself. Even so, he knew he shouldn't have grown angry at something that was ultimately inconsequential.

The boy had elicited in Sedge a reaction he couldn't comprehend.

On the way out he passed the room beside the *genkan*. Glancing through a narrow opening between the sliding door and a wall, the hallway light illuminated a pair of shelves inside, a display case, and a table filled with Kutani-ware and their *tomobako* storage boxes. There was no question but that the ceramics were her husband's.

"Why do you have all this?" he said, confused.

"What do you mean?"

"He abandoned you. Why do you want these reminders of him?"

She smiled with something like patience. "I used to keep all of this in the kura, but Riku broke a lot of pieces there. I had to move them here."

"Riku purposely broke them?"

"I'm not sure what to do with them," she went on, not answering his question. "Sometimes, when I wanted to give someone who visited a gift, I chose a piece from this room. But people thought it unseemly of me. Others said the items were too valuable to give away. So I stopped."

Sedge hesitated before saying, "Do you mind if I take a look?"

She opened the door for him to walk through and turned on the overhead light.

All around the room were pieces of the three traditional Kutani-ware styles: *aote*, with its fired green glaze; the five-colored *iroe*; and a few of *akae-kinrande*, with gold painted on red backgrounds. The majority, however, were *aote*, whose deep greens and yellows, and dark blues and purples, suffused the room. They were of better quality than the Kutani-ware he and Nozomi had sold in their shop. He'd seen pieces like them behind glass at museums in Kanazawa and Daishōji.

There was a supreme delicacy to these porcelains, but also a liveliness. The flower and bird designs looked so real they might at any second lift from the pieces they'd been painted on. Their shapes and uses astonished him: square and circular dishes; shallow and footed bowls; square cups and gourd-shaped sake bottles; water ewers; incense burners; eating utensils; two-tiered boxes; vases and jars. The room overflowed with her husband's mastery of *kutaniyaki*.

Noticing Mariko beside him, an awkwardness washed over him. His mind raced with questions, but he was unable to ask a single one. His unexpected admiration for the talents of the man who'd run away with Nozomi rooted him where he stood.

"How long has he made Kutani-ware?" Sedge said.

"Since he was twenty-one or twenty-two. He started in Fukui, making Echizen-ware. But he was forced to leave and ended up here. He mastered *kutaniyaki* in Yamanaka Onsen."

She pulled out a small wooden chest from beneath a table. Inside it were more *tomobako*, stacked evenly atop one another. She placed a few upon the table and showed Sedge their contents: exquisite pieces covered with bluish-white enamel, various decorations appearing under blue slip. They were much older than the other pieces in the room.

"*Ko-kutani?*" he said, bending down to inspect what he assumed was "ancient Kutani-ware." Potters in this area, along with Arita in Kyushu, had produced a unique form of decorated porcelain from the mid-1600s to the mid-1700s, then suddenly stopped making it. No one knew why the kilns had been abandoned. *Kutaniyaki* was revived in the early 1800s and was what one commonly found in shops throughout this part of Ishikawa.

"He collected or was given a number of pieces. Museums and researchers have come to see them."

"They're extraordinary."

"Kōichi used to say he was like *ko-kutani*. At first I thought he meant he had a hardness like enamel and was in some ways very traditional. But he meant something different. He was referring to the times he left us. He said he might disappear for one hundred years before mysteriously coming back."

"He joked about it?"

"Not often. But I remember when he did."

Sedge couldn't believe her husband had said something so hurtful.

At the *genkan*, Sedge tugged his wet socks and shoes back on. Mariko followed him outside, past the carport beside the house where a black K-car was parked. Behind the small car was the long flowerbed and gravel path he'd noticed from inside. Rain still fell, but lighter than before.

"Thank you for teaching me," she said. "I apologize again about Riku."

"You don't have to apologize. It would be natural if he didn't like me. After all, he probably sees in me the reason why his father left. He knows who I am, doesn't he?"

She nodded. Looking at him inquiringly she said, "Is that what you see in him, too?"

Her question stopped him. He had only considered it from the boy's perspective. Part of him recognized the ugliness of having judged the boy so harshly, and after meeting him only once. Did he dislike Riku because he reminded him of what he'd lost? Because Riku forced him to deal with Nozomi's abandonment all over again? No, he had been put off by the boy's behavior and because Mariko didn't react to it the way he would have had he been in her shoes. Surely it was as simple as that.

"Will you come again next week?" she asked.

He hesitated to say yes. Although he wanted to teach her again, the way their evening had ended left him uncertain. "I'll have to check my schedule," he said, picking up his umbrella.

She started to say something but stopped herself. "Please, take this," she said, trying to slip some money into his hand. "For teaching me like you did."

He pulled away and looked at her in surprise. "I came because I wanted to."

As if to hide the slight blush that came over her, she bowed to him. "Goodnight. Be careful walking back to town."

"Goodnight."

Starting down the street, he looked toward the kura, whose gable-roofed, two-story silhouette gleamed wetly under the sky. Despite the darkness, he saw Riku leaning against its entrance.

A light burned dimly behind him and reflected off birdhouses hanging from the clay-tiled eaves. Riku hesitantly raised a hand and waved goodbye.

Sedge pretended not to see him.

🖒 🖒 🖒

The next morning, Sedge carried his breakfast tray to the hallway outside his room. As he pulled open the front door, a small package leaning against it fell toward him. He lowered the tray and looked down the hallway. A couple was admiring the mini-exhibition of Kutani-ware against a wall one room away. He took the package inside.

Kneeling on his futon, he shook out the package's contents: a note, a small wooden box, and a plastic container that held a slice of apple pie.

The note was short, written in Japanese.

> Sedge-sensei:
> Thank you for teaching me last night. And thank you for being kind to Riku-kun. Last night after you left I baked an apple pie. If you like it, I'll give you more. Also, Riku asked me to give you a bird he made this morning. He says you're a nice man.
> Mariko

Sedge pried open the wooden box. Inside was something white—an origami crane. He plucked it out and lifted it before his eyes. It was surprisingly realistic—and, considering its origin, exquisitely made.

9

Yuki stood with several staff outside the ryokan entrance, bowing to a departing family and waving until their shuttle was out of sight. She broke off from her staff and approached Sedge on his way for a morning walk.

"Where are you off to?" she said.

"I was going to cross Ayatori Bridge. On the opposite side of the river there's a path you probably know that climbs from the Bashō Hut to a shrine up the slope. I've never been there, but since the weather's nice I thought I'd go."

She smiled at him. "Are you happy with your classes?"

"They've gone smoother than I expected. I've been happy to see some staff try to speak English with the foreign guests."

"Yes, so have I. By the way, I hear you're taking on private students."

Sedge assumed she was referring to Mariko and was surprised she knew he had taught her. "Are you concerned I might be making money? I only have one outside student. And that person pays me nothing."

"I think it would be great for you to earn money while you're here. But please be careful about cultivating relationships outside of work. We spoke about this before, didn't we?"

"I don't know what you mean." As soon as he said this, he remembered her and Takahashi warning him that people might spread rumors about what he did in his private time.

She sighed and said, "I mean Mariko."

"What about her?"

"Like we said, if she wants to study with you, she can do so here the same as the other staff do. They also have busy lives, and longer commutes, most of them."

"Anyway, that's not why she asked me to teach her at her home."

He was about to explain when Takahashi emerged from the ryokan and asked Yuki about her schedule. "Did I interrupt something?"

"No," Sedge answered. "I was explaining my teaching arrangement with Mariko."

Takahashi's face darkened and he looked at Yuki. "Didn't we tell you that wasn't a good idea? The only thing we've asked of you in return for your room and board is that you teach our staff. But that means here, where they work. Not in the privacy of their homes."

"I'm sorry, but what are you worried about?"

Takahashi assured him that he wasn't worried about anything.

"You're free to do as you please," Yuki said. "We just ask you to be careful. And mindful of your associations."

"What you do in town reflects on our ryokan," Takahashi added sternly. "We emphasize this regularly to all our staff, not just to you. But as a foreigner, you're more visible than them."

Sedge hoped this would be the last word on the subject. He resented the implications of what they were saying and worried they would confront Mariko more severely. In their disapproval he heard an echo of their conditions for letting him stay there.

"Don't let us keep you from your walk," Yuki said encouragingly. "It's so nice today, it would be a shame to waste even part of it. Besides, Takahashi and I need to go back to work."

Sedge cut his walk short. After returning to the ryokan, he was soon back in the tea lounge. He wanted to see if Mariko was there and ask if Takahashi and Yuki had spoken to her. If she was upset, he would leave the lounge immediately and not make matters worse for her. But she wasn't there when he arrived, nor did she come that afternoon. She wasn't there the next day or the day after, either. Finally, unable to get through to her on his phone, Sedge inquired about this with the woman who had replaced her.

Ms. Ozeki was one of his students. He ordered tea from her, and when she brought it to his table by the window he said, "How do you like working in this lounge? I don't remember seeing you here before."

"The lounge gets few guests, so it's a little boring. And most just want to sit or take a nap, or they buy drinks from the vending machines and bring them here."

"Where were you before this?"

"The laundry facility, mostly."

"I'm not sure where that is," Sedge said.

"It's in a separate building. I enjoy it there because the staff are nice and it's relaxing. I was told this is only temporary. I guess it's nice to do something different."

"When you say it's temporary, do you mean the person you replaced here now works in the laundry building?"

"That's my understanding. I don't know the reason why, but sometimes it happens."

She disappeared into the small kitchen behind a hanging *noren* curtain. In some ways Sedge welcomed Ms. Ozeki's news, for he saw he had become attracted to Mariko. But it was an attraction that remained indistinct; he hadn't completely lost his love for Nozomi, despite what she'd done and the passage of time. And he was married to her still, just as Mariko remained married to her husband. Neither of them had taken steps to end their respective marriages, though he was confident they would one day. He didn't entirely trust his attraction to Mariko because

of what had happened with Nozomi, and this made him grateful
he couldn't run into her so easily every day.

But the next day she was there again, dressed as always in
her light green staff kimono. She shuffled to his table, looking as
pleased to see him as he was to see her. He had taken a table hidden from the front desk, where Yuki and Takahashi often worked.

"I thought you disappeared into the higher echelons of management," he said, keeping his voice low.

"I would never survive so high up."

"How was working in the laundry? Ms. Ozeki told me you
were transferred there."

"It wasn't bad. I got to know the people there better, and it
was a nice change of atmosphere."

"When you're not here, it's not worth visiting." He took more
pleasure than usual in her smile.

"I've worked in every position imaginable here. You shouldn't
be shocked if I enter the men's baths while you're there to clean
the changing room and put the washing areas in order. It's not my
favorite job, but then I don't know any of the men bathing. In any
case, I try never to look at them."

After so long in Japan, it didn't bother him when female staff
entered the men's baths while he was dressing or undressing, or
when cleaning himself at the washing area and soaking in the hot
water. While he and Nozomi were dating, they had visited same-
sex baths at Nyūtō Onsen in Akita, and Hōshi Onsen in Gunma,
and his nervousness being there had evaporated as soon as they'd
entered the baths and submerged themselves. It was as it had
always been done in old times.

"Promise to forewarn me if you get transferred to the men's
baths while I'm here."

"Promises are so boring. I'm afraid I can't promise you
anything."

Sedge realized that they'd crossed a line they'd been tiptoeing along. But if word got back to Yuki and Takahashi about their flirtation, he knew their disapproval would be stronger than before.

He stayed in the lounge all afternoon, hidden by a large panel on which hung an old calligraphic scroll. The only people who could see him were those who entered the lounge and walked toward the window. The only person to do that, however, was Mariko.

👍 👍 👍

When Sedge returned to Mariko's house for their second English lesson, he was impressed by how much she had calmed her stepson. Riku was waiting for Sedge's arrival from the kura door, and this time when he waved to Sedge, Sedge waved back. Riku jumped down from the wall and ran to the rear of the house. He opened the front door from inside before Sedge rang the bell. As Sedge removed his shoes at the *genkan*, he saw Riku struggle not to say anything. Preferring this version of the boy to the one he'd met before, Sedge smiled at Riku but didn't encourage him by starting a conversation, either.

"*A-ra-ra*," Mariko exclaimed upon seeing Sedge. "I was waiting for the doorbell. Riku let you in, did he?"

Sedge gave Riku a chance to answer, but he remained silent. Whereas he'd appeared happy a moment before, his face was now darker. Sedge had no idea what he was thinking.

"I was surprised he recognized me," Sedge said, smiling. "I guess I don't blend in well with the people who live around here."

Riku's expression didn't change.

As Mariko and Sedge sat where they'd studied before, Riku settled himself at a low lacquered table in front of the Buddhist altar. He started working on his homework while Sedge and

Mariko began their lesson. Whenever she laughed, Riku jerked his head up and stared at Sedge.

The only time he spoke was when an hour had passed. "Your lesson is over," he told Mariko, jumping to his feet and coming up behind her.

"You were good while we studied," she told him. "Thank you."

Riku looked from her to Sedge and said, "Can I ask you a question?"

"Of course."

"What's your favorite bird?"

"My favorite bird? In the world?"

Riku shook his head. "That you've seen around town."

"There are far too many to choose from."

"No, there aren't. There are far too few." He had grown excited, but when Mariko touched his arm he calmed down. "My favorite is the kingfisher. But every week it changes."

"That's an admirable choice."

"I know. So what's yours?"

"Since coming to Yamanaka Onsen, I've been interested in the Asian gray heron."

"Everyone knows what that is," Riku said, and began listing some of its characteristics. He was particularly keen to talk about its courtship patterns. He also described its monogamy and parenting, which he said he'd learned about on TV. Sedge added to what Riku said—how they sometimes use bait to catch fish like fishermen do; how powder-down they produce from special feathers in their plumage make them water-repellant; and how those same feathers never stop growing, but fray rather than fall out—without saying all he might have.

"Have you seen the movie *Milky Way Railroad*?" Riku asked.

"No, but I've read the book." Sedge had read it several years ago, a strange, wondrous novel by Miyazawa Kenji about two boys who run away from a summer festival in their rural town to ride a train that travels through the stars. Regretfully, he'd forgotten much of it.

"Do you remember the part where a man boarded the train at the Cygnus constellation carrying bags stuffed with birds? The first bag he opened was full of herons. When they flew above him he simply raised his arms in the air, and just touching their feet made them drop all around him." He lifted his own hands toward the ceiling, showing Sedge how he imagined the man did it. "I don't understand how, but he said they were made of sand from the Milky Way."

Riku's mention of the bird-catcher brought the scene back to mind. But Sedge and Riku remembered it differently. "I thought the herons were made of candy and weren't real."

"You're wrong," Riku said, excited again. "The man's bag of wild geese tasted like candy, but all his birds were edible. Before the herons could be eaten, he had to hang them under the light of the Milky Way or bury them in the sand. His other bags were full of cranes and swans, but the boys in the story didn't eat them."

"It sounds like a sad fate for those birds," Mariko said.

Riku shook his head in disagreement, then turned back to Sedge. "What's so special to you about herons?"

Mariko was watching Sedge with equal interest. "Is it because of what happened at Kenrokuen back in March?"

Riku shushed her. "I asked him first."

"It's not because of that," Sedge said. "Maybe it's because of their majesty. But if I had to be a bird, I wouldn't choose it. I'd rather be a powerful seabird. But herons are beautiful. And there are many in this part of Japan."

Riku was listening to him intently; perhaps struggling to choose from among a thousand things he wanted to say.

Sedge said to Mariko, "I should go. If we continue studying together, I'd better leave on time."

Mariko led him to the front door. "Are you worried about Takahashi and Yuki?"

"Only for your sake. I don't want rumors spreading about us."

That she didn't respond made him think he'd offended her. Sliding the door open she said, "Please be careful walking back in the dark."

He nodded toward Riku and said in a low voice, "I enjoyed his company tonight. Whatever you told him after our last lesson, he clearly listened to you." He stopped himself from saying: he doesn't resemble his father as much when he behaves well.

"He's good around people he trusts," she said happily. "It's as much because of you as either of us."

She called to Riku: "Do you want to say goodbye?"

But Riku only stared at them, his face dark again and unreadable.

"Goodnight," Mariko called from the doorway as Sedge stepped into the street. Like last time, she tried to pass him a small money envelope.

He waved it away and started walking toward town.

"Thank you for your lesson," she called to him.

☙ ☙ ☙

Late that night, as Sedge was preparing for bed, someone rapped on his door. When he opened it he found Yuki there, staring at the ground.

"It's nearly midnight," he said. "Not that I mind, but this is late for you, isn't it?" His immediate thought was that she had news about Nozomi.

She lifted her gaze tiredly. "An hour ago Takahashi's mother called. His father had another stroke. He's been moved to an intensive care ward, but Takahashi hasn't been able to speak to any doctors there yet. Since he's still your father-in-law, I thought you'd want to know."

His stomach knotted and no words came to him right away. "Of course I do. Thank you for telling me." He paused, aware of the double-absurdity of her sharing this news—the obligatoriness on her part and his thanking her for it on his. It was how strangers might behave. "Is there anything I can do?"

She shook her head again. "If there is, I'll let you know. Takahashi drove to Kanazawa. When he comes back you should talk to him."

"I'll make a point to find him tomorrow."

She hesitated before saying, "He asked me what we should do about Nozomi. I told him I had no idea."

Sedge leaned against the doorframe and looked at her helplessly.

"It's ridiculous that she cut us all off," she said. "It's not like *we've* done anything."

Sedge let her barb pass as inadvertent. "I haven't spoken to any of our mutual friends for a long time. I can check again to see if they've heard from her, and if so, ask that they tell her about her father."

"You can if you think it might help. But Takahashi and I have been searching for her every day. Personally, I think she should suffer the consequences of leaving like she did. At her parents' ages, surely she realized this could happen. It's like she wanted to precede her father on his way to leaving this world."

Sedge stiffened, and she quickly apologized. She added: "I told Takahashi the other day that you should hire a private firm to track her down."

"But what for?"

"Most of the money she took was yours, wasn't it?"

"Yes." His attitude toward the money she took had turned less forgiving.

"That's not the only reason I said that. You need to be sure she's been as selfish as you believe before you turn away from her forever."

Sedge was unsure what she was getting at. "I don't think I can see the situation as clearly as someone on the outside. Perhaps you're right, though."

She made to depart but turned back. "Maybe this isn't the right occasion to ask, but do you feel you're capable of moving on from her? After all she did . . ."

The question had arisen in his own mind many times. "Things are getting better. Didn't you tell Takahashi that a person needs fifty days to accept a loved one's death? It's been much more than that for me—maybe because I'm not mourning her actual death. But somewhere along the way I've learned to accept what happened."

She brushed her hands on her kimono sleeves, dusting them off. "I'm sorry I bothered you so late. I only came at this hour because I thought you should know."

He watched her walk down the hall and turn the corner.

On the following morning, while brushing his teeth over the small sink in his room, he heard a rustling at his front door followed by footsteps hurrying down the hallway. He opened the door and found another envelope. Like the one before, it contained an origami figure and a note that said only: "Your favorite bird!"

Sedge shook the paper figure from the bottom of the envelope.

A gray heron fell into his palm, perfectly executed. Riku had not only folded the paper into the exact shape of a heron with its head hunched into its shoulders, its long neck shaped into an 'S,' but even its plumage overlapped and was reflected in the different colored paper he'd used.

For a young man tormented by angst, there was no denying the existence as well of an extraordinary artistic sensibility. And a sensitivity, too, buried somewhere the boy was extremely protective of.

10

Takahashi and Yuki spent more time in Kanazawa to be with his father, whose condition had destabilized. Sedge was unable to obtain any details about his health, and out of consideration didn't push for them. Surely Takahashi or Yuki would tell him whatever he needed to know.

Their absence from the ryokan emboldened him to devote more mornings and afternoons to the lounge where Mariko was working again. He still sat where the front desk staff couldn't see him, and he brought a laptop to search for jobs.

"I like working here when you visit," she told him, "but I'm thinking of requesting a transfer back to my old job of cleaning guestrooms."

Hearing this disappointed Sedge. His time at the ryokan would be harder to endure if he couldn't see her here most days. "You don't like it here?"

She glanced toward the front desk, where a tourist group was checking in. "All the long-timers know that when a woman is transferred here it's usually so Takahashi can keep an eye on her. Eventually he tries to seduce her, but when she refuses or no longer satisfies him, or when he starts worrying that Yuki will find out, he gets rid of her."

"Are you sure it's not just a rumor?" But even as he asked this, he remembered Nozomi's stories about his womanizing.

"I witnessed it once. With a new girl on staff as she was supposed to be tidying a room. I peeked past the half-shut door and saw her sitting on his lap—I don't know how she got there, but he wouldn't let her go. I withdrew and loudly announced to an imaginary person down the hallway that I'd keep my eye open for Takahashi. A moment later he burst from the room, demanding to know who was looking for him. I answered that Yuki was, and without another word he hurried toward the elevators. A few days later the girl was let go. And he acted suspicious of me afterward for a long time."

"Old Ms. Ozeki, too?"

"He mixes the rotations so it's not obvious."

"What about you?"

She looked toward the front desk again. "He's tried it before. When Kōichi ran off or chased us away from the house. But he didn't succeed."

Anger welled inside Sedge, not only at Takahashi but also at Nozomi for never opposing this behavior. Both were guilty of thinking that whatever they did was beyond condemnation. "Tell me if it happens again."

"What will you do if it does?"

"I don't know. But I want you to promise to tell me."

Mariko nodded, though her expression suggested there was no point in it. And perhaps there wasn't.

On Saturday afternoon, Mariko approached Sedge's table. He nearly touched her leg as he'd once touched Nozomi's. The desire to do this took him aback. She stood so close to him, he wondered if she felt the same thing, or if he was simply reading her wrong. Nozomi had sometimes accused him of being *kūki yomenai*—unable to read the air.

"Something unexpected came up," she said. "I'm afraid I can't study with you on Sunday evening."

"That's all right." The curtness in his voice was unintended, but for some reason her announcement upset him. "What if we met earlier?"

She looked at the dusky blue sky in which the treetops shook.

"Do you mind going for a picnic?"

It hardly sounded like an environment to study English, but he quickly agreed. "Just us?"

"Riku will spend all day with a village woodworker. I have to speak with the man when I pick Riku up and it might take a while."

"There may be no better day for a picnic."

She smiled, and he realized she was being patient with him. "Let's meet at Yamanaka-za at ten a.m. I'll prepare the picnic tonight."

With that she left him in the lounge.

At 9:59 a.m. Mariko pulled up to Yamanaka-za in her K-car. The morning was already hot. She was wearing a light blue sundress that reached just past her knees, and he saw for the first time her calves and the slight swell where her thighs began. Her arms, too, were bare beneath the light covering of a shawl.

"Good morning," she said. "I hope I'm not late."

"You're a minute early. I bought us cold tea at the Family Mart."

"Thank you." She pointed to a cooler on the back seat. "I made bentos for us. It'll be the first time you've eaten my cooking."

"You made me pie once. Or a slice of it. Afterward I wished I'd had the whole thing."

"That was only something sweet," she said, pulling back onto the road. "I've looked forward to cooking you something more substantial."

He turned again to the back seat. "I'm tempted to eat my bento now."

"No, you can't yet. Or haven't you eaten breakfast?"

"I did," he said, his attention now on the traditional confectionery shops, antiques and crafts stores, and small restaurants they were driving past. "It's just that you've made me hungry again."

"Me?" She laughed. "I guess you meant my talking about food."

He turned to her. "Which meaning would you have preferred?"

She glanced at him with more laughter in her face.

Rather than turn right toward the tunnel that would take them in the direction of Kanazawa, she continued westward through sparsely populated villages known for their crafts, too, as well as small lumber mills, Shinto shrines set back from the road, and eventually rice fields that shimmered into the distance under the bright May sun. Sedge asked if Riku had made it to the woodworker's on time, and their conversation soon turned to the boy's future.

"Is this arrangement with the woodworker something he asked to do?"

"Yes. He likes making things with his hands. But I don't know if he wants to do what his father did. Especially if he won't be as successful. He wants to do something he can surpass him in."

Sedge was pleased to learn about Riku's ambition. "He likely won't find what that is right away."

"You don't think it's possible?"

"Possible and likely are different things. He'll need to be patient. And I'm not sure that's his best quality." When she didn't respond, he added: "And from what I've gathered, he hasn't figured out how to get along with other people. That's the most important thing."

She sighed and shook her head. "Honestly, I'm not sure what he can do. I don't think he'd survive long in a company. Not more than a day, in fact."

"You've really become his mother."

She glanced at him. "I don't think either of us feels that way completely. I'm not sure that's even what I want. But I don't have a choice. And neither does he."

As they passed rice fields in whose standing water crows and herons fed, Sedge watched the smoke from a farmer's refuse fire turn part of the blue sky gray.

"Do you wish you and your wife had started a family?" she said after a moment. The question caught him off-guard, though it was natural to ask considering they'd been talking about her stepson.

"There were times I did," he answered. "We talked about it but never made specific plans. But after what happened, it's better that we didn't."

"Sometimes I wish Kōichi had taken Riku with him. I guess he always knew he'd have a better chance with other women if his son stayed behind. I feel sorry for Riku. More than anything, I suppose that's the main feeling I have for him."

Sedge didn't know what to say. He pitied Riku, too.

"That must sound terrible of me," she said after a moment. "I'm sorry."

"It's understandable. I'd feel the same way, and I'm sure anyone else would, too."

"Riku probably knows deep down how I feel. I think it's one reason he misbehaves so much. He can't help it, you know. And I'm partly to blame."

"Who says it's fair to you to have to live like this?"

"But like I said, I don't have a choice."

She looked at him again. Sensing that she wanted him to confirm this, he gazed once more into the watery green expanse that stretched to faraway farmhouses. He could see she was stuck with Riku and that it was disruptive for them both.

"Let's not talk about it anymore," she said, as if she knew what he was thinking.

A new topic of conversation didn't come easily. They arrived at Katano Kamoike bird sanctuary a few minutes later, having hardly said another word to each other.

🐦 🐦 🐦

Sitting on a bench side-by-side, they peered at the pond before them through telescopes mounted in the sanctuary's indoor observation room. Speakers in the marshy grass captured the cacophony of frogs and various birds. Sedge aimed his telescope to the side, where several herons stepped gingerly through shallow water. A moment earlier, Mariko saw an osprey pluck a fish from the pond and disappear into the tops of the surrounding broadleaf trees. She had cried out, hoping the fish would wrest itself from the osprey's grasp. She was now trying to identify all the birds at the pond's far end, perhaps a half-kilometer from where they sat: ducks, cormorants, kites, and—based on a choice of three birds Sedge named—what she guessed was a golden eagle.

"There are garganeys and grebes out there, too," he said.

"I don't know what those are."

He focused his telescope on an area closer to them. "Look through mine." She scooted toward him and he leaned slightly into her. Her bare arms were soft and warm.

"How do you know them so well?" she said, her eye pressed to the telescope.

"Maybe I was a bird in a previous life."

"I wonder what kind."

He laughed. "Probably a working-class bird, like a sparrow or barn swallow. Something most people don't get excited about."

"You're being modest."

"In Japan, maybe I'd be a rare bird. But it would probably be common in America."

She withdrew from the telescope and laughed, her shining eyes lingering on his.

Two young families entered the sanctuary. The noise of their children, excited more by the telescopes than by what they helped them see, hastened Sedge and Mariko's departure.

"I was getting hungry anyway," he said as they walked back to her car.

"I'm afraid I packed chicken for lunch."

"It's okay. The ospreys and hawks we saw won't judge us badly."

She drove them to a tall, wooded hill amid rice fields with no houses around. From the shoulder of a country road where they parked, he spotted an overgrown path to its top. A *torii* gate stood there with a weathered *shimenawa* rope stretched across it, indicating a Shinto shrine. She said that from the top, such a cloudless day would give them a perfect view of the sea.

"How do you know this place?" he said, lifting her cooler from the back seat.

"In high school, I once wrote a history paper on local Shinto shrines. I researched about a dozen before choosing this one. Its location and the spiritual feeling I had when I visited drew me to it. My mother drove me here on her day off work. She said it was one of the nicest shrines she'd ever been to. She loved the view of the rice fields and ocean, and the breeze that cooled us on the hot day we went. It made her happy to come here, and she was almost never happy. It was like she discovered a different world. We came here a few times, and our visits may be the nicest memories I have of her."

"What made her unhappy?"

"My father."

That was all she said about it as she led him up the hill. He could almost believe that Mariko's childhood visit was the last time anyone had come here. Stepping in front of her, he brushed away the cobwebs hanging over the path. Somewhat out of breath, they made it to the *torii* and bowed toward the shrine at the end of a short approach.

When they reached the shrine, Mariko waved him to a narrower path he hadn't noticed, which wound behind the shrine and through a copse of *sugi* trees. In a minute they emerged on the opposite side of the mountain, lower than where they'd been. Here the view opened even more. Despite the highway near the ocean, where cars were small as ants, he sensed that no one in the world could find them here.

"Riku told me once that the rice fields below, and the Daishōji River in the distance, are breeding grounds for herons this time of year." She pointed to where she meant. "That's another reason I wanted to take you here. Can you see them?"

Two or three herons stood in each field, and there were perhaps thirty fields altogether unfurling toward the sea. Even the river, miniaturized by distance, had herons circling above it. Sedge gazed out below them in wonder, then pointed further into the distance. "They must nest along the Daishōji where those trees cluster together."

"Do you suppose they're here in winter, too?"

"They're here year-round, but in winter their numbers decline. In the colder months they sometimes fly to Okinawa. They leave but come back." He paused. "This vantage point is incredible."

"I'm glad you like it."

She led him to the shade of a large tree out of sight of the shrine, to a place presumably no longer on its grounds. They laid out a plastic sheet where they could sit and eat. She handed him a bento and took one for herself. She had made small portions of grilled chicken and sliced omelet, shredded cabbage and tomato, macaroni salad, two small *onigiri*, and a single slice of orange. Between them she placed their bottled teas.

Gazing over the landscape while they ate, she laughed unexpectedly; smiling at her, he asked what was funny.

"I came here once with Kōichi. But we didn't make it to the top. It was raining and he only had *geta* on his feet. You can imagine how hard it would be to climb this hill in the rain wearing wooden sandals." She paused. "This is the kind of place he and Riku might have come to, though. Just the two of them."

"Why is that?"

"I don't know. I guess he had a hard time being with me."

They were quiet for a moment. "Even when Riku wasn't around?" Sedge asked.

"When he and I were at home together, Riku was usually there, too. It was only at night that we were ever really alone. When we went to bed, I mean."

Sedge tried to think of what to say—to connect her husband's difficulty being alone with her to their usually being alone only in bed—but in the end he didn't need to.

She continued: "He was never able to satisfy me was why, I think. When we went to bed, he was usually too drunk to do anything but collapse beside me and fall sleep. And he was too selfish to spend just one night a week not drinking." She shook her head, and Sedge wondered if she regretted the life she'd wasted with him. "Then he found your wife, which I must admit amazes me. One thing that makes me feel less bad about him leaving is that

I know he won't satisfy her, either. Maybe you've noticed that I never call her his lover. It's not just to spare you. I'm sure it would be a misnomer." She grew more serious. "But maybe he's different with other women, and that's why he runs off with them."

This news was not unwelcome, but it made Nozomi's disappearance even more difficult to understand. Why would she run away with someone who drank as much as Mariko said, and couldn't—or could only rarely—satisfy her physically?

"Riku swears he'll kill him if he comes back to us."

"Do you really think he would?"

"It's hard to know. Riku hasn't learned how to control his emotions. Their reuniting isn't something I want to witness."

An invisible passage through the air seemed to connect the river in the distance with the rice fields surrounding their hilltop. Several herons flew between them as Sedge and Mariko finished their bentos.

"Do you expect your wife to come back?" she asked him.

"It doesn't matter to me anymore," he said, only half-sure of what he was saying. Watching the herons he'd been tracking grow smaller, he added: "It's hard to believe she could have severed her connections to everyone. No matter how much she might have wanted to get away, to put her life here behind her—it doesn't make sense."

"You didn't get drunk every night, did you?"

"No," he said. "We never had issues being alone."

She laughed lightly, uncomfortably. "Lately Riku has become curious about sex. It's not something I was prepared for. I've only been a mother—a stepmother, I mean—for five years."

"He's sixteen; it's natural. But how do you know?"

Although she'd raised the subject, she hesitated to explain. Her hesitancy made him wonder if Riku's sexual interest involved her.

"I recently bought him a membership to Yūyūkan, the baths near our house," she said. "There was a reason for that." Last month, she explained, when she was soaking in the bath at home, Riku started passing back and forth in front of the glass-paneled door. And though the glass is clouded, one can detect movement through it, and one can see the colors of a person's skin and hair. Soon after this started, she discovered his semen on the shower floor two days in a row. There was no question in her mind that he'd meant for her to. And once, after Sedge had come over to teach her English, Riku tried to get in bed with her, saying a centipede had crawled into his futon and he was afraid to sleep there. When she made him leave, he had an erection. "There was no missing it because he stood staring at it for several seconds. I told him that if he ever did that again he'd have to find somewhere else to live. He quietly left, but a moment later the front door opened and slammed shut, and I knew he went into the kura to bash whatever he could find there. I thought he learned his lesson because he's been better behaved the last few weeks."

"That's a terrible situation for you to be in," Sedge said angrily. He was upset but somehow unsurprised by what she'd told him.

Tears started to collect on her cheeks. "It's not that I mind him becoming a man," she said. "He nearly is one already."

"But it's not normal to direct one's sexual urges towards one's stepmother," Sedge quickly said.

"I just wish I hadn't had him foisted onto me. Kōichi guessed right that if he abandoned Riku, I'd take care of him. All I ever wanted was a normal marriage. A man to say he loved me once or twice a year, a man who wanted to satisfy me if only just occasionally."

They were the saddest words he'd heard her say. "Is that all you really want? You don't feel you deserve more?"

"Deserve more? But that would mean I don't appreciate all I already have. And I don't want to be that kind of person."

He put his hand on hers, and she leaned into him, her weight knocking them both to the plastic sheet. Their tea bottles spilled and rolled down the hill as she steered him on top of her, and in confusion he positioned himself to protect her from a cascade of leaves and branches that never came.

His eyes stayed open to take her in as she pressed her mouth against his and her hands shot up and down his arms and shoulders. She forced them under his weight to his chest then back around to squeeze his buttocks. Her hands as they worked over him brought him dizzily into her world, here on a wooded hill, while below them herons filled the distance between the water-filled rice fields and the blue rippling sea.

She sat up to undress, and when she had unbuttoned the top half of her sundress, she hurried it down before grabbing his belt and undoing it. He stopped her momentarily, because even with her passion unleashed he didn't want them to race through this moment.

The scars from rescuing herons that she had told him about stood out raised and pink on her skin—two navel-like puckerings between her stomach and ribs, a slash beneath a breast, a furrow high on one thigh—and she fell toward him, preventing him from gazing at them longer.

They hadn't fully undressed before he found his way inside her. She came so quickly it was almost impossible to think her husband had been unable to satisfy her.

He waited for Mariko to finish convulsing before pulling out of her. When only a small stream spilled forth from him she lunged toward him again, still hungry to give everything of herself. Her vigorousness surprised him, and he wondered if her husband had taught her to be this way, that she had to work so hard to elicit a response. He drew her closer so there was intimacy instead of only the act itself.

He was struck by how unlikely this moment was. And yet there was an inevitability to it, too. And a desperation that propelled it. Both of them were lonely and needed someone who understood that hollowing-out which being abandoned had made them suffer. He knew that what they were doing was healing to them both.

Afterward, as they lay in silence, he didn't feel they had made love at all, though his feelings for her had come to approximate that.

Her hand traced a circle on his ribs. "We should go back in half an hour." Almost as soon as she said this, her hand dropped and he realized she'd fallen asleep against his shoulder.

With her pressed against him, warm and half-naked, he nodded off, too. But a heron's croaking soon awakened him. A white streak passed overhead. He could have sworn the heron was staring down at them, and that its cry had been one of surprise.

11

On Wednesday morning, after returning from the Bashō museum in town, he found slipped beneath his door a small envelope. He took it to the table by the window. Assuming that Mariko had brought it, he was surprised that it had come instead from Yuki.

> I hate to bear bad news, but Takahashi's father passed away early this morning. I'm sorry, but that's all I can tell you now. We have to go to Kanazawa immediately. When there's more to tell you, we'll be in touch.
> Yuki

Death had come for his father-in-law sooner than Sedge had imagined. Had he been so gravely ill, or had there been unforeseen complications? He and Nozomi's father had never really been close, yet they'd always treated each other respectfully. Her father had liked to drink, and there were occasions when he and Sedge sipped sake together at his house, in an *izakaya*, or during visits to the ryokan. He wondered again if Nozomi had known he was hospitalized, or if she knew now that he was dead.

The note on the table drew his attention. Yuki and Takahashi sometimes slid notes under his door when he wasn't around or didn't want to inconvenience him. And though they had been in a hurry to drive to Kanazawa, he resented that they hadn't at least telephoned him with the news. Perhaps they hadn't wanted to invite his questions, or deal with a possible request to accompany them, but until he and Nozomi divorced he would view himself as part of her family. So short a note pained him; it offended him that they could simply cast him aside the same way Nozomi had and that her mother seemed inclined to do. Was it a last hope they had cut him off from? A disparagement of their connection to each other's lives? Trying to suppress his anger, he reassured himself with Yuki's final comment that they would talk to him about things later.

But as the day wore on and he heard nothing, he was even surer he'd been forsaken. At the same time, he didn't want to force himself on a family crisis in which he was unwelcome, where his presence would make things worse for himself than they already were. What disappointed him the most was the implication that he was to blame for what Nozomi had done. To him, this was what being kept at arm's length by her family meant.

His father-in-law's death distracted him from planning his English lesson and from the job research and apartment hunting he had gotten in the habit of doing. Rather than go to the tea lounge to see Mariko, he stayed cooped up in his room all day, not even bothering to have lunch.

By four p.m., though, he wanted to be outside. On his way to take a bicycle ride, he detoured to the front desk for any news about Takahashi and Yuki's return. To his surprise, Yuki was there, busying herself with the check-in ledger.

"Did you just get back?" he said, coming up to her.

"About twenty minutes ago. I had to check in a tour group that arrived at the same time."

"How is Takahashi?"

"He's taking it hard, of course. He'll stay with his mother tonight, and I'll go up again tomorrow first thing."

He noted her black mourning dress and remembered that he had a suit in his room, but it was navy, not black. He would have to find a more appropriate one to wear when the time came. "Did the doctors think his father was in such danger?"

"He clearly wasn't well. But they expected him to recover. It was a shock to everyone."

"I guess the funeral will happen soon."

Yuki nodded. "Takahashi and his mother are planning it. The body's been moved to a prefectural morgue. Soon there will be a small ceremony and viewing, followed by his cremation. If I'm gone for the next few days, that's why. I've already notified our managerial staff, and they'll let the workers know the situation, too."

Sedge tensed at hearing her plans. "You said you'll likely be gone for the next few days?"

"Depending on what Takahashi needs from me. Once he and his mother arrange what's necessary, I'll go to Kanazawa to lend a hand."

"What will my role be?"

"Your role?"

Her confusion made him doubt the accuracy of his Japanese. "Am I not invited to help or to attend? He was my father-in-law, too."

"The viewing will be public. A few of our staff may go. You could join them if you'd like."

"You're lumping me together with your staff? Surely I should be given some meaningful responsibility."

Her tired eyes widened. "I'm the wife of the family's first son. Doesn't that explain why my role is greater than yours?"

"I understand that. But am I no longer part of the family? It would be nice if I could grieve with the rest of you and had the chance to say goodbye to Nozomi's father."

"I don't make these decisions. But frankly, I don't think that now is the right time to get angry."

He lowered his voice, though he didn't think it had grown louder. In any case, he thought his anger was justified. "And when might that be?"

From the corner of his eye, he saw the front desk staff shift their weight and shuffle papers uncomfortably on the counter.

Yuki's voice cracked with emotion. "I keep thinking that if Nozomi were here, I'd tell you to take it up with her. But she's not, so I can't. It makes me wonder why you can't keep your anger directed at her and not at the rest of the family. I hope you'll reconsider your feelings before Takahashi comes back. Your self-ishness at such a sensitive time is beneath you, don't you think?"

He paused to let her words circle back to her. But now that they'd left her mouth, she failed to consider how they applied to her. "If anyone could be accused of that, it's all of you," he told her, as calmly as he could. "Until Nozomi and I are divorced, I'm still part of the family."

"I think we should stop talking," she said, her own anger discernable beneath a forced smile. "Surely we both have more important things to do than bicker at such an unfortunate time."

Sickened by how things were unfolding, and no longer trusting himself not to inflame matters, he nodded and returned her bow. She disappeared into a rear office without another word.

As he stepped outside, he wondered if he had lashed out at her because of Nozomi's absence. But it was hard to dismiss the feeling that she and Takahashi had shown him little sympathy aside from letting him live at the ryokan. He wasn't sure how much credence to give to what Yuki had just said, as she could hardly claim to speak for Takahashi or his mother.

Before he knew what he was doing, he returned to the lobby. He wasn't finished talking to Yuki, though he hoped that being surrounded by ryokan staff would ensure a degree of civility between them.

She had changed from her black dress into her normal work kimono, and stood again behind the check-in desk, speaking with a guest about a series of Meiji-period photos hanging in a corridor. When she spotted Sedge, she stopped speaking momentarily. He waited for the guest to leave before approaching her.

"Can I help you with something, Sedge?" she said, her voice outwardly pleasant but her countenance stiff.

"I forgot to ask how I can send Nozomi's mother my condolences. I thought you might be willing to advise me."

"I don't know that they're necessary, but I'll ask Takahashi when I see him. If you'll excuse me . . ." She turned away again. He raised his voice to make sure she heard him.

"Can you tell me what Nozomi plans to do about the funeral?"

Before she looked around at him, he glanced toward the tea lounge. Mariko was watching him while cleaning the surface of a table. He imagined she was too far away to hear their conversation clearly.

"I can't believe you think we have any idea where she is."

"She's on my mind at a time like this. I'm sure she's on all of yours as well."

"Since I've made it clear that I can't help you with her, you'll need to find someone telepathic. But maybe Nozomi herself is, and there's nothing for you to worry about. In that scenario, she would already know her father is dead."

Her boldness gave Sedge pause. And in that moment, she continued.

"We have no idea what's happened to Nozomi. Only that she left you and took more from you than she had any right to. I promise that at this very moment Takahashi and his mother are beside themselves trying to find some way to reach her. Have you made any new efforts to?"

Sedge acceded her a certain point, but he was no less angry for being made out as the villain in all of this. Yet he was aware that by arguing with her he risked his welcome at the ryokan. Had he already overstepped his bounds?

"Again, please let me know how I can send Nozomi's mother my condolences. Or if there's anything else I might be allowed to do."

Yuki nodded, her body relaxing. "I will," she said. "I can't promise when, but I will."

He returned to his room, having given up the idea of a bike ride. Instead, he grabbed a small and large towel and went downstairs to soak in the hot baths, eager to clear his mind. For the first time since coming here, he was troubled that he'd stayed too long. But if he didn't remain for the foreseeable future, where was he to go?

Still hot from the baths, he couldn't stop sweating. He sat directly in the air conditioner's stream, blotting his face and chest with the hem of his open *yukata*.

He had managed to focus his energy on two language-school interviews he'd lined up for next week. He considered the work a step down from the shop he'd run, but he recognized he was more likely to be hired as an English teacher than in the field of Arts Management he'd studied and worked in. None of the ceramics shops in Yamanaka Onsen, most of which were family run, had any need for him. On the off chance he was offered a position at either school, the work wouldn't start right away. If he was lucky, a better job would present itself in the meantime. He had little faith in that happening, however.

Mariko came by after finishing her work. She had only visited before to deliver his meals or to change his bedclothes. It had been over a month since she'd last come. She entered his room quickly, looking over her shoulder as he shut the door behind her.

"This is unlike you," he said, kissing her. It was an awkward exchange, but she looked happy afterward. It was their first kiss since she'd taken him to the hilltop. "Isn't it dangerous coming to my room like this? My dinner will arrive soon, you realize."

She looked around them, and he remembered again that she and Riku had stayed here once.

"I wanted to know if everything was okay," she said.

"Why wouldn't it be?"

"I saw you arguing with Yuki. It must have been about something important since it happened in the lobby. I've watched her get angry before, but never where guests might see. It worried me."

"My father-in-law died this morning."

"I know. An announcement was made in today's staff meeting."

"We weren't particularly close, but I like to think we had a decent relationship. He was helpful to my wife and me during our marriage, and as he got older we tried to do as much as we could for him. Of course, there's going to be a funeral for him . . . Buddhist services . . . a cremation. All important family events."

Her eyebrows nearly came together as she concentrated on what he'd said.

"Takahashi and his family—I don't know who exactly—are keeping me at a distance. So I had it out a bit with Yuki earlier today. Or she had it out with me."

"I heard you both from the lounge, but I couldn't make out anything. That explains why you looked upset."

"Shouldn't there be some acknowledgment or clarification of my position within their family?"

He knew she couldn't answer why they were excluding him, though she could guess at any number of reasons as easily as he.

"Maybe it's time I consider leaving," he said. "I can't right away. But I've been contacted about two teaching jobs and will interview for them soon. One is just outside of Kanazawa, the other in Fukui. I doubt I'll be the first choice at either school, though. If that's the case, I'm back at square one."

They turned toward the door as someone hurried down the hall.

"I thought I heard Yuki mention your wife's name," she said.

He looked at her. "I've decided to contact the bank from where she stole my money and talk to the police. It's a place to start, though it's hard to believe it took me almost a year to do. And even if Takahashi and Yuki asked me not to involve the police in what she did."

"I always hoped you would."

"I'm doing it partly for you."

Mariko's eyes widened. "For me?"

"To prove I'm over her."

"You don't have to prove anything. Not to me."

She leaned into him with her head curled into his chest. He could feel her breathing, and her hand pushing up to wipe at her eyes.

He kissed her again in the *genkan*.

When she opened the door to leave, she gasped. Ducking her head, she half-ran down the corridor and out of sight. Yuki watched her go.

"I never took you for an eavesdropper," Sedge said.

"Are you saying Mariko was here long enough for the two of you to be eavesdropped on? Really, you should both be more careful. Especially her. We don't pay her to visit our guests privately."

"What did you come here for?"

"Not for what Mariko came for."

He didn't say to Yuki what he wanted to—he was at a disadvantage, and Mariko even more than he.

"I was going to apologize for what I said about Nozomi. I

thought your memory of her was still painful. Apparently, I was mistaken."

"She was only checking on me. She heard our argument in the lobby this afternoon."

"You don't have to explain."

Despite what she said, she stood in the doorway as if she expected him to tell her everything that had passed between them. The silence grew.

"Next time there's something to tell you," she finally said, "I'll have Takahashi come do it."

Behind her, the cart with his dinner came rattling down the hall. Yuki stepped aside as the man delivering it approached Sedge's door.

"You're certainly being well fed," she said, and the surprise on her face looked genuine. "Bon appétit. Enjoy it while it lasts."

12

Sedge was winding down from his English class, sitting by the back window of his room, which he'd pulled open so only a screen separated him from outside. Crickets and frogs were competing over who could make more noise, and through the wire mesh a pleasant breeze blew.

Outside, insects gripped the screen, and as he gently flicked them off, his room phone rang. The only people who called on it were Yuki and Takahashi, but normally they didn't bother him this late. His students had told him that Takahashi was due back from Kanazawa tonight. Sedge, however, hadn't seen him. A minute later his cell phone rang. Takahashi's name flashed on it, and Sedge picked it up.

"Sorry I didn't answer the room phone. I have a headache and didn't want to move."

"That's all right. I may have some pills if you think they'd help."

"I'm self-treating with a couple drinks."

"Sake?"

"I bought a bottle of Tengumai from the gift shop."

"How about coming to the lounge? I can pour us a drink from my own stock."

Though exhausted, Sedge realized that now, when most of the staff had gone home and Yuki was probably in bed, was an ideal time for them to meet. He agreed, and Takahashi said he could be there in fifteen minutes.

"It'll be like the old talks we used to have," Takahashi said. "When you stayed here with Nozomi but it was only the two of us, late at night drinking and soaking in the *rotenburo* outside. Times have changed, haven't they?"

In the lounge, Sedge sat at a different table than normal, within clear view of the check-in desk. Normally at night two people manned it, but with no guests present they had stepped into a lighted office to the rear. Takahashi greeted Sedge as he walked past him into the lounge kitchen.

"I haven't seen you in a while," Sedge said after Takahashi returned with a bottle of sake and two glasses. "I was shocked and saddened to hear about your father."

"His condition was worse than the doctors realized. They assured us he didn't suffer. I guess that's a silver lining if any exists."

Takahashi told him about his father's second stroke, and about how his mother had been at his side when he passed.

"I asked Yuki how I might send your mother my condolences," Sedge said. "She told me that one of you would let me know later. It was too bad I couldn't take part in what the family organized."

Takahashi let out a long sigh, and Sedge winced. He knew Takahashi had heard criticism in his words. But Sedge had spoken gently, and less confrontationally than he'd spoken with Yuki.

"I can share your condolences with her. There's nothing you really need to do beyond that. I'm not sure how much she remembers what specific people have done."

"I'm not asking because I think she expects it. It's something I want to do on behalf of your father, whom I loved and respected."

Takahashi lowered his head and nodded solemnly. When he raised his head again, his eyes glistened. "It's traditional to give some money, but in your case it's not necessary."

"Is my case that I'm close family, or that I have no money?"

Takahashi smiled tiredly. "Both, I suppose."

Sedge continued to speak in a quiet, sincere tone. "Because if I'm considered close family, it would have been nice to attend his Buddhist ceremony or even his cremation."

"You understand, of course, that it wasn't possible. Yuki said she explained it to you. I don't know why you want to talk about it with me, too. I'm exhausted, you realize."

"I want to talk about it with you because you're now my main connection to the family I married into."

Takahashi gazed into his sake glass for a long time before mumbling, "To my mother, Nozomi's being away for a year with another man means the two of you are divorced. She didn't want you there without Nozomi because it might have started people talking."

"But that's ridiculous."

Takahashi didn't say anything and Sedge saw that arguing about it further was pointless.

They drank in silence, gazing out the window at the pond and the night that had long ago settled around it. Takahashi glanced at the registration counter several times, and Sedge anticipated an excuse to cut their conversation short. Finally, Takahashi turned back and, finishing the sake in his glass, bent his head over the table and sighed again deeply.

"It would be nice if Mariko were here, don't you think? I'd like to sit back and let her pour for us."

Sedge didn't know how to respond. Was Takahashi taking him into his confidence, or was he setting him up so he could knock him down a notch?

"She works enough as it is."

"Yes, she does," Takahashi agreed. "If anything happened to Yuki and I was left on my own, Mariko would be top of my list to replace her." He laughed, though Sedge didn't feel like he'd made a joke. When Sedge frowned in distaste, Takahashi said more seriously, "She's a sight for sore eyes, anyway. It's one reason I like her working where I can see her. I assume you feel the same way, otherwise you wouldn't come here every day. Or keep teaching at her house after I asked you not to."

"Is it really any of your business what I do?" Sedge said.

Takahashi glanced up from the table at Sedge, his face set hard. When he sat up again, his features returned to normal.

"Another reason I invited you here for a drink," Takahashi went on, not bothering to answer the question, "was because of things I've heard about your English classes."

"Oh?" More than what Takahashi had said about Mariko, the comment caught Sedge off-guard.

"I had a staff meeting before any of this with my father happened. I guess it was a week and a half ago. I asked how everyone's English skills were progressing, and though it was a casual question, one I didn't really expect serious answers to, the floodgates opened. All I heard were complaints. One or two staff members said you prepared well, but everyone agreed that they didn't want to continue with your classes."

Sedge looked out the window again. The darkness over the pond had deepened suddenly. "I see. But why did no one approach me about this? I would have been happy to make changes."

"I wondered the same thing. They said you were unapproachable."

Sedge couldn't make sense of it. Nothing had ever indicated that his students were dissatisfied with his classes, and he constantly asked them for feedback. Three weeks ago, after he'd finished his first month of teaching, he had even given them a short survey to fill out anonymously and return to him. Their only complaints were that the class met late and that the classroom was either too hot or too cold. He distrusted what Takahashi said. His skepticism grew as he recalled Takahashi telling his mother during their last visit together that he'd been doing an excellent job of teaching his staff.

"I don't know what to say. Maybe I can have a heart-to-heart talk with them next week and try to meet their expectations better."

"Yuki and I think it's too late for that. Once the staff makes up its collective mind, it never goes back. We've decided that tonight's class was your final one."

Sedge stared at his empty sake glass. "That's not premature?"

"I'm afraid not. I think the students might have felt this even from your very first class."

Sedge knew he was lying now. He guessed what was coming next, and he looked up at Takahashi as the anticipated words tumbled from his mouth.

"Since we've reached this decision about your classes, and you've been here long enough to get back on your feet—long enough to form a serious relationship with Mariko, I understand—we think it's better if you leave the ryokan. Yuki suggested one week from today, but I'll give you a few days more."

"Of course," Sedge said, trying to swallow the tremor in his voice. "I'll start looking for a new place immediately."

"We're glad you understand. It's one of those things that can't be helped."

Sedge stood as Takahashi poured himself another glass of sake. Standing over him, Sedge calculated that by the time he moved out he'd have lived here for nearly two months of the four they'd promised him. He could hardly complain. Had they not been so generous with him, he didn't know where he might be now. He was doing his best to remain positive.

"Again, I'm sorry about your father. If you decide there's anything I can do . . ."

Takahashi set down his glass and bowed to him.

As far as Sedge was concerned, they had nothing left to talk about.

"Good night," he said.

Takahashi echoed his words, which floated over Sedge's shoulder as he left him alone in the lounge.

13

Sedge stayed up past one a.m. emailing friends as far away as Kyoto, Tokyo, Fukuoka, and even Sapporo, hoping they might have leads for jobs and places to stay. Eventually he fell asleep, but even by the next afternoon he hadn't received a single reply.

His breakfast came as it always did, and though he remained grateful for it, it was of a different quality now: a hard-boiled egg, slice of toast, and coffee. It was more than enough; even so, it proved his time here had come to an end. That Takahashi or Yuki had instructed the kitchen to do this struck him as unnecessary. He didn't need reminding that this was their ryokan and they were in charge.

Over the next few days most of the staff kept their distance from him, and his dinners came to resemble his breakfasts. The most uncomfortable development was that Mariko had again been transferred, and he had no chance to see her in the tea lounge. Even the bicycles stored in the parking garage were fitted with cheap chain locks, whereas before they'd been left unsecured and anyone could borrow them. He had been one of the only guests to make use of them. With the weather, especially in the afternoons, marked by torrents of rain, he couldn't make it to the places he most liked to go.

Sunday, however, was sunny. After being told that the ryokan's bicycles needed maintenance and couldn't be used, Sedge found a tourist office that rented them, and he paid to use one until tomorrow.

His intended destination was the bird reserve he and Mariko had gone to. He knew it took an hour to ride to the sea, and since the reserve was only a mile before it, he thought he could make it there and back without exhausting himself, and with time to wash and eat before teaching her.

Although the way to the reserve wended through a string of rural villages and towns, he avoided the major roads as much as he could, riding down asphalt paths between rice fields. All the while he worried about what he would do when he left the ryokan in less than a week. He could probably rent an old apartment in town with what little money he had, but it would only prolong his situation and perhaps leave him with nothing, finally, as the long winter approached.

The afternoon grew hot, forcing him to stop once for cold tea at a vending machine in the shade of an abandoned community center. Along the way were irrigated rice fields that mirrored the bright summer sky.

At one point, however, perhaps halfway to the bird reserve, he spotted a gray-white mass thrashing about on the shoulder of a road. When it paused, as if tired, he realized it was a heron.

He looked around for help, but there was no one in the surrounding fields. A small service truck was parked up ahead, and a tractor stood with its wheels half-sunk in the corner of a nearby plot, but whoever the vehicles belonged to was nowhere to be seen. On an afternoon as hot as this, anyone smart would be indoors. There was a reason, he understood now, why he hadn't seen anyone else bicycling.

On his phone he looked up the bird reserve, but when he dialed it he couldn't get through. He tried Mariko's number, too, but she didn't answer, and over the next few minutes she didn't call back.

Four crows on a telephone wire stared down at the injured bird. Beyond them, an equal number of hawks circled in the sky. A vehicle must have struck the heron within the last half-hour, but in that time none of these birds had finished it off. If he left it, however, he expected they would.

He spotted a cardboard box on a dike two rice fields away. After shouting a warning to the crows, he ran to check its condition. Though not as stiff as new cardboard, he hazarded that it was sturdy enough to hold the injured heron. As luck would have it, a pair of muddy work gloves had been left twenty feet away. They were small, but he pulled them on enough to protect himself if the bird attacked him with its sharp beak.

He ran back to the road. Two crows had dropped from the telephone wire and were hopping around the heron, only a few inches from its head. Sedge waved the box to scare them off. Now that he was within a few meters of them, they flapped lackadaisically to their former perches.

The heron squawked as Sedge stood over it. It swung its head to stab at his shoes, and he stepped backward, wondering how he would transfer a bird its size into the box and carry it on his bicycle, all while keeping it from lashing out at him.

He removed the shoelace to one of his shoes. Circling slowly around the heron, thinking his pace would partly determine the bird's panic level, he sought an angle from which he could safely lunge toward it, for the first thing he had to do was tie its beak shut. From directly above its head he reached for it. The bird's beak opened in a deafening squawk, but as soon as it snapped shut he gripped it like he would a stick. He knotted the shoelace around it. Holding the beak with one hand again, he carefully slipped his hand beneath its body. Considering its size, and the deceptive power he knew it possessed, he was taken aback—as he had been in Kenrokuen—by the bird's lightness. Using the underside of his arm like a stretcher, he lifted and slid the bird into the box. He wished he had something with which to cover its eyes, but this would have to do. The bird reserve was still far away, and even if he rode there he wasn't sure they could help him.

The bird lay in the box, its injuries unclear to Sedge. Remembering that Mariko had experience helping injured herons, he decided to bring the bird to her house. He rode with it balanced atop the bicycle's handlebars, steadying it with one hand. He went slowly, sweating more than he had all day, and hoped it wouldn't start raining.

Sedge worried that the heron would try to escape, but he soon saw this was unwarranted. And luckily the raised sides of the box kept it from falling, even while it slid back and forth. He pedaled carefully so his unlaced shoe wouldn't fall off. If it did, he would have to move the bird again to retrieve it, and he wanted to keep it where it was.

The rice fields brought him back through a succession of villages. As the houses and buildings increased, so did the people driving in cars, playing with their children in the shade of their houses, and gardening in their yards. Thankfully no one said anything to him, no one asked where he was carrying an injured heron with a shoelace tied around its beak, nor did he stop to ask them for help. He was afraid of becoming a spectacle, which would only frighten the bird more and result in losing time he might not have to lose. Now that he was more accustomed to balancing on his handlebars a large bird in a rotting cardboard box, he increased his speed until hitting another stretch of road.

Eventually he reached the outskirts of Yamanaka Onsen, where traffic was greater and the roads more often needed repair. Whenever possible, he veered onto side streets parallel to the main road he needed to follow, and in a few minutes he arrived in the middle of the town.

He had never considered Yamanaka Onsen a busy place, for

compared to Kanazawa it was *inaka*—the countryside—but it was more crowded now than he could ever remember, and dangerous to ride a bicycle in. He finally came upon Yamanaka-za. Because tourists congested the sidewalks, he stayed in the road, forcing cars and tourist buses to drive around him.

A mile or so later, he turned left and had in his sights Takase Bridge as it crossed Kakusenkei gorge. Where the road curved right, at the bottom of the mountainside, he only had to climb uphill a little farther.

The heron was no longer struggling, and when its eyes blinked they stayed closed for longer. All he hoped now was that Mariko could help when he showed it to her.

Even before her house came into view, Riku cut into his line of vision, running back and forth in the street. He was chasing dragonflies, or simply following their flitting overhead.

"Rik-kun!" he cried out.

Riku stopped and turned to Sedge. His eyebrows lifted as he peered at whatever was lying in the box atop the handlebars.

"Get Mariko," he said. As he slowed the bike down and put both feet on the ground, the boy stumbled toward the front door. Riku slid it open until it slammed against the wall. "Okaasan!" he shouted.

Mariko stepped outside. Riku ran past her into the street, eager to see the bird.

"The poor thing," Mariko said. "Your bicycle couldn't have done that to it. Did someone hit it with their car?"

"It could have been a dog," Riku speculated.

"I don't know what happened to it. I'm sorry, but I didn't know where else to take it." He explained how he'd found it and that he'd tried to call the bird reserve and then her.

Mariko patted her clothes and admitted that she must have left her phone upstairs. "I'm sorry. I never imagined . . ."

Sedge handed her his phone. "Do you mind calling the reserve and leaving a message?"

She took the phone from him. He watched her dial, and to his surprise someone picked up on the other end. It was clear from what Mariko said that the veterinarian wasn't there and that nothing could be done for the bird right away. She thanked the person and hung up.

"The vet will be back tomorrow morning," she said. "It's just as well you didn't go there."

"Can we keep it here tonight?" Sedge said.

"Of course. We'll watch over it until morning. And before I go to work I'll drive it to the reserve. How far away did you find it?"

"Maybe forty minutes from here."

"I'll build it something," Riku said. "I can make it a cage big enough to stand and spread its wings partway."

This was more of a plan than Sedge had, and he let Riku lead them to the kura.

Carrying the box, he followed Riku behind the house and up the short steps to the kura, ducking beneath the row of hanging birdhouses to go inside. Despite visiting Mariko at her house half a dozen times, he'd never been inside the storage building. He had been led to believe it was Riku's private space.

Riku obviously didn't mind them entering to check for materials with which to make the bird a temporary shelter. Past the entryway was a flat stone step that led into the kura itself: two floors of storage space, the interior made of earthen walls, thick wooden pillars, and overhead beams. A single light bulb lit the first floor. The near corner had a workshop of sorts, along with scattered manga, school textbooks, magazines with bikini-clad women on the covers, and a box overflowing with paper cranes. In the opposite corner lay a narrow futon enclosed by mosquito netting.

Mariko brushed against Sedge in the cramped entryway, and he returned his attention to her and Riku. "The bird was lying on its back in the road," he said, "so its injury is probably there. But it could be injured anywhere: its head, wings, even its legs."

Riku stepped inside through the kura's heavy sliding door. "Can you give me about an hour?"

Anticipating the noise Riku would make, Sedge and Mariko carried the heron back outside.

"It was good of you to help it," Mariko said.

"Crows and hawks had gathered around it. They were waiting to finish it off."

"I'm glad you didn't let them," she said, rubbing his sweaty arm. "You look a mess."

He set the cardboard box on a wooden bench beside the house. "I'm afraid I can't teach you tonight."

She snuffled a laugh into the crook of his neck. "Go clean yourself up, will you? Tonight I'll cook all of us dinner, and we'll take turns looking after your heron."

"You're not upset I brought it here?"

"It's the last thing I expected, but I'm happy you thought to do so. I told you before, I've tended injured birds several times. And for Riku, this may be a good distraction after his stint as a woodworker's apprentice ended prematurely. He's been difficult lately."

Mariko went back inside to prepare Sedge's bath and collect things for the heron: a towel for it to sit or lie on, a hot water bottle to warm it in case it was in shock, dried cat food softened in water, and an eye dropper to give it fluids. When she came back, he went to clean himself up. She had laid out for him a towel and what were apparently an extra pair of clothes belonging to her husband. He showered and rinsed off thoroughly before entering the hot bath; through the outside window as he soaked, he listened to Riku hammer wood and use an electric drill. In the moments when Riku fell silent, Mariko's voice as she sang softly to the bird was as memorable to him as anything that had happened that day.

Sedge didn't stay in the bath long. Uncomfortable wearing her husband's clothes, he put his own clothes back on and returned to the side of the house.

She laughed when he approached. "You just defeated the whole purpose of taking a bath. Didn't you see the clothes I put out for you?"

"I don't want to wear your husband's clothes."

Her smile faded. "But they're clean. You've just made yourself dirty all over again."

The bird was standing now, a towel wrapped around its body. In its box were some of what Mariko had gathered for it. A meter and a half separated it from her, and it made no move to get away.

"Our guest looks better already," Sedge said. The heron stared toward the *sugi* forest behind the kura, above which the clouds had thinned since Sedge arrived. The sun had fallen behind the trees.

"It was active when you were away. Your presence has calmed it."

They observed it quietly together.

"Now that you're back," she said, "I'd better make dinner. You'll eat with us, won't you?"

He nodded and thanked her.

"Riku will probably want to eat out here," she said, "so he can watch over the bird."

"It might not be a bad idea."

She ran her fingers through his wet hair. "I won't be long," she said, and made her way back inside. Riku continued to hammer at the cage he was building.

The heron began squawking and looking for a place on the ground to jump to. Sedge placed himself wherever it leaned toward, and soon it moved back to the other end of the bench. He watched it from the low wall of Mariko's flowerbed.

Out of the moribund day, as a crow flapped by overhead, new and unwelcome questions flashed through his mind: Did the heron have chicks that relied on it to survive? Did it have a mate that worried why it hadn't returned to its nest? If so, would it risk leaving its young alone to search for it? Although Sedge had learned about herons over the years, these were questions he couldn't answer. When he looked at the bird again, he saw it with these unanswerable questions in mind, and he became more determined to help it. Even if it had chicks that wouldn't survive its absence, at least this heron might survive and be given another chance.

Fifteen minutes later Mariko came back through the carport and down the gravel path. "It's early," she called, "but can you eat now?"

He nodded.

"Come inside. I'll let Riku know dinner's ready, too, and check on what he's been doing."

When she returned with Riku, the boy's shirt was covered in sawdust. "He made a big cage for the heron," she said. "It has bars in the door, but he needs to add hinges."

"That was quick work."

"I can make anything if I have time and materials."

"He says he'll eat outside with the bird. Come on, Riku, let's get you some food."

Sedge and Mariko sat at the dining table. Through the veranda's windows they could see the bench where Riku and the bird shared each other's company.

"The gorge here, Kakusenkei, literally means 'immortal mountain of cranes,'" Mariko said, writing the kanji for Kakusenkei on the table with her finger. "But it's the mountain that's immortal, not the cranes—or herons, for that matter. I hope it recovers."

"If it gets through the night," Sedge said, "I think it stands a decent chance."

Although Sedge looked often toward Riku to make sure he didn't touch the heron or feed it—he had told him not to give it food until they could determine it wasn't in shock—his situation at the ryokan pushed into his thoughts and he asked Mariko if what Takahashi had said about his English class and students a few days ago was true.

She looked surprised hearing the news. "I've overheard the staff talk about your class often. Maybe not after every class, but probably three or four times a week they talk about it with each other. I've never heard anyone complain."

"You don't believe what Takahashi said?"

"It sounds unlikely to me. Maybe it was only one person—someone who decided they didn't like you, or didn't like having to study after work, and they claimed to be speaking for the entire class."

"I've thought about those possibilities."

"But why would Takahashi lie?"

Sedge told her that Takahashi had asked him to leave.

Her face blanched and she spoke with new seriousness. "What are you going to do?"

He leaned back and shrugged. "I still have a little money. It's enough to rent someplace cheap for a few months until I find a job."

"Why did you wait until now to tell me?"

"I didn't want to worry you. Anyway, you haven't been in the lounge recently. Even if you had been, I thought that looking for you might jeopardize your situation."

She glanced at Riku and the bird. "Why don't you stay here tonight?" she asked Sedge.

The offer pleased him, but he worried what Takahashi and Yuki would say if they found out. Not that it was any of their business. "I've never done that before."

"But you might as well now. And early tomorrow morning we'll go together to the bird reserve."

"I'd better call the ryokan to cancel my dinner, though they may have already made it. And breakfast, too. But I'm mostly worried about you."

"But I haven't done anything wrong."

"No," he agreed. "And neither have I. Nothing that can't be forgiven, anyway."

She shook her head dismissively. "I don't care what they do. I might be able to find a different job. Though I wouldn't have the same salary, and with all the low-wage foreign workers Japan's brought in, there aren't as many openings as before. But I'm sure it won't come to that."

Sedge didn't want her to lose her job, but she reassured him repeatedly.

"Has Takahashi done anything I should know about?"

"Nothing so far."

From the corner of his eye he noticed Riku staring at them through the window. The bird continued to stand at the end of the bench, with a towel on its shoulders like a customer at a spa.

After dinner, Riku finished building the cage. He had done a good job, and Sedge trusted it would keep the bird safe overnight and make it easier to transport in the morning. After coaxing the bird inside, they closed the cage door and slid a latch to keep it shut. The heron banged against the bars for a few minutes, but soon gave up its struggle.

The workmanship of the cage was sturdier and of a more complex design than Sedge expected. He was impressed, too, with the speed at which Riku had completed it.

"Thank you for this, Riku. If the bird recovers, you'll be a big reason why."

Riku peered inside the cage. "Do you think it will be all right?"

"It depends on its injuries."

"I guess I'll stay with it tonight."

"Outside?" Sedge said. "You'll get eaten by mosquitoes."

"I don't mind."

The next thing Sedge knew, Riku ran back to the kura. He returned a moment later with a blanket and pillow.

"You don't have to stay," he told Sedge. "You can trust me, you know."

Mariko arranged a futon for Sedge two rooms away from hers. In the middle of the night, however, she tiptoed into his room, slipping under his covers and hugging him. "Riku's watching over the bird. He won't hear us."

When Sedge woke up with sunlight streaming through the *shōji* windows, she was gone. The house had filled with the smells of toast and coffee and also with the thumping of footsteps on the first floor.

He went downstairs and into the dining room. In the veranda, Riku was looking through the window at the bird. He had stayed beside it until Mariko awakened him. The bird, sitting on its towel as if on a brood of chicks, its yellow eyes level with the hump of its back and pinned on Riku's movements, was more lethargic today than yesterday, which worried all three of them.

"Did you hear it in the middle of the night?" Riku asked. "I untied its beak and it started squawking. I had to open the cage and retie that old shoelace around it again."

"Why did you untie it?" Sedge said, glancing at Riku's hands. "It could have cut you badly with its beak."

"I wanted to give it water and food. Anyway, I grabbed it quickly, before it could peck me."

"It would have given you more than a peck. You were lucky."

"Good morning," Mariko said as Sedge walked into the kitchen.

"Good morning." They were careful not to be affectionate in front of Riku, who was observing them. "What time do you want to leave?"

"Riku has to go in an hour. I thought we'd leave then, too, if that's all right."

An hour later Riku left the house; Sedge stood in the kitchen listening to the uneven clomping of him running down the street to meet his bus. When he was gone, Mariko came back from seeing him off. She ran into Sedge's arms. Almost immediately the bird started banging against it cage.

On the way to the bird reserve, Sedge pointed to a road slightly below the one they were on. "That's where I found it." He wanted to inform the veterinarian of this, so when the time came to release it into the wild, they might try to do so as close to there as possible.

She dropped him off with the bird and the bicycle he had rented yesterday, apologizing again for having to leave him alone. She walked the bicycle to the entrance of the observation building while he carried the heron in Riku's cage.

"When will I see you again?" she said.

"It depends on where the ryokan assigns you."

She peered down the road they'd taken here. "I thought I might talk to Riku at dinner this evening. I think he might like having you around more. He seems to have more in common with you than with other men he knows."

"If you think that's best," he said. However, he was unsure why she needed to do this.

"I'm sorry, that's not quite what I wanted to say."

He waited for her to continue.

She didn't speak again right away, perhaps hoping he would understand without her explaining herself. "You said you have to leave the ryokan in several days. But there's no way you'll find anywhere to move to before that. For the time being, I thought you might want to move in with us."

He set the heron down and came closer to hug her. His commitment to her was complicated by the fact that neither of them had explicitly shared what they wanted from each other. He enjoyed being with her and found her as giving and supportive as anyone he could hope to meet. That seemed as good a place to start as any.

"Thank you. But I don't want to move in if he's going to resist. Even if you don't always feel like his mother, the fact is that you are."

"I'll talk to him tonight. I'm sure he doesn't want you to live on the street."

"I don't think it will come to that."

She left him, promising she'd find a way to help him.

After dropping off the heron with the bird veterinarian, Sedge bicycled back to the ryokan feeling happy about the help they'd given it, but his mind kept coming back to Mariko's suggestion that he move in with her and Riku. He didn't want to take advantage of her or hurt her if he struck out on his own eventually, but he also wanted the opportunity to get to know her over time, like he'd had with Nozomi when they worked together for a year at a bilingual arts magazine in Tokyo before they started dating. But was he only using Mariko to replace her, and to salve the scars deep inside himself she had caused? He didn't know.

Moving into Mariko's house would be scandalous to those who knew them—a Japanese woman with an American man, the two of them still married to spouses who'd run off with each other. But perhaps he and Mariko would pretend to have a renter-boarder relationship, as people sometimes did. The bigger concern was Riku. Sedge knew the boy liked him, and at times Sedge felt an affection for him, particularly when they came together over some interest they happened to share. But he also knew Riku had violent tendencies and might feel his claim to his stepmother was being threatened.

If he didn't have to consider the boy, Sedge knew what he would do.

14

Mariko's offer and Sedge's deepening feelings for her encouraged him to research what divorcing Nozomi involved. He learned he could do it without her participation, though it would take time and be difficult. It would also cost more money than he had.

Over the next two days, Takahashi and Yuki were rarely at the front desk, though he knew through Mariko that they weren't necessarily in Kanazawa. Sedge suspected they were avoiding him. Pained by this, he hoped they would all resolve their differences before he left, yet he had come to accept that they probably wouldn't. He was clearly on the outside of Nozomi's family now.

He wondered how much Takahashi's attraction to Mariko had influenced his decision to make Sedge leave. There had been times when Takahashi betrayed his jealousy over Sedge's relationship with her and viewed him as a rival. Sedge didn't want to become Takahashi's enemy, however.

With his departure fast approaching, Mariko came to his room again when she finished work. He let her inside quickly and shut the door. She said she could only stay "a New York minute." He laughed and asked where she'd learned this expression.

"The other staff taught me. They said it had come up in one of your lessons and they found it funny. They use it with each other sometimes and substitute New York for small Japanese towns like this one. They've even used it with foreign guests."

"I guess my teaching wasn't completely wasted on them."

"Not at all." She looked away from him momentarily, her face troubled. "Can you come to dinner tonight? I want you, me, and Riku to talk."

Sedge set out for her home two hours later. He arrived carrying a bundle of dried larkspur he'd bought at a flower shop along the way.

Already the dining table was set, and half the dinner Mariko had prepared was sitting on it. Riku, she told him, was tidying the kura to show them both later. She had put a bottle of local Harugokoro sake where Sedge would sit and was pouring ginger ale for Riku and homemade plum wine for herself.

"I've never seen you drink alcohol before," he said as she set the plum wine on the table.

"The chance just never came up. I don't like being drunk, but I enjoy celebrations. Please don't let Riku drink. Kōichi used to insist on it, and Riku often vomited all night afterward."

When Riku came in, Mariko warmed up the food that had cooled while she and Sedge were waiting for him.

"Have you heard from the veterinarian about the heron?" Riku said by way of greeting, sitting down at the table.

"Not today, no."

"There's been no news since he told you about its broken wing and vertebra?"

"He called once to say it's taking food and water, which usually means that, barring a setback like an infection or a new break in what needs to heal, it will fully recover. But it's still too early to say."

"And if it doesn't? Will they put it down?"

"Only if it's suffering and has no chance to survive. Otherwise, there's a 'Bird Paradise' in Nagano where permanently injured birds can live out their natural lifespans. He said he knows someone there and could get it in if necessary. So far it looks good for the bird."

"What about my cage?"

"Do you want it back?" Mariko said, serving Riku.

"I want him to keep it if he thinks he can use it in the future."

"Maybe you can visit sometime and talk to him about it. Maybe he'll ask you to make more to have on hand in emergencies."

Riku shrugged, as if his only concern was the heron he'd helped.

When they finished dinner, Riku was eager to show them the changes he'd made to the kura.

"In a minute," Mariko said. "You know why we asked Sedge to dinner."

"I don't know anything," he mumbled. "*You* asked him here, not me."

Mariko watched him, her smile fixed, poorly camouflaging her anger. "Okay, but since you agreed to what I suggested, it amounts to the same thing, doesn't it?" She turned to Sedge. "If you'll have us, we'd like you to consider living here. Riku's about to show us the kura he's fixing up to live in, and he says he doesn't care which room you take in the house as long as it's not the same as mine."

"Thank you," Sedge said. "Just so you know, I have no idea how long it will take me to find a full-time job. It could be a few weeks, or it could be longer. I've been unlucky finding decent full-time work. Not even souvenir shops here or in Yamashiro Onsen want to hire me."

"There's lots of work around the village and town," Riku said. "Handyman jobs and company drivers, for example. I could help you look for one if you want."

Riku's unexpected offer touched Sedge. "Thanks, Riku. But for the next few weeks I'm going to look on my own."

"Why not let me help?"

Sedge smiled at him. "Because I'd feel better with myself if I did it on my own."

"Well, I'll ask the people I know, anyway. They often talk about those kinds of things."

"Was your answer before a 'yes'?" Mariko asked Sedge.

"It's a tentative 'yes.' It means I appreciate the offer, and I genuinely want to, but I need more time to convince myself I'm not imposing on you."

"We wouldn't ask you to if we felt you were. And besides, you don't have more time."

Embarrassed by his need, he had been avoiding Mariko's eyes. Meeting them now, they shined with what he interpreted as worry and hope. "Then yes," he said.

"You'll move in with us?"

"I'll move in with you."

She leaned across the table and grabbed his hand.

"Why are you holding his hand?" Riku said.

"Because I'm happy," she said, still looking at Sedge. "You should be, too. Our lives are about to get better. You'll see."

There was something funny in how quickly Sedge's desperation disappeared once he accepted her offer—and in how he had somehow avoided a scenario he feared more than any other. He had told her before that he would never be forced to live on the street—which probably meant sleeping in all-night internet cafes—but it had been only his second-greatest worry. His greatest worry was that he would have to leave Japan, which meant, possibly, never returning. He mentioned this to them now.

Riku laughed and looked at him in surprise. "Why are you worried about returning to your country?"

"I'm getting too old to return and start over. And my life is here now. I want it to stay that way."

Frowning, Riku said: "Who wants to see what I've done with the kura?"

"Sure," Mariko said, unwilling to let go of Sedge's hand. "Why don't you lead the way?"

Sedge was impressed by the energy Riku had devoted to renovating the kura on his own. With money Mariko had given him for materials, he had covered the length of one earthen wall with stucco, leaving the vertical, evenly spaced support beams in it visible. Half the overhead beams had been sanded and polished dark brown, and one could see a wooden support he had added to the stairs. Looking past this, it seemed he had also installed lights in the second-floor ceiling.

"You have serious talent as a carpenter and designer," Sedge said, his enthusiasm real. "Where'd you learn to do all this?"

"I taught myself. Do you really think I did all right? I'm not finished, you know."

"I had no idea you'd made this kind of progress. You're as skilled as a professional."

Riku and Mariko laughed.

That night, Mariko explained that in exchange for making it livable she had to promise to buy Riku the best video game console he could find and let him install it there.

In the house, with Riku living in the kura, Sedge would have his own room. Until a bathroom was installed in the kura, Riku would come and go to use the one at the bottom of the stairs. When he needed to bathe, he would go to the hot spring baths at the edge of their village.

Except for using the bathroom and taking his meals, Riku had no reason to share the house with them, though Sedge suspected loneliness would sometimes bring him inside. Finding Riku more grown-up today, he would talk to Mariko later about how the three of them could regularly spend time together—not as a family, because they were far from being that, but as allies in the wearying search for love that wouldn't risk again what they'd already lost.

He hoped the boy would learn to become more independent, and perhaps even find a girlfriend. But when Sedge raised the latter subject, Riku turned sullen and disappeared into the kura. The thuds and crashes that carried into the house made it clear he was tearing down much of what he'd fixed in order to live there. Sedge realized then that Riku must have thought he'd tried to humiliate him.

15

Sedge stayed at Mariko's house every night while keeping his room at the ryokan, and now ate breakfast and dinner with Mariko and Riku. But he wanted to spend part of his days at the ryokan still, hoping he might repair his relationship with Takahashi and Yuki. He held no grudges against them; on the contrary, he was thankful for all they'd done for him after Nozomi disappeared.

At the ryokan he continued to frequent the tea lounge even though Mariko wasn't working there now. He wanted Takahashi and Yuki to see him, as this might give them a chance to reach out. But as his last day approached, he realized the responsibility would fall on him.

On the day before they expected him to leave, Sedge approached Takahashi while he stood in the corridor, making space among the ryokan's Kutani-ware exhibition for the two sake cups he had sometimes brought to Sedge's room.

Takahashi looked up as Sedge came over.

"May I talk to you for a minute? If you're busy, I can come back later."

"Now's fine. A large tour group will check in soon, but I have a couple minutes."

Sedge was about to suggest they go somewhere and sit down, but a vague apprehension convinced him to say immediately what was on his mind. If things went well, maybe they could sit and talk more later.

"I wanted to thank you and Yuki for everything you've done for me. I don't think I'd have made it to this point without your support."

Takahashi returned Sedge's bow.

"You and Yuki asked me to move out by tomorrow. But since I have a place to go, I decided to clear out a little early."

"You're moving today?"

"I'll move what's left in the next hour or two."

"May I ask where you're moving and what you'll do?"

"For now, I think it's better if I don't say."

Takahashi turned to the Kutani-ware he'd been rearranging. "You mean for Mariko's sake . . ." He looked back at Sedge, blinking rapidly. "What do you two intend to do about your spouses?"

"I can't answer for Mariko. But I'm looking for ways to divorce Nozomi. It won't be easy, but I've been told it can be done."

"I see. I guess that becomes inevitable at some point. Even so, I can't say I'm pleased by your involvement with Mariko. Nor is Yuki. In fact, she's been dismayed by your relationship with Mariko for longer than I've been."

"There's nothing to be dismayed about." He thought Takahashi was only voicing his jealousy over his involvement with Mariko.

"Of course there is. From the outside, what the four of you have done looks like an exchange of spouses. With a child involved, no less. And also our ryokan. Do neither of you see how potentially damaging it is?"

Sedge wasn't sure what to say.

"It was bad judgment to get involved with Mariko while you're still legally married to my sister. And it's bad judgment on Mariko's part, too. By the way, will you help her raise her stepson?"

"She's letting me use a room in her house. The boy has nothing to do with me."

Takahashi stepped forward to check the small change he'd made in the Kutani-ware display. "You realize, I suppose, that whenever Kōichi comes back she'll choose him over you. He's still husband and father in their home, after all, no matter what problems they have together. You could easily find yourself with nothing again. And what will you do then?"

It was true Sedge was unsure how Mariko would react if her husband returned. He wanted to ask Takahashi what Yuki would do if she found out about his infidelities, but he held his tongue. Takahashi's concern sounded genuine.

"I'm sorry we've had this so close to your room the whole time," Takahashi went on. "But we agreed to exhibit it before you arrived."

Sedge looked at him, not understanding his apology. "What are you talking about?"

"I thought you knew these pieces were made by Mariko's husband. That's his photo and biography on the wall. Unfortunately, it came undone and has been lying face-down behind the glass for some time . . ."

Sedge turned toward the display. He tried to remember the photo Mariko had shown him on her phone at Kenrokuen back in March, which was clearer in his mind than her husband's face when he'd come to their shop. This photo was obviously from a long time ago. Now that he knew it was him, he saw Riku emerge in the features.

Sedge had stopped to admire the Kutani-ware before; because he didn't like being reminded of the ceramics store he'd been forced to close in Kanazawa, and felt bitter that no such stores in Yamanaka Onsen would offer him work, he hadn't paid much attention to it. Knowing now that it had been just outside his room for all the weeks he'd stayed here nauseated him, as did the memory of having drunk from Koichi's sake cups. Had Mariko wanted to spare him, and thus never mentioned the display? He couldn't imagine how having to see it every day affected her.

"What did I do to make your family push me aside?" Sedge said, his voice brittle.

He had nearly said "Nozomi" instead of "your family," and

he felt himself redden. Had the way she'd left him made him lash out at her family? Or were his feelings about them justified? At the moment, all he knew was an all-encompassing resentment.

He was disgusted with Takahashi and wondered if it had pleased him all along to keep the secret of the Kutani-ware from him. "My arguments with you and Yuki only happened because I respected your family and was hurt when I saw I was being scapegoated for what Nozomi did." When Takahashi didn't answer, Sedge added: "And what did I do wrong in my classes? All the students I've spoken with contradict the story you told me."

"I'm sorry you heard something different, but everything I told you was true." Takahashi glanced at his watch. "If you don't mind, I need to get back to the lobby."

Sedge imagined he was no busier now than when he had approached him a few minutes ago. "Look, I don't want to end on a bad note with you or Yuki. I'll be staying in Yamanaka Onsen, at least for the time being, so if you want to get in touch or have a drink together, you can reach me at the number you have. Thank you both, again, for everything. I'll always feel indebted to you for the kindness you showed me these last two months."

"And we hope you'll find your way to something better soon. Thank you for coming to talk to me before you left."

Takahashi bowed formally to Sedge before disappearing down the corridor.

Sedge turned toward his room, but the Kutani-ware display caught his eye again. He stepped closer to it, determined to read the small, lengthy text beside it, which with effort he managed to do. It was a typical artist's bio, detailing years of education and training, followed by exhibitions and local and regional awards he'd received. The bio praised the artist's tones and color schemes, comparing his porcelain to snow and cream, and singling him out for his mastery of tradition as well as for pioneering new forms and styles. Although his Kutani-ware had been designated an Intangible Cultural Property, he had quietly rejected it, saying that such prestigious honors and awards would suffocate his drive. His bio ended with a quote from the famous twentieth-century artist Rosanjin Kitaoji, who had spent time in Yamashiro Onsen:

> Born alone, die alone.
> Arrive alone, depart alone.
> Learn alone, proceed alone.

The quote resonated with Sedge in a way that had nothing to do with the man in the photo, who looked so much like Riku, but with himself. He had felt hopelessly alone after Nozomi left, even after Takahashi and Yuki had opened their ryokan to him. Mariko, however, had extended all of herself to him, pulled him into her life, and saved him. Was it love that had made her do this?

Feeling a deeper gratitude toward her, he returned to his room.

Fifteen minutes later someone knocked on his door. A newly hired staff member—someone he'd never had the chance to teach, and therefore whose name he'd never learned—handed him a thick envelope and said it was from Ms. Yuki. When the young man left, Sedge emptied out the envelope's contents.

A thin stack of ten-thousand-yen notes wrapped in traditional Japanese paper fell onto the table. A short message was written in Yuki's hand: "Despite our original agreement, we always intended to pay you for your teaching. We hope this comes in handy."

Was this their way of apologizing? Or, at the least, of trying to make amends? Or were they still trying to ensure that he wouldn't turn on them if given the chance? Whatever the case, it was clearly a final gesture.

There were fifteen bills in all. The amount would have covered one month's rent at the apartment he and Nozomi shared in Kanazawa. In Yamanaka Onsen it might cover five. At Mariko's house, where he would stay for free, it would cover whatever she asked him to pay for the expenses he incurred by living there.

❧ ❧ ❧

"This is so unexpected," Mariko said, covering her mouth with a hand. She was staring at the pendant Sedge had bought after leaving the ryokan that afternoon. "What did you do this for? And when you don't have a steady income. Please, I don't want you spending even one yen on me."

He appreciated her carefulness over his money, but he enjoyed much more her reaction to his gift. She couldn't hide from him that she liked it.

"The ryokan paid me for my teaching when I left. I've always wanted to get you something, but it wasn't until today that I could."

The white wings of the hand-crafted ibis, raised in flight, were set off beautifully by the color of her skin at the base of her neck.

"I told the neighbors today that we were taking in a renter. Most of them had seen you and were pleased to know you speak Japanese. They assumed you only spoke English. Riku went with me and told them about the heron you brought home and the cage he built for it. They were impressed you'd done such a thing."

"I hope you told them not to look for me if they find an injured heron in the road."

"They appreciate that sort of kindness. You'll see that many villagers refuse to kill bees, even though there are aggressive species here that can seriously injure you."

Sedge knew this already. Some of the craftsmen in town protected the bees' nests, even when the bees built them under the rooftops of their homes. In wintertime, when the bees returned to the forests, the craftsmen would have large, perfectly round hives they could lacquer and make last several hundred years. People protected barn swallows, too, because they believed they brought good luck. Some villagers even opened the windows of their houses for the birds to fly inside and build nests out of harm's way. More common were nests at the entrances to homes, beneath which the owners placed boxes they filled with newspapers and regularly changed. The only creatures the villagers killed were centipedes. Even stinkbugs, which were ubiquitous for half the year, they widely tolerated.

Riku returned to the house for dinner. He brought a backpack with towels and a hairbrush to take to the baths after eating. When Mariko bent forward to set their food on the table, the ibis swung before her neck, appearing even more to be flying.

"Where'd that come from?" Riku said, reaching for the pendant and pulling it toward him, forcing Mariko to lurch forward against the table.

"Let go," Sedge commanded, grabbing Riku's other arm.

Riku did as Sedge told him to, but his scowl made clear he disliked Sedge raising a reproving voice and touching him. Surely he knew he could have upended the table and hurt his stepmother, and that he might have broken the pendant or its chain. Before Sedge could demand that Riku apologize, Mariko insisted that everything was fine.

"You should know better than to act that way in front of others," she told Riku.

Sedge said, "He shouldn't act that way, period."

There was hardly any table conversation that evening—only the sounds of Riku forcing his food down as quickly as possible. When he finished, he pushed his rice bowl away and stood up. He surveyed the mess he'd made, which was more salient beside Mariko's and Sedge's organized bowls and dishes.

"*Gochisō*," he muttered, announcing he was finished. After retrieving his backpack, he returned and said to Mariko, "I need some money."

"You're going to the baths?" she said. "There's a thousand yen on the shoe cabinet. Take that if you want. But I've already bought you a pass. You don't have to pay to get in."

He left the table without explaining his need for money. At the *genkan* he stuffed it in a pocket, stepped into his shoes, and disappeared into the darkness outside.

"He's a complicated kid," Sedge said. "But it's easy to see he craves attention. And it's obvious there's nothing worse to him than being criticized—even if you're not explicit about it."

"He's not all bad, though. If he were, I'd force a different living situation on him."

"How would you do that?" Sedge refrained from asking why she hadn't done this yet if there had always been this option.

"His paternal grandparents live in Echizen. It's not so far from here. Riku goes there every summer for the O-bon holiday and stays the first week of the New Year. Last year, they told me they could take him off my hands if he became a problem. They're good people, but Riku isn't the boy they know from the past. He's nearly an adult now, and they've both grown frailer. They could use Riku's help on their small farm. Although he's fond of them, he's at an age where they couldn't control him. I'm afraid of what he'd do."

"What do you think he'd do?"

"I mean the havoc he might wreak. They're well into their

seventies. He would never suspect the damage he was inflicting on them."

"And how is the situation here acceptable for you to deal with?"

"He's my responsibility. And when he's being good, I love him very much and want to be as good a stepmother to him as possible. Weren't you difficult at his age? I know I was sometimes disrespectful to my parents."

"Of course I was. But there were lines I knew never to cross, and I didn't. With Riku, if there are lines holding him back, he either can't see them or doesn't respect them."

"He does have an awful temper. And he gets so jealous sometimes. It's awful when it happens because it takes him a long time to calm back down. I hope you'll be understanding with him. I'm sure he'll be some trouble, but he needs time to adjust to you being around. Even if he doesn't see you as being his father—which he won't, of course—you're still a figure of authority in his eyes. I'm afraid he'll project his feelings toward Kōichi onto you. But I've told him many times that you're not the same person, and he always assures me that he understands."

Sedge made a silent promise to exert a positive influence on both their lives.

He didn't tell Mariko, but he'd begun to worry about what problems might result from moving in with them. Who could say that she and Riku, and even the entire town where they lived, wouldn't eventually reject him the way Nozomi's family had? What was more, who could say that what Nozomi had done to him couldn't happen again with Mariko? With Riku between them from the start, their relationship had become even more fragile than when Sedge was living at the ryokan.

Although he disliked thinking this way, the fact that both Mariko's parents were dead, and only an estranged brother remained in her life, reassured him. He and Mariko only had each other to rely on. If not for Riku, he would trust more not only her but also the kind of future that was opening to them.

Riku largely left them alone over the next few days. He clearly relished the privacy of the kura, especially after finishing dinner and returning from the baths, as well as Mariko's agreeing to let him transform it from a two-story, Taisho-period storage building to his own living quarters. Although he had recently destroyed much of the interior in a fit of anger, because he had started to view it as his own, he was slowly developing a more adult attitude about taking care of it. Whether he disliked the house's atmosphere with Mariko and Sedge always together, or if he was being respectful of their own need for privacy, Sedge didn't know. But Sedge was heartened by his early days there, and indeed Riku showed signs of the "good kid" Mariko had described.

On the second floor of the house were three rooms. The largest was Mariko's bedroom, its wooden floors, white walls, and exposed ceiling beams a sign of recent renovation; the other two were traditional tatami-floored rooms that no one used, adjacent to one of her bedroom walls. She suggested that Sedge use the farthest room from hers so Riku might believe they were close but never intimate. She also suggested that she and Sedge go to bed at different times in case Riku ventured upstairs and had a chance to confirm their living arrangement. In the middle of the night Sedge and Mariko always found their way to one another's futon and slept together until an alarm went off at half-volume, a half hour before Riku awoke to prepare for school. The separate room and nighttime schedule were pretenses Sedge agreed to, though he knew Riku would inevitably learn the truth.

Like most people in the village, Mariko didn't lock her front door if she was home, even if she was sleeping. There had never been a need to, for the village was safe. After his first week living there Sedge insisted they lock it at night, however, and instead leave the back door unlatched. It was closer to the kura, which would make it easier for Riku to go to the toilet. They installed a motion-detecting light facing the back door, too, as a safety precaution.

Sedge bought a used bicycle and rode into town when the weather permitted, getting them takeaway sushi from Saraku and going as far as Ōkami-no-Ie, behind the Yamanaka Lacquerware Museum, to buy pastries for their weekend breakfasts. When it rained, he walked with an umbrella to Yamanaka-za, which allowed him to peer inside the sake and crafts shops along Yugekai Road, to stop occasionally to buy local vegetables, honey, and fresh croquettes and talk with the friendly shop owners, and even to soak up the atmosphere at the shrines and Buddhist temples he passed. He avoided Takahashi and Yuki, though he expected to bump into them sometimes in a town as small as Yamanaka Onsen. But this never happened, and a part of him was glad for it.

One of the job interviews he'd arranged was canceled at the last minute, which depressed him for several days. The one he went to, in Fukui, proved a troublesome commute without a car, and when that interview went poorly he celebrated his failure with a one-cup of sake on the train home. He had received no responses to other applications he'd sent two and three weeks earlier.

These developments left him with no clear options going forward. He worried this would bother Mariko, too.

16

Sedge and Mariko fell instinctively into a routine in which they did things together when time allowed—before and after her workday, and on weekends when she wasn't running errands or taking care of Riku and her house. Lying together at night, Sedge felt her speaking for him as she explained that his presence was an endless source of excitement to her, and how everything they did together made her happier.

"I feel the same way," he said.

One after another, they recounted what these instances included: their evening walks to the village Hachiman shrine and its two-thousand-year-old *ōsugi* trees; the elaborate meals they cooked; their gardening in the small plot between the back of the house and the kura; their visits to the sake bar in front of Hasebe Shrine where they drank, made friends with local people, and watched old samurai movies the owner played on a small TV; their birding competitions in the village.

"I wonder if the time we're spending together bothers Riku," he said. "My being here has turned his life with you on its head."

"He does seem lonely. But I always ask if he wants to join us and he only ignores me. I suppose he thinks I should know what he wants and how he feels without my asking him."

"He chooses to be like that. Nothing we do will change it."

"I'll continue to ask him, though. It's the least I can do. I want him to be happy, too."

On a Sunday in the middle of June, however, she failed to ask Riku to join them on a birding trip around Wagatani Reservoir.

"Why didn't you invite me?" Riku griped. He was in the

dining room finishing breakfast and had been talking to them about turning the kura's second floor into a bedroom, reserving the first floor for exercising and playing video games.

"You can come if you want," Sedge said, though he hoped Riku wouldn't. He had a feeling the boy only wanted to complain about how much time he and Mariko had been spending together.

"Yes, you're welcome to join us," Mariko said. "We just didn't think you'd like our company, especially when you already have plans."

"I only said I was going to do that stuff because I had nothing better to do. Now you tell me I can come along, but I know you want to be by yourselves. Just like everything you've been doing since he moved in." He began enumerating all the things they'd done without him. Sedge was unaware that Riku had been keeping tabs on him and Mariko and knew exactly how often they did things together.

Sedge interrupted him, trying to be conciliatory. "It was my fault we didn't ask you. I thought you'd be bored with our company and embarrassed to be seen with us. Why don't you come, too? I'm eager to learn from you about the local birds."

Perhaps Riku was only waiting for a more forceful invitation from Sedge, because his attitude brightened and he quickly forgave his stepmother.

He ran to the kura and returned with binoculars and a sunhat that trailed behind his neck. When Sedge asked what was inside the daypack on his shoulder, he said, "On one side peanuts, and the other side breadcrumbs. The peanuts are for me."

Mariko drove the short distance to where the road met the reservoir. From there they followed the long loop around the emerald-green water below. Along the way, Riku leaned forward from the back seat and asked Sedge when he first became interested in birds.

"I don't remember the very first time," he said. "But I've had the interest as long as I can remember. My parents bought me binoculars when I was in elementary school so I could spot birds in our trees more easily."

The question reminded him that it had only been when he met Nozomi, and they encouraged each other to spend time exploring nature, that he became what most people would call a birder. Due to the little free time they had, they went most often to places they could easily reach from their apartment. Year-round, in good weather, they bicycled to two separate heronries on the Sai River, followed by the bird sanctuary and bird-rich dunes of Kenmin Seaside Park.

Now that he was in Yamanaka Onsen, with only his feet and a used bicycle to get around, he made his sightings locally, in the rice fields and vegetable plots on the edges of town; around the temples and shrines ringing the valley; and along the banks of the Daishōji River. He had already filled a notebook with bird sightings—the kinds of birds he'd seen, their behaviors and locations, and sketches of them if he could manage it. He pulled it from his own daypack and showed it to Riku.

They passed bicyclists and cars parked at a trailhead, while a handful of people foraged for herbs and mountain vegetables up the nearby slopes. Despite Riku suggesting they stop in various places, Mariko didn't do so until they'd reached Suginomizu, a small village hemmed in by *sugi* and pines that had been revived recently for tourism, but that tourists had only slowly discovered. With few people around, they could comfortably explore the area, including a rocky stream that meandered through the village. There was also a café and a treehouse built inside two kura; Mariko wanted to show them to Riku so he might get more ideas for renovating the one he'd moved into.

When they opened their car doors Sedge directed Riku's

attention to the birdsong around them, but he was curious about other things.

"Look," Riku said as he approached a monument above the stream. "It's to the village's war dead. It says they were killed in World War II."

"How many names are there?" Sedge asked, standing with Mariko behind him. He couldn't imagine there would be many. The entire village was within sight of where they stood, and though he didn't know how many houses might have been here seventy or eighty years ago, there were now fewer than a dozen.

"Did anyone in your family fight against the Japanese?" Riku asked Sedge.

"The war was ages ago." Mariko's tone was impatient, almost angry. "You can't possibly mean Sedge's immediate family."

"Your grandfathers or great-grandfathers, I mean," Riku corrected himself.

"One of my great-grandfathers fought in World War I in Europe," Sedge said. "Afterward he moved with his wife to America. People in my family have led peaceful lives for as far back as I can remember. But that's only me. I can't speak for other Americans in Japan."

Riku scrutinized the monument, as if trying to imagine the era when these villagers had fought and died. A moment later he continued walking. He broke into a run where the road curved and a few more houses stood behind a small bridge. As he ran, the shortness of his legs caught Sedge by surprise; they gave an impression of even greater strength and balance than Sedge had previously noticed. From a distance, had he not known Riku, he might have mistaken him for someone twice his age.

"Where on earth is he going?" Sedge asked, wondering if they should call him back. They started walking slowly in the direction Riku had run.

"It's better to let him be," Mariko answered. "He'll come back when he's ready."

"Has he been here before?"

"Two or three times. The last time was with Kōichi. I don't remember what brought them here. But it turned into one of their fights."

"You mean they argued?"

"Kōichi didn't have the patience to argue. He would get mad and strike whoever had angered him. He didn't always do it to hurt the person; I don't think he ever put all his strength into it."

Sedge wondered again what had attracted Nozomi to such a man.

They soon reached a small bridge crossing the Sugimizu River, so narrow it seemed only a stream. Cement walls two meters high and covered with moss lined both banks.

"Did that include you sometimes?"

"Kōichi never hurt me. He might have abused me verbally, but he was never physically violent. And he was only that way when he was drunk. When he was sober everyone could see he adored me. At those times he treated me as well as he could."

"For some reason I thought he hurt you," he said as they crossed the bridge into the shade of a tall mixed forest. To their left stood a scattering of old farmhouses.

"Not me. Riku."

"He spared you but not his son?"

"He said he'd never do anything to mar me. And he didn't. But Riku has always been a strange boy, and Kōichi found every reason he could to bully him. Which isn't to say he didn't love Riku, too. And Riku knew this, and I think was conflicted in how he felt about him. He was both hugely relieved and hugely despondent whenever Kōichi left us."

"He has a lot of scars inside."

She nodded somberly. "I remember one time he beat Riku.

It was right before he left us two years ago. Some older boys at Riku's school had been making fun of him, and during a break between classes one of them swiped his pencil case, ran into an empty classroom, and threw it out the window, three floors down. Riku told the boy to fetch it, but the boy, knowing his friends were watching, only laughed at him. Riku had one of his episodes, as we used to call them, and launched himself at the boy. He not only knocked him to the ground, but by the time a teacher came in to break things up Riku had gone through two of his three tormenters. The last one had been a local judo champion, but I'm not sure he would have lasted much longer against Riku. But when Kōichi found out, Riku, as always, met his match. He beat Riku worse than Riku had beat the kids in his school. He kept telling Riku there was greater dignity in walking away, that later in life he'd never think of it again, and if he did he'd be grateful for the life lesson. By fighting he lowered himself to their level. But he said this all while punishing Riku, who cowered at his feet. I don't think Riku learned a thing from him. Other than his hypocrisy."

Riku let out a far-off whoop, interrupting Mariko. It had come from where the crumbling path they were on curved to the left and disappeared. As Mariko went on speaking, Sedge led her to a bench above the river, under a row of cedar trees but bathed in sunshine.

"For the next few days Riku stayed home from school. On his last day home, when I returned from work, he had just finished making one thousand paper cranes and stringing them together. They were a peace offering to Kōichi, but more than that, I think he believed he might win his father over with them. And Kōichi was moved. When he first realized what Riku had done, that the cranes were for him, he actually shed a few tears. But he never thanked Riku. And he never apologized for beating him.

"About a year ago," she continued, sitting on the bench they had come to, "another group of schoolboys bullied Riku. Know-ing about his love of birds, they put a dead baby sparrow they'd found under a tree into his desk, and when he opened it and saw it, he picked it up and immediately left the classroom, right in the middle of class. It apparently caused a commotion among the students who saw what he had in his hand. After burying it in a park near the school, he waited outside the main gate for sev-eral hours until the students who had pranked him passed by. This time he didn't leave a single foe standing. Again there were three boys in the group, and two had to be taken to the hospi-tal, both with broken ribs. Because the boys admitted to bullying him, Riku was suspended for one month rather than expelled. When Kōichi found out and tried to teach him the same lesson as before, Riku was a year older. Instead of cowering under Kōichi's blows, he stood and took them. And when Kōichi tired, he fought back. He turned the tables on him, until he heard him begging that he stop. I was beside myself, not knowing what to do. But in a way Kōichi solved everything for us, because a few weeks later he left and never came back."

It was hard for Sedge to imagine such scenes playing out in their peaceful village and inside the house where he now lived.

"Riku made one thousand paper cranes again, but this time he gave them to the students he'd beaten up. That made his pun-ishment at school slightly less severe, but it also made the bul-lies stop picking on him quite so much. Riku told me later that making the cranes had taught him something. When I asked him what, he said that for some people the cranes meant nothing at all. But for others, they made a difference in his relationship with them; they made forgiveness easier. Even now, he has a collection of paper cranes and adds to them sometimes. I guess he thinks he might need them again in the future, though I hope he won't."

Looking up, Sedge saw two crows chase a Japanese

sparrowhawk across the sky. Trying to process what Mariko was telling him, he watched them disappear beyond a wall of faraway trees.

"Immediately after Kōichi left, a few men dropped by out of the blue. The last one was an older man from Komatsu City, a ceramicist like my husband. It was during the last big snowfall we had. Riku and I were struggling to shovel it all, and though we'd cleared some off the roof, we couldn't reach every part of it. Kōichi's friend realized this, and he pointed out a section, warning that it was on the verge of collapsing. I discouraged him from climbing to the roof, but when he took this as flirtation I got angry and let him go. He climbed our ladder and hadn't walked ten steps along the roof before he slipped and slid right off it. He fell into my flowerbed; had there not been so much snow he would have broken his back, or maybe even died. I brought him inside and got him feeling well enough to go home. He came over again a week later, this time by taxi. He was drunk, and another incident ensued. A relatively small one, thankfully. The man didn't know what Riku, who had a strong dislike for him, was capable of. I think he hurt the man worse than when he fell off the roof. When he stumbled away from our house a final time, he didn't act at all angry with Riku. Instead, he cursed Kōichi."

Sedge picked up a stone at his feet and bounced it down the steps to the river. "What made you think that marrying him would make you happy?" he asked.

"He was good to me at first, and no one before him had shown an interest in marrying me. Also, for some reason I was ready to trust him more after seeing all the beautiful things he made and noticing how people fussed over him. I was wrong to think his Kutani-ware reflected his soul, but I was younger then, less experienced, and that's the kind of ridiculous idea I had."

No one Sedge had met in the village ever mentioned Mariko's

husband to him. An outsider could be forgiven for thinking he never existed, except for these stories, and for the shadows he cast over Mariko and Riku's lives—and Sedge's, too. Something like a drill began to bore inside him as he reflected on what Mariko just told him. And from the hole it left, which pained him, what emerged was a question he needed her to answer.

"You asked before if I expected my wife to return. You should know that I'm trying to find out how to divorce her. What about you? Will you divorce your husband? What will you do if he returns?"

She lay down on the bench and draped her legs over Sedge's thighs. A terrible sadness floated in her eyes, and he saw that mentioning this possibility was the worst thing he could have done. But he soon realized what her expression meant. "I won't know until it happens," she said.

Her words shocked him. He hadn't believed Takahashi's warning just before he'd left the ryokan, but hearing this threw everything into doubt. His old fear of Mariko abandoning him, of all they'd committed to each other amounting to nothing, reared its head again.

"Why would you want him again?"

She considered his question for a long time. Finally she sat back up and said, "It's not that I think he'll change. Or that he'll ever be good to me the way you've been. But I'm not getting younger. And I don't know who would want to marry me after him. Play around with me, sure, I'd have plenty of takers if that was all I wanted. But it would be worse for me if I did that. I guess I'll have to wait and see what happens."

Hearing this made his apprehensions mount. "But you know I'm not playing around with you, don't you?"

They both looked toward the bridge they'd crossed earlier. Riku had charged across it back to the main street and, after a moment looking around, spotted them sitting by the river. He turned back and headed toward them.

"That's what I want to think," Mariko said, standing up. "And maybe you want to think that, too. But neither of us can say how things will turn out. We both know it's impossible to predict the future. Don't we?"

Riku hurried over to their bench and pointed to where he'd run off to. "I found a clearing behind those houses. A bunch of birds were flitting around, so I dumped all my breadcrumbs on the ground. I bet a ton of birds are there now. Come on, I'll show you." He was already walking backward, waiting for them to follow him.

Sedge felt Mariko looking at him, waiting for an answer. Was it really impossible to predict the future when they both wanted to do the best they could for each other?

"Let's go," Riku said. He stepped forward again, taking Mariko's arm and pulling her away. Sedge trailed behind, rewinding through the conversation he and Mariko had just had.

❧ ❧ ❧

That night, lying in his futon, Sedge gazed at a four-paneled screen across his room. Flowing down each panel was Buddhist calligraphy so old even Mariko couldn't read it; the screen had originally belonged to her grandparents. Electric light from the street penetrated the *shōji* windows to his left, illuminating an alcove at the end of the room where a scroll of a woman chasing fireflies hung. To his right were the sliding doors that separated him from Mariko.

In the dim room, listening to the old wooden house creak in the wind, he waited for her to message him on his phone. Finally, it buzzed; on its screen were the words: "Come to my room now."

He made his way quietly to her room and slid into her futon.

Mariko pushed her head into his chest and took a quick breath. Slowly she got up and stood over him, letting him gaze at her nakedness in the moonlight before kneeling beside him and peeling off his t-shirt, which she pressed into her face and inhaled. She dropped it beside the futon and her hands moved to his boxers, pulling them down his legs. When they were both naked, she curled up next to him. She breathed in as he entered her, reaching behind to pull him more tightly into her body. She climbed on top of him and, after finding her desired rhythm, soon gasped that she wanted to come. When she said this the same feeling welled inside of him. Afterward she fell forward on top of him and they held each other for a long moment.

The wall they faced glimmered with moonlight.

"Let me see you in the light again," he said.

She stepped back into it and turned to face him. Her breasts, the tuft of hair between her legs, the hourglass of her body, her eyes smiling down at him. Suddenly her smile vanished and she glanced out the window.

The walls lit up from a light outside. Mariko jumped back to the futon. At first Sedge thought Riku had directed a powerful flashlight at the window, only to remember the motion detector behind the house. He told Mariko this, but it didn't calm her down.

"Either way, I'm sure he saw me."

"Riku? He probably just needed to use the bathroom downstairs. With the motion detector where it is, this might happen every night—at least until the kura has its own bathroom."

Mariko went to put her ear against her bedroom door. "He never came inside. He must have been at the kura entrance when I stood up."

"Anything could have turned it on. It might have been an

animal. You've told me before about the neighborhood cats that wander around at night, and even the times you've seen stoats, and *tanuki*, even boar and their young, tearing apart your garden."

But she wasn't listening. The light outside had shut off again, and he could barely make out her putting her nightclothes back on.

"He must have heard us. Or he knew all along we do this sometimes."

Sedge guessed it was one-thirty a.m., possibly even two.

He had followed Mariko into her room earlier that night, before either of them had gone to bed. It was only to see a book she wanted him to read, but he remembered looking out her window and spotting Riku kneeling at the kura entrance, staring up at him. Sedge had flinched at the sight of him, and never mentioned it to Mariko.

Had he been there ever since? Had he instinctively known Sedge would return?

Sedge stayed beside her until she fell asleep. When he was sure he wouldn't wake her, he slipped out from under her blanket. At her window, the moon illuminated the kura. There was no sign of anyone outside. The only thing Sedge noticed was that the sliding door of the entrance was ajar. Through that space it was completely dark.

Before he crept toward his room, he saw that the moon was far above the kura's roof, still shining in Mariko's window.

17

Yuki called to tell Sedge that among the ryokan's mail was a letter addressed to him. That she sounded breathless and had skipped a customary phone greeting could have meant anything—all the more so since her tone sounded friendly. "If you're still in town, can you come and pick it up? Or would you like us to forward it to wherever you are now?"

He was surprised she didn't offer to send it to him through Mariko. "Is it about a job?"

"No," she said. "It's from Nozomi."

Her answer stopped him cold. "I'll come by later today," he said quickly.

Yuki was at the front desk when he entered the ryokan. He greeted her and the staff—all were his former students—standing on either side of her. He looked toward the tea lounge for Mariko. She was in the back, polishing empty tables by the garden window. In the middle of the room, Takahashi sat on a sofa watching her.

"How have things been here?" Sedge said to Yuki, resting his hands on the counter and looking for Nozomi's letter.

"Everything here is fine. You haven't been gone long enough for things to change. But of course there have been changes with you, and I hope you're doing well."

"You called me about a letter . . ."

"We got one, too. Takahashi has the one she addressed to you. I think you saw him in the lounge. He's expecting you."

Sedge walked toward Takahashi. Mariko glanced at him and he smiled at her, but neither of them said a word to each other.

He sat across from Takahashi and leaned forward, waiting to be acknowledged.

Sedge didn't want to discuss Nozomi within earshot of Mariko, but that was for her sake, as he had nothing to hide. He couldn't help but wonder if Takahashi had arranged to speak to him in front of her, though. Takahashi was both smart and considerate—he had to be to run a successful ryokan—and when he failed to be the latter, he likely intended it that way.

"Thank you for coming," Takahashi said, capping a pen he'd been twirling between his fingers.

"Everything looks impressive, as always."

Takahashi glanced around them and smiled. "How is it being back in the real world? Have you found a job and started working?"

"I've had interviews. And I'm scheduled to have more. Hopefully I'll get an offer soon."

"A bigger city might support your qualifications more."

"Even the cities are turning me down."

Takahashi waved Mariko to their table and told her to give Sedge a menu—which was unnecessary, since he already knew it by heart. She immediately handed one to him and stepped back to wait for his order. Although he and Takahashi were being civil to each other, which he was glad for, he had difficulty controlling his nerves. He wished now he'd come at night, after Mariko had gone home.

Before he could order, Takahashi said, "We were surprised by the letters Nozomi sent. They relieved us, though, and we can't wait to see her next week when she comes back. She wrote that she wants to see you most of all. But that was in her letter to us. I have no idea what she wrote to you. It's here on the table; I must have hidden it with this ledger."

He lifted the ledger and slid the letter toward him. The envelope was thin and could have just as easily contained nothing.

"I'll have what I always have," he said to Mariko. "Or what I always used to have."

She bowed expressionlessly and hurried into the back kitchen. She must wonder if her husband would be returning, too—or did she already know? With Mariko away, he asked Takahashi about him.

"Nozomi didn't mention him," Takahashi said. "But that she's apparently done with him should be a relief, I'd think. Of course, we don't know the situation yet."

"A relief to whom?" Sedge said.

"Well, to me and my mother, certainly. And probably to you as well."

Sedge picked up the envelope and slipped it into a pants pocket. Takahashi shifted uncomfortably in his seat, as if he had expected Sedge to open and read it in his presence.

Mariko returned with their drinks on a tray: black coffee for Takahashi and a ginger tea for Sedge. After setting them on the table, she tucked the tray under her arm and stood by the window a short distance away.

"You'll have to excuse me," Sedge said, "but I have lots to do. Maybe we can talk another time."

Takahashi raised a hand as if to halt him with it. His voice was placating. "Wasn't the whole reason you accepted our offer to stay here so you could find a way to bring Nozomi back into your life and fix your marriage?"

"At the time I had nothing. No money, no job, no income, no place to live. You gave me time and space to get back on my feet."

"But we helped you with the understanding that salvaging your marriage was still a priority."

"Things have changed."

Takahashi stared at him uncomprehendingly. "I know she hurt you very badly. But she's still your wife and she's coming back. In her letter to me, she said she was eager to set things right with you again, however difficult that might be. Wouldn't you like to give her that chance?"

Takahashi's calm, reasonable tone unsettled Sedge. Was he being genuine? "After what she did? Why would I?"

Takahashi fell silent, his fingers tracing the stitching of his ledger's leather cover. After a long moment he said, "I remember not so long ago when you said that despite what she'd done, you'd be willing to give her a second chance. That was why you hadn't pursued a divorce or contacted the police about the money she took."

"You made me promise not to. That was one of your conditions for letting me stay here."

"You must have misunderstood me." Takahashi glanced at Mariko, then turned back to Sedge. "Do you really think the two of you will find what you and Nozomi once had? And could have again, potentially?"

Angry that Takahashi had pulled Mariko into their conversation, Sedge stood up and said, "There's no point in our talking more. I have no idea why you're being this way."

Takahashi remained seated and turned to look out the window again. "Thank you for coming. It must be nice to hear from Nozomi after all this time. That's certainly how my mother and I feel. It's a relief to know she's all right. And that she's coming back."

Sedge hoped Mariko would see the disappointment in his face, but she was staring at the ledger Takahashi was repeatedly opening and closing.

As soon as Sedge stepped outside, he hopped on his bicycle and rode to Yamanaka-za, where he sat at an empty table and tore open Nozomi's letter.

Dear Sedge,

I'm so sorry I did what I did. Only a saint wouldn't hate me now, but I hope you'll at least find the goodness to read my short letter to the end.

I was contacted recently by a Mr. Kawasaki, of Kawasaki & Suzuki Law in Kanazawa. I couldn't believe he was able to find me, for until then no one had. He said you asked him to start divorce proceedings and wanted to know if I would cooperate to make it go smoothly or if I intended to fight it. I told him I haven't decided. I think it's better if you and I meet first. You have every right to be angry with me, but please understand that I'm probably more fragile than you are now. Part of it is the result of learning belatedly of my father's death. I always knew something like that could happen, but I didn't expect it to before I came back from this period of needing to be on my own.

Also, I find myself in a bit of trouble these days. It has nothing to do with you, but rather with where I've been and some people who the police there said viewed me as an easy target. I know it's asking a lot, but I would feel more settled trying to reconnect with those I left behind without the pressure of explaining.

I don't know where you're living now, but because I expect you're still in contact with my brother, I've sent this letter in care of him. I'm including a separate note to him, asking that he relay this to you. I'll be in touch with you again soon, after returning to Ishikawa. Even if you've decided I can't be forgiven, I hope you'll suspend your judgment of me until after we meet—if you'll be so good as to see me when I'm back.

Nozomi

A thrill coursed through him that confused him at first—the sort of boyish excitement of learning that a beautiful girl has reciprocated one's obsession with her. But he realized that his feeling was more complicated. He was relieved to know Nozomi was all right, and beneath that was the hope that her return might allow him to put his life back in order, initially by hurrying their divorce, and perhaps even by having the money she'd taken returned to him. A more convincing apology might be nice, too, but it was the least of his concerns.

His anger at her began percolating inside him again, and he wondered if Mariko would ever be capable of doing to him what Nozomi had.

18

Mariko returned home in time to meet Riku at the bus stop down the street, something she rarely did. To Sedge's dismay, she didn't enter the house first to greet him but waited in the small bus shelter for Riku to arrive. Out the kitchen window, as Sedge marinated fish and cut vegetables to make dinner, he watched them walk home together, neither of them talking.

He guessed what was on her mind after she'd overheard Takahashi talk about Nozomi. He expected her to doubt him now—his constancy if nothing else—even though she had admitted the possibility of taking her husband back one day.

Riku entered first and disappeared inside the bathroom. Mariko grabbed the small broom she kept in the *genkan* and stepped back outside to sweep in front of the house, though Sedge had recently done it himself. He walked to the *genkan* to welcome her home.

"I'm sorry you had to be there for my talk with Takahashi. At the time, I know, it was awkward. But on reflection I'm glad you were there. I hope you believed what I said and feel reassured."

"I guess you'll have to meet her when she comes back. Your wife, I mean."

Sedge didn't answer. All afternoon he'd been thinking about Nozomi's proposal to meet and wasn't sure what he'd do when the time came to see her. He'd come so far since meeting Mariko.

Riku emerged from the bathroom and asked Sedge, "Are you making dinner? The house smells like miso."

"I just stir-fried some eggplant and ginger with miso, shiso leaf, and sake. I thought I'd do my part for once and make dinner tonight."

"Thank you for doing that," Mariko said, stepping back inside and laying the broom against the wall. "I'm not feeling all that well."

"There's a kid at school who was talking about fasting. He says it helps build muscle and sharpens your mind, even though you're starving your body. I thought I might try it sometime."

"Is that your way of saying you don't trust my cooking?" Sedge said.

Riku laughed.

"I won't let you do it," Mariko said. "Not while you're living with me, anyway. You're still growing. It's absurd to think you don't need to eat."

"I live in the kura now," he said. "I can do whatever I like."

"If that's what you think, you can pay rent and half our bills, too."

"What about Sedge?"

"Sedge, too."

"If we both pay half, you'll be doing really well."

"You're right. I wonder why I'm working in a ryokan when I'd clearly be more successful as a businesswoman."

Riku laughed again and, saying he had no money to pay her anything, left through the front door. After he stomped across the gravel in the walkway beside the house, it was quiet again where they stood.

"I was horrified to be there this afternoon," she said.

"I know you were. I'm sure he planned it with that in mind."

"When you left, he told me we reflect badly on the ryokan. But aren't we just a scapegoat for it not doing as well as he'd like? There are rumors that the ryokan's in financial trouble and Yuki wants to cut back staff. I'll probably be the first to go if it happens.

Lately Takahashi and Yuki disapprove of everything I do. But they only became that way when you started teaching me."

Sedge was sorry to hear about all of this. "Takahashi said he knew nothing about your husband. He seemed to be telling the truth."

"I've heard nothing myself. Who knows where he is or what he's doing."

They stood awkwardly in the *genkan*. "Does Takahashi often go to the tea lounge now?" Sedge asked.

"Since you left, he comes every day."

Sedge checked his anger. "I made tea. Come have some."

She shook her head. "I'm going to lie down upstairs. Can you call me when dinner is ready?"

An hour later Riku came back and announced that he was hungry. Sedge had set the table and was nearly finished making dinner, so he asked Riku to call Mariko to join them. From the bottom of the stairs Riku shouted to her.

"Why don't you go up and tell her instead of breaking everyone's eardrums like that? She's not feeling well, you know."

Riku answered him seriously. "Because she told me I wasn't to come upstairs anymore. Now that I've moved out, I'm not to go up to your rooms. I have no choice but to shout."

"That's a silly rule. It's better to agree to be respectful."

"But she's like my father: there need to be rules, and the rules must be obeyed."

"She's nothing at all like your father. You know that."

Sedge listened to Mariko's footsteps above while Riku wandered to the table to inspect his cooking.

When they all sat down to eat, Riku told them what he'd learned at school that day about Matsuo Bashō. "Everyone in Yamanaka Onsen knows he spent time here in the seventeenth century. But all those *kuhi* in town with his poems on them are hard to read, and most of my classmates aren't interested in literature. But today our teacher showed us his route when he walked all over the country writing poems. He spent time not just here, but also in Kanazawa, Komatsu, Yamashiro Onsen, and Echizen. He even wrote a poem about Natadera temple."

A docent at the local Bashō museum, a woman born in Natamachi where Natadera stood, once proudly explained to Sedge the poet's haiku immortalizing the temple's white rocks. "But one thing I don't understand is why he walked all over Japan," Sedge said. "Why did he bother traveling for months along that 'narrow road to the deep north'? It might have been interesting at times, but most of his journey had to have been unpleasant, and dangerous, too, with bandits in so many places. And didn't he die on his last trip?"

"Wasn't it to get inspiration?" Mariko asked. "He must have found it, otherwise he wouldn't have written so many famous poems."

Sedge accepted Mariko's answer, but he didn't think it explained Bashō's perseverance in such difficult times. What had set him upon his first journey, all alone at times and probably without real expectations of what it would be like? It must have looked to outsiders like suicide at the time, or hopelessly irresponsible. He turned to Riku for his opinion.

"He did it to escape the pain and sorrow of this world," Riku said, his tone dismissive of Sedge's questions. "At least that's what my teacher said."

"I forgot he was a devoted Buddhist," Sedge said. "A Zen Buddhist, wasn't he?"

But Riku was already on to something else. He had apparently memorized some poems as a class exercise, for he began to recite several that were attributed to the period Bashō stayed in Yamanaka Onsen.

"My favorite Bashō haiku has nothing to do with his time here."

"Which one is that?" Sedge said.

Riku recited this one, too.

> In the late spring rain
> A crane's legs
> Grow ever shorter

"I've seen this happen in the fields," he said. "It's hard to believe he wrote about something I've seen many times here. It makes me want to write haiku, too."

When Riku had said all he wanted, Sedge turned to Mariko and asked if earlier she'd fallen asleep upstairs.

"I did. I dreamed about you, actually."

Riku lowered his soup bowl from his mouth and said, "What about?"

To Sedge she said, "It was very realistic. I dreamed that you left us."

Riku glanced between the two of them. In a low voice he said, "Why would he do that?"

"In the dream, he decided to leave for some reason. It wasn't just that, though. He was leaving and said he would never see us again. We kept telling him it wasn't necessary, but he only nodded and insisted that it was. Right when you called me, Riku, you and I were watching him on TV. The news was reporting something he had done, and everyone was celebrating. But it wasn't the local news we always watch. He was in a big city far away."

"Most dreams don't mean anything," Riku said.

"The funny thing is," she went on, ignoring Riku's remark, "I was crying when I woke up. Everyone on TV acted so happy for him. But in my dream I'd burst into tears." She looked away for a moment. "Now that I've told you about it, the dream is losing its vividness. How strange." A short, startled laugh escaped her.

"You're putting too much stock in that dream," Sedge said, shaken by what she'd described. He imagined that Nozomi's return had provoked it. He couldn't ask if she'd appeared in it, too. "Even if you've taken me in temporarily, I have no plans to leave soon."

"But you will eventually," Riku said.

"You will," Mariko said. "I didn't realize it until just now. Not the full reality of it, anyway."

"How am I supposed to defend myself from what you saw in a dream?"

Mariko laughed, wiping her eyes. "I'm sorry. Riku, we shouldn't make him feel bad. After all, he cooked a great dinner for us, didn't he?"

"I like your cooking better."

Sedge laughed, too. "I promise to stay long enough to perfect my cooking in both your eyes. That should be worth something."

Riku finished his dinner quickly and without a word left the house.

"I upset him," Mariko said. "He's fond of you, you know."

Sedge wiped Riku's place with a napkin. "I don't remember myself being so sensitive at his age. Or at your age, either."

"Neither of us wants to be left behind again," she said. "You understand, don't you?"

Sedge nodded. He understood that worry all too well.

Sometime after midnight, lying on his futon and thinking of the quiet night he'd spent downstairs alone, he saw a message light up his phone. It was from Mariko.

"I'm still not feeling well, so I think I'll go to sleep now."

He walked softly to her door and stood there for a moment. The door had no lock, and she always kept it ajar; this was the first time since he'd moved here that she had shut it. He sat in the doorway of the middle room that separated them and listened to the night through the thin windows and walls. The cicadas had fallen quiet, but, following a short rainfall after dinner, the frogs were louder than ever. The winds remained from the storm, and Mariko's house, as it always did, creaked in their battering gusts. It was a lonely feeling, sitting in the dark by himself and listening to the sounds of an old mountain village.

He didn't hear Mariko rise from her futon and walk to the door. When she opened it and stepped into the hallway before the doorway where Sedge sat, she gasped.

"What are you doing there?" Mariko entered the room and kneeled in front of him. She was wearing a summer *yukata*, clutching its opening to her chest.

"You said you weren't feeling well. But when I came to check on you, I thought you might prefer being alone."

"I never want to be away from you. It's your absence that made me ill. Come here."

She led him into her bedroom. Of the three curtained windows along her walls, only the one behind her futon had been left open for the sky to pour its light inside. It was enough to see her figure when she slid her *yukata* off, light and darkness moving over her body: her nipples, her navel, the space beneath her armpits, the barely visible bars of shadow between her ribs, the constellation of scars—the sea of skin that surrounded these things, like water keeping islands afloat.

She lay down and pulled him beside her. Her hands never left him, and even for a time her feet became hands, she was everywhere pulling him into her body; they would have been pummeling each other if not for the sweetness of it. Eventually the violence of their union settled into the slow and steady rhythm they had taught each other to follow. Their breathing marked the realness of their existence, and when they came together it felt like falling through stopped time. As always, it had passed too quickly. He wanted more of her but would have to wait.

She lay on her back beside him, and he turned to her, letting his fingers find her scars in the dark like a code they wanted him to decipher. He closed his eyes but opened them again when she pushed her body into his and drew in an anguished breath.

"What is it?" he said softly.

"I thought we closed the door."

Sedge looked across the room. The door was wide open, exposing a rectangle of darkness where the outside light couldn't reach. He glanced around them. A silvery light still illuminated their bodies, the futon, and the back window, beyond which stood the kura. The wind howled, knocking the glass windows against their frames.

"We did," he said. "I pulled it shut. It must have opened in all the wind."

He stood to shut the door again and when Mariko called to him, "Stop!" he turned around to see what she meant.

He never saw Riku rush into their bedroom, nor did he hear him—not clearly, anyway. Mariko shrieked as Sedge crumpled under the force of Riku launching into his back. Together they toppled to the floor in an explosive thud that shook the house.

At first Sedge thought an overhead beam had crashed down on him, but he quickly realized it was the boy. Riku had pinned him down. With his chest pressing on Sedge's curled-up body he smashed his head into the floor and kneed him in his back. Sedge was sure he'd be killed if he didn't find a way to fight back.

Flailing with the one arm not trapped beneath him, he pulled

Mariko's discarded *yukata* toward him, thinking he would shove it between his head and the floor, but as Riku's position shifted and Sedge's other hand came unstuck, he managed to wrap the *yukata* around the boy's neck. He twisted it quickly and pulled it taut. As Riku grabbed at it, Sedge rolled out from beneath him but kept close enough that he never relinquished the *yukata*. Perhaps it only distracted Riku, or put fear into him, but in another moment Sedge had reversed his disadvantage. They now faced each other. Sedge crouched naked beside the futon, blood trickling down his face and into his mouth. The boy sat on his buttocks and flung the *yukata* from his neck.

Riku stood and hovered over Sedge. "Get up!" he shouted. "I'll kill you! I should have killed you when I saw you together like that!"

Perhaps the clouds parted then, but the light from outside brightened slightly. Sedge kicked at him in a warning, aiming for his legs and not caring if he hurt the boy. He struck his knee. When Riku toppled forward a little he kicked him again, this time in the chin. Riku fell and rolled to his side, and with his legs pulled to his chest began sobbing. Sedge didn't think he had hurt him badly. From what he could tell, Riku had only given up.

Mariko ran along the wall to the room light and switched it on. She stared with Sedge at the scene. Sedge stepped into his boxers and picked up his t-shirt to wipe the blood from his face. He tossed Mariko her *yukata* and she wrapped herself in it again.

Sedge didn't know where the instinct came from, but he bent down to Riku and pried the boy's fingers from where he gripped his own body. Riku relented, and Sedge brought him to a sitting position. He hugged the boy, bringing his face to his shoulder and palming the back of his head.

Mariko hovered in the doorway, her hands over her mouth, clearly unsure what to do. "You're both bleeding. Are you okay?"

"Bring some wet towels and a medical kit if you have one. Our injuries aren't life-threatening."

When she was gone Sedge pulled Riku's face from his shoulder. "Why did you attack me? Were you watching us from the door the whole time?"

Riku's tear-soaked eyes blinked in the room's bright light. Sedge repeated his question. Riku only nodded.

Sedge listened to Mariko as she ran around the first floor and hurried back upstairs. Her hands were full of the things he had requested.

"He was sleeping down there," she said, "not in the kura. There's a futon in the room beneath the stairs."

"He must have heard us. He came up to confirm his suspicions. And when we stopped and I walked toward the door, he couldn't control his anger and attacked me. Isn't that what happened, Riku?"

When he didn't answer, Mariko screamed at him: "Riku!"

The boy nodded again.

Sedge let go of Riku as Mariko checked the gash on the boy's chin. It trickled with blood, but she didn't think he needed stitches. "Let's apply some pressure to it, and when it stops bleeding we'll bandage it."

She turned to Sedge and grimaced. "Look at you."

"I'm fine," he told her.

Riku's cut soon stopped bleeding. They led him downstairs, Mariko ahead of him and Sedge behind, and sat on either side of him as he lay back down to sleep. Sedge suggested that Mariko try to sleep, too. He would stay with Riku, and in the morning she could deal with the incident however she wanted. When she came back downstairs, it would be his turn to sleep.

She pulled Sedge into the hallway. Stepping behind the sliding door of the room where Riku lay, she hugged him again and started to cry.

19

Sedge arrived early at the hotel's streetside café, opposite the apartment he and Nozomi once lived in. He guessed she had chosen this place to appeal to his nostalgic side. Had their life together proceeded as he once believed, they would still be here in Korinbō, and from his table inside the café he might now be watching either of them through their apartment window.

He recognized a resident from the building cross the street, and he looked away, not wanting to be seen and recognized himself.

How had he and Nozomi appeared in other people's eyes all the times they'd crossed that intersection hand-in-hand; spent their evenings wandering along the rivers and through the old geisha districts; or attended Kanazawa's many festivals? What did the owners of the *izakaya* they frequented say about them after they left? The café workers where they spent their weekend mornings? The mutual friends they ate and drank with? Had he overlooked what all of them might have seen clearly? Upon learning of her leaving him, had they been as astonished as he?

Nozomi entered the lobby at the exact time she'd suggested they meet. Removing her sunglasses and sunhat, she turned into the café and spotted him. Tentatively she smiled.

Although she'd been gone a year, inside him their time apart contracted suddenly, and that she hadn't outwardly changed both confounded him and seemed inevitable. In addition to being shorter, her hair was also lighter, a chocolatey color it might have become after exposure to the sun. She paused at his table and gave a long, low bow. Her hair fell from behind her ears and hung straight down, causing her sunglasses to drop from the neck of her dress to the floor. A waitress behind her knelt to retrieve them. People at the surrounding tables had turned to watch Nozomi's unexpectedly formal behavior. It was like a performance, Sedge nearly said aloud.

She sat across from him and asked the same waitress for a glass of water and a cup of coffee. The waitress looked at Sedge, who had put off ordering until Nozomi arrived. "I'll have the same," he told her.

Nozomi set her sunglasses on the table. Almost immediately she took them back and placed them in her lap, where she turned them over repeatedly. The clacking of their earpieces was the only noise between them.

"Thank you for meeting me," she finally said. "I realize it can't be easy for you."

Her voice was stronger than he expected—different from before, or different from how he remembered it. Hearing it confirmed that she was real and in front of him again. Even so, he remembered—he consciously reminded himself—that he had nothing to celebrate by seeing her. Though he tried to conceal his careful observation of her, he noticed she was thinner, her cheeks and the line of her shoulders just prominent enough to indicate this. Had she lost weight because she'd been taking care of herself, or because of worry or even illness? She wore little makeup, which wasn't unusual, allowing him to see she wasn't hiding any bruises. His mind raced wildly. He could barely speak.

"Is this easy for you?" he managed to say.

"Of course not. But I'm relieved we're together again like this. I was extremely nervous until I saw you sitting here."

"And you're not now?"

"No, I am. Would you like to feel my pulse?" She held out

an arm, beautifully white with perfect green-blue veins running through it.

He shook his head.

"Your face is bruised," she said, leaning forward. "What happened?"

"I got in a fight."

"You? You never fight. Who was it with?"

"It doesn't matter."

She reached across the small, marble-topped table between them and took his hand. He wanted to draw it away, but the inclination was only a mental exercise. Her hand was warm; or his was unnaturally cold. He only pulled his hand back when he could no longer control its trembling.

"Are you moving back to Kanazawa?" he said.

She paused, and he saw her trying to process his tone. "I don't know yet. It depends partly on what my mother and brother ask me to do. If anything."

When she turned to look out the window, his eyes scrambled over her body, which appeared thinner as well. That another man had taken it from him, had probably discovered every secret pleasure it had once bestowed only on Sedge, infuriated him. And yet he had discovered similar pleasures with that very same man's wife. None of it made sense.

"Have you seen them yet?" he asked.

"Yes. I stayed at Takahashi and Yuki's ryokan my first night back. For the last two days I've been at my mother's."

Sedge could hardly believe she had been in Yamanaka Onsen at the same time he was living with Mariko. He wondered if the two women had seen each other. Mariko never mentioned that she had, but it would also be like her to shield him from this, just as she had shielded him from her husband's Kutani-ware in the hallway outside his room.

"I was sorry to hear about your father," he said. "Your family kept me at arm's length after he died. They distrusted me, and your mother was sure I'd chased you off. That hurt me, but I came to understand where I stood. I'm afraid I pushed them hard to be included in his funeral and cremation. You've probably heard about it by now."

"Why would they distrust you?"

"They didn't say?"

She shook her head.

"They worried that I'd press charges against you. It's true they helped me, but they weren't concerned with my well-being. More than anything, they were afraid about what might happen to them."

She looked down. "I'm sorry. I made it awkward for everyone."

"You're lucky they're so forgiving with you."

The waitress came back with their drinks and slid a cakes menu onto their table. By the time she bowed and stepped away, Nozomi was looking at him again.

"I'm not sure which I regret more: leaving you how I did or being unreachable when my father passed away. At least I'll be able to help with the *shijūkunichi* soon. That consoles me a little."

Sedge had forgotten about the forty-nine-day death memorial that her family would hold, but it no longer mattered to him.

She continued: "The man I ran away with, Kōichi, insisted that I hold off contacting anyone, even my parents. He took my phone the moment we left Kanazawa and wouldn't give it back. In the end, he threw it into a river and just laughed. You may not believe it, or not want to hear it, but it's been difficult for me, too."

"What do you mean?"

But she didn't answer, and he wasn't prepared for what she said. "I don't want to go into it now, but Kōichi wasn't who I thought he was. He took the money I'd taken from you, and I had to beg for everything I needed."

"What did you need it for?" The question nearly burst out of him. "Why did you have to take everything?"

"He told me to. And I didn't want to disappoint him. He said we needed it to live on."

Sedge closed his eyes and kept them shut until she spoke again.

"One time he just . . . went crazy," she went on, her voice quieter—or perhaps it was the competing noise of the café that made it harder to hear her.

"What did he do?"

"He frightened me. The things he said were . . . they were unforgivable."

"And that's why you came back? Because he took your money after you'd taken it from me and spoke unkindly to you? Neither of you must have loved each other if it all came crashing down so easily."

"I never loved him, Sedge."

He didn't believe her. It would complicate things more if he did. He asked again why she came back.

"I came back because . . . I couldn't experience what I wanted to."

"Which was what?"

"In the end I suppose it was an illusion." She smiled as if to prepare him for a riddle that has no answer. "Before I say anything, you have to realize that I can't explain it so you'll understand. I wish I could, but . . ."

"Try me first before telling me I won't understand," he snapped

"Okay. But it won't be easy for you." She studied him for a moment before continuing. "I left to atone for my past."

"Your past when?"

"My past before I met you."

Her words were a poisonous effusion, washing away every thought he had. "You mean your first boyfriend who killed himself?"

She nodded. "Yes, I mean Tetsuya. Kōichi came into our shop the first time almost three years ago and we spoke for a while. A week later he texted me to invite me out for coffee. He said you weren't to come. When I asked why not, he explained our connection to each other: Over the six months I dated Tetsuya, Kōichi had been his best friend. He knew all about me. Tetsuya had mentioned Kōichi to me only a few times that I could recall, and I'd never paid attention to it. But once he told me, I remembered who he was. He wanted to talk about what had happened between me and Tetsuya twenty-five years ago. Because I still felt guilty about it, I agreed.

"We met at an old *kissaten* near the train station, where the half-blind granny that ran it played *enka* tunes all day and the interior was dark with stained wood and years of tobacco smoke. It was the perfect place to meet secretly, where we could say anything and not worry about being overheard. In fact, we were the only ones there that day. And just about every other time we went there, too."

She paused and Sedge said, "How many times did you meet there?"

"At the *kissaten*? Half a dozen, I guess. On the same days our shop was closed or when I had appointments in town. We started meeting in other places, too. Hotels, mostly, I'm sorry to say. Anyway, on about our third meeting there, after we'd reminisced about Tetsuya's life and our lives with him, he said I was to blame for his suicide. That hit me hard, especially since everything we'd talked about before had celebrated his life. I knew it was true. Other people back then had circled around saying the same thing, but I knew what they were accusing me of. Kōichi convinced me that if I'd suffered for my wrongdoing when Tetsuya was alive, he'd still be with us."

"Kōichi is a sonofabitch."

"I know that now. But I believed he was saying all the things I'd needed to hear for twenty-five years. Somehow he cast a spell over me. Luckily, it didn't last."

"It didn't last?" he said sarcastically.

"It could have been longer. And worse in the end."

Sedge was sure she was right, but that she considered herself lucky after she'd nearly ruined his life angered him. "Why do you still think you were to blame? You only ended the relationship. That happens all the time. And you were only fifteen then. You were both children, basically."

"Tetsuya found out I'd been seeing other guys when we were together. I cheated on him many times. And Kōichi was the one who told him."

"Clearly he never should have. But even so, no one's to blame for what Tetsuya did. Not even Kōichi."

"I wasn't just a jerky teenage girl, Sedge, but something more repulsive—the things I said and did even after he found out. I . . . I even suggested he kill himself once. Of course I said it out of anger or frustration and didn't actually mean it."

This was the first time she'd admitted this to Sedge. "Of course you didn't mean it."

"I've been living with the thought that he killed himself because of me, and I was so selfish and clueless about everything. I think that was why it took so little for me to accept Kōichi's accusation. And he convinced me very quickly that he was the logical one, the only one, who still connected me to Tetsuya. From there, he had me in a vulnerable position."

Sedge rubbed his temples with his fingers, trying to process what she was telling him. He couldn't help but think of stories he'd heard about former cult members—people who had been manipulated for sex, or money, or other things—who were desperate to expiate sins they believed they were guilty of. He never would have believed that Nozomi, his own wife, whom he'd known for ten years, could sound like this.

"And that's when you and he became lovers?"

She turned to look out the window again. A moment later she nodded. "I'm sorry," she said, barely audible.

"Why did you decide to leave together? Why didn't you simply continue seeing him on the side?" He was surprised to hear himself suggest it would have been better to cheat on him without leaving. It pained him to ask, but he had no choice.

"I didn't want to keep deceiving you. And we thought it would be easier for me to suffer how I needed."

Responding to the question in his face she said, "I don't remember which came first, my asking for this or his suggesting it. But we both agreed on it. We had no specific plan at first, but I felt I was making a sacred commitment, I suppose. I don't know how to explain it except to say I found it necessary. I thought I had to do it . . . to get my life back on track."

"But it was always on track."

"That's what you never understood."

Sedge watched Nozomi turn her cup in its saucer. Its grinding sound made him want to knock it to the floor.

"You mean you feel that way still? I thought you said he only tricked you."

"What I mean is you never understood how I felt. That my guilt was taking me to a place I could never return from. I did feel that way, Sedge. And although I left to atone for my past, I did it with the wrong person. I have a lot of thinking to do now. But I guess that goes without saying."

"Where did you expect you'd be able to atone for Tetsuya?"

"Far away, obviously. I thought the mountains would be best, but it turns out I'm not suited to them, especially in the winter. Then I thought an island, the remoter the better, would suffice, but I wasn't suited to that life, either."

He came back to what he'd said before. "What kind of suffering were you looking for?"

"I didn't know in the beginning. I assumed we'd eventually figure it out, but we had to leave our lives behind first."

He scoffed at this. She had thrown away him and their marriage to try to absolve herself of a tragedy she wasn't responsible for. She had set out with an impossible goal to attain. It still made no sense to him.

Her plan to suffer with Kōichi recalled sordid tales of lover's suicides—a staple in old Japanese movies and novels, yet not unheard of today—and group suicide pacts and online suicide clubs headlining the news in more recent times. Of course, these phenomena didn't only exist in Japan, but they seemed to find particularly fertile ground here. "Were you two planning to die together?"

She shook her head vehemently. "I never wanted to end my life and I'm sure Kōichi didn't either. We never discussed it."

This, at least, relieved Sedge.

In an almost defensive voice she said, "No, I only wanted to suffer. I wanted to see how far I could push myself, to learn what I was capable of bearing up against. I wanted to be deprived of everything I loved, everything that mattered to me, every comfort and joy—so I could get closer to what Kōichi and I thought Tetsuya had felt. Because those were the things I'd taken away from him." She paused, looking up at the ceiling and closing her eyes. A moment later she looked back at him, her eyes shining with tears. "I could never have done that with you, Sedge. But with Kōichi, it was easy. The problem was I couldn't rely on him. Too many times he . . ." She trailed off, shaking her head miserably. "Anyway, in the end, when I had nothing, and when I thought my life might be in jeopardy, my mother and Takahashi promised to help me. I became afraid, Sedge . . ."

He stifled the question he wanted to ask: Why didn't you come to me? Instead he said, "What do you mean?"

"When I demanded that we move again, he turned violent. It wasn't just his words this time."

To hear her talk about how she had suffered, despite what she'd done to him, confused him. An unexpected tenderness washed over him, and the hurt in her eyes made him want to forgive her. It would be so much easier than continuing to hate her. She smiled as if embarrassed by what she'd told him.

Sedge's hands had started shaking again and he dropped them to his lap. He glanced at the backpack beside his chair and at the folder he could see through the open zipper at the top.

"You can't understand it, can you, Sedge?"

"No. I can't."

"You would if you had suffered more."

"What are you talking about? I've suffered plenty since you left me. For a long time, pain was all I knew."

She shook her head even before he'd finished speaking. "I don't want you to think I'm diminishing your grief. But that's not what I'm talking about. At bottom, you see, what you just described is selfish. You've never suffered because of the pain another person has gone through or what they've lost. You've never suffered from guilt. Not the way I have, anyway. We've talked about this before."

"I know we have."

"And you never sympathized with me. In all the years you knew me, and knew about Tetsuya, you never understood me from that perspective. The perspective of my suffering. So no, I can see you don't understand me. You're too wrapped up in what I did to you. Which is fair. Your suffering is entirely my fault. And I'm sorry for that."

Again he found himself confused. "So the only way I could sympathize with you is if I did something that resulted in someone's suicide?"

"Are you making a tasteless joke or are you really so unimaginative?"

Nozomi had always been more direct with Sedge than other Japanese people he knew. But today, in the context of their discussion, it made it more difficult to understand her.

"I'm having a hard time with this is all. Kōichi clearly brainwashed you, but that couldn't be all there was to it because he left his whole life behind, too. And he had a reasonably good life, from what I've pieced together."

She shook her head slowly but didn't contradict this.

"Maybe you're right and it's impossible for me to understand your reasons," he said. "But why did you do it *the way you did*?"

"I'm not really sure. I know I didn't want to draw it out. I thought it would be better if we just woke up one day and saw that the other was no longer there."

"Why did you need to run away with him?"

"I told you. Because I thought he could help me. He was the connection to Tetsuya I needed. It couldn't have been you or anyone else."

Hearing this sickened him.

She continued. "He made me believe that his helping me, and my trusting him to, was the foundation we needed to start a new life. But I was foolish to believe him. Even what I set out to do, though at the time I embraced it with almost religious fervor, I now see was utterly wasteful. Utterly mistaken. For a time I must have lost my mind."

She reached again for both his hands where they now rested on the table and dropped her head in a half-bow, almost violently. He detected something broken in the gesture. Or was it something inside her? He hoped that there was, for what was broken could perhaps finally heal.

The people on either side of them had stopped talking. From the corner of his eye he saw them watching Nozomi.

"You never answered my question," Sedge said when she looked out the window again. "Where exactly did you run off to?"

"It doesn't matter, does it? I'm not going back."

"Tell me anyway. I'm trying to piece all of this together."

"In the end we went to Fukushima."

"Fukushima? Why?"

"After the nuclear meltdown, the population in many places bottomed out. We thought it would be easy to start over there, without anyone looking at us strangely or getting into our business. If that didn't work out, we talked about Okinawa, or even somewhere overseas where it was easy to get a visa and stay for as long as we wanted. But in Fukushima it fell apart quickly and—"

"I don't want to hear the rest. I just wanted to know where you thought would be better than here."

"I wasn't looking for better. You were that all along."

Sedge stared at her, not knowing what to say.

"Takahashi said you contacted the police about the money," she said.

"It was preliminary paperwork; I've waited all this time to avoid submitting it. I'm willing to let it go as soon as you return what you took."

She gazed at her water glass, finally reaching for it and drinking several quick sips.

"What do you suggest we do about it?" he said.

She bowed to him again. "I'm sorry for the trouble I've caused you, Sedge. My family suggested I borrow money from them to pay you back. My mother and brother were able to loan me only a little of what I took, but it'll have to do for now."

She removed from her handbag two regular-sized mail envelopes and placed them on their table.

"They're full of cash. I hope you don't mind doing things this way."

"What about the rest?"

She shook her head. "I have nothing, either, Sedge. Yuki suggested we invest this in a new shop. But Takahashi said you'd never go for that, and I agreed that it wouldn't work. But if you thought it would be a way forward . . ."

"If I did that," Sedge said, "how would I trust you again?"

He picked up the envelopes and dropped them into his backpack. Afterward, he lifted out the folder he'd brought with him and handed it to her. "It's a copy of the divorce papers from my lawyer. You can read over them and stamp your *hanko* seal on the places he marked. I can do it without your cooperation, but if you give it to me it will go more smoothly."

She hesitated but took the folder he held out to her.

"Would you stay with me tonight if I got us a room here?" she said. "I feel like we have a lot more to work through. Wouldn't it be easier to do that now that we've seen each other again? We're here already and . . ."

Sedge lacked the resolve to stand up and walk away; he considered what it would mean if he went upstairs with her.

They sat in strained silence. Then, out of nowhere, he thought again of her going to hotels with Mariko's husband. Had they ever come together to this one, right under his nose?

Instead of answering her he asked, "Where's Kōichi?"

"I don't know. I assume he's still in Fukushima."

"He's not back in Yamanaka Onsen?"

"I have no idea. I don't want to know anything about him now."

They were silent again for a long time. Nozomi suggested again that she ask the hotel if they had a room available. "I'm willing to reserve it for two or three days even, if you want me to."

"I don't think that's a good idea."

"What wouldn't be good about it? We could make it good."

"I don't know. I just don't think . . ."

"Why not? I'd do anything to make you forgive me, Sedge."

"It wouldn't be right, that's why."

"I don't understand."

But what he meant when he said it wouldn't be right had to do with Mariko. It wouldn't be right to her.

"I want to make it right, Sedge. I want one little chance. Do you really feel so vulnerable with me?"

Nozomi's suggestion was what he'd wanted for so many months. What if he went upstairs with her, just for one night? What did he care if Nozomi suffered for it later?

At that moment he grieved for her. For if what she'd told him about her suffering was true, he had the advantage over her of being able to leave her here and find stability, even love, in Mariko. Without her, he knew he would go upstairs with Nozomi and lose himself in her, which was to say lose everything all over again. He understood with rare clarity that he owed Mariko a debt of gratitude and maybe more.

"Why does my forgiveness matter?" he said, feeling anger well in him. "Because of the money?" When she didn't say anything he continued: "Don't you see you've only set yourself up to feel about me—about us—the same way you felt about Tetsuya for all these years? You've done the same thing, and you'll never get out of this cycle you're trapped in. You sacrificed me—us—for a wisp of the past you failed to chase down. You turned what we had into Tetsuya."

She stared out the window a long time. "I understand why you think that, but it's different. For one thing, you're alive. And I hope we can find a way to move forward somehow. With your for-giveness, initially . . ."

Tightness formed in his chest and he massaged it as he replied: "I don't believe you're sorry for what you did. And you don't want us to be back together. Though I wish you did. It would make me feel better even if it were hopeless for us to move in that direction."

"No matter what I do, there's no way I can fix things?"

"Fix them how? How do you fix something that's been smashed to a million pieces?"

She sighed and shook her head. "I don't know."

"You still haven't explained why you did what you did, sac-rificing our happiness for the sadness you went through twen-ty-five years ago, without so much as talking to me about it. I was forced to leave that apartment we lived in for how many years together—six? I had to close our shop by myself and pay our taxes with money I could only get by selling everything we had and begging the rest from my friends. I was forced to live in Yuki and Takahashi's ryokan and feel indebted to them in the most miserable way." He paused before adding, "But one good thing came out of it."

Nozomi's eyes pulled away from him. "My brother told me."

"It was poetic, don't you think?" He waited, cruelly he sup-posed, for her to answer. When she didn't he said, "She and I are still together, you know."

"It may be unfair of me to say, but I don't want to hear about it."

For the first time since he'd seen her again, he wanted to

laugh. But he refrained from this, and also from telling her more about Mariko. He had nothing to gain by hurting her.

"I'm alone now, Sedge. If you don't want to see me anymore, I intend to leave again. It's easier to start over where I can reinvent myself."

Her talk of leaving again pained him despite his resolve to move on from her. "It's not easy for me, either. Even now. Even after I've found someone else."

"Do you love her? More than you loved me?"

"Don't ask me that. There's no point, is there?"

"There could be . . ."

They were silent for a long time. Finally Sedge realized he had nothing more to say. He pointed to the folder he'd given her. "There's an address inside for you to send those papers to," he said, overcome by an exhaustion he saw in Nozomi, too. "Don't forget to take them with you and *hanko* them all. You can email me when you're ready to return the rest of my money. I'll tell you where and how to send it. It's better if it's not in person again."

He lifted his backpack and stumbled through the other tables to the counter. As he pulled out his wallet to hand the waitress what they owed, he noticed that his hands had stopped shaking.

On his way to the exit, Nozomi hurried to him and held him by the arm.

"The registration desk is over there. Let me get us a room, then come upstairs with me. You can leave whenever you like. Just give me a chance to earn the smallest bit of your forgiveness. Maybe it will show us a way forward."

She pulled him back from the door. He could see her trying to smile at him. She pulled his arm again and they began walking toward the registration desk.

When the staff there greeted them, Sedge stopped and shook

his arm free. He had remembered their conversation in Hegurajima when she said she wished he had suffered more.

"Not after what you did. I'm not the same person I used to be.
But you, I'll never have a way to know."

He glanced back at her before he left the hotel. As she watched
him, and he observed again that face he'd once loved with all he
could give, he wondered with both fear and sadness if it was ever
possible to know what another person was capable of—for the
love of another, or for the love of oneself.

20

Before coming to Kanazawa to meet Nozomi, Sedge had arranged to spend the weekend at the home of his friend, Shinji, who would be out of town. He had given Sedge permission to invite Mariko. Riku, who hadn't seen his grandparents for several months, would visit them in Echizen at the same time. Mariko agreed that getting away for a couple of days would be healthy for all three of them. She planned to come to Kanazawa the day after Sedge met Nozomi.

Shinji lived beside the Asano River, between the Tenjin and Asanogawa bridges. The front of his tenth-floor apartment peered over a row of four-hundred-year-old black pine trees toward Mt. Utatsu, while from the bedroom in back one could see parts of Kanazawa Castle and Kenrokuen. The neighborhood was more residential and traditional than where Sedge and Nozomi had lived; from what he recalled, in the Edo period, before the West forced Japan to open, it had been home to Kanazawa's "undesirables": prostitutes, leather workers, handlers of the dead. Now, however, the area was desirable. He looked forward to staying here for two days and nights, away from the general bustle of Korinbō and far from where he had made most of his memories of Kanazawa.

Meeting with Nozomi had deeply unsettled him. He now wished they had communicated by writing rather than in person. They could have told each other the same things, and probably much more, and he could have received the money she'd returned through Takahashi. Yet he was grateful for having seen her again.

That afternoon, wishing Mariko were already with him, he

strolled along the Asano River, finding it visited by fish and birds. He sat on the riverbank near Tokiwa Bridge, watching loaches dart through the shallow water; and the wagtails, thrushes, swallows, and kingfishers that flew down to its stony edges; and the osprey, kites, and herons that glided above the low mountains or circled overhead. Mariko would have been thrilled to see them all.

And what would Riku think of this place? Sedge imagined sitting here with him, just the two of them together birdwatching. As he imagined this, Nozomi's accusation that he wasn't sympathetic to other people's suffering came to rest before this image of Riku. There was no denying that the boy had suffered more than most, but Sedge's resistance to him wouldn't accommodate any sympathy yet.

Try as he might, he couldn't imagine the boy continuing to live with them. He had made sexual overtures toward Mariko and attacked Sedge after sleeping with her. For Sedge, this wasn't a battle over who would be dominant between them. He was convinced Riku was trying to claim more than he had a natural right to. He couldn't trust the boy around her now and wanted to find a way to put distance between them. How was he to be sympathetic to him now?

He still carried the backpack that he'd brought to the hotel, along with the envelopes inside. Their weight in a bottom pocket reassured him, bumping against his back as he walked. He was glad for the money and would be gladder for the rest; having it would rid him of an enormous obstruction in his life. And he would no longer have to rely on Mariko for a place to live, though he hoped he wouldn't need to move out right away. This last thought made him question how selfish he'd been with her. But they weren't becoming such significant parts of each other's lives, and he hadn't chosen to live with her, merely out of convenience.

She had opened her life to him. She had taken more risks than he, and if one day their relationship ended, he knew the consequences for her would be worse.

Mariko arrived late the next morning. He'd been eager to see her since yesterday, and he hardly let her out of his sight after ushering her inside the apartment. She had brought groceries to cook for them, but Sedge wanted her to relax, to treat her time in Kanazawa as a vacation. He hadn't told her about the money Nozomi returned, but he planned to spend more than usual of what he had on her. There was no reason for them to cook, he assured her.

"I was in too much of a hurry to eat breakfast," she said. "Will we have lunch soon?"

"I made a reservation at Kenrokuen. I thought it would be nice to go back."

Kenrokuen was only a fifteen-minute walk away, and after entering through Katsurazaka Gate they strolled along a wooded pathway, looping back to Hisagoike pond. Peeling away from the crowds, they crossed another path to Miyoshi-an, the restaurant where they would eat. It was perched on the pond's northern edge, framed by a wooden trellis whose intertwined vines shaded the tables at the restaurant's long window.

A waitress led them to a table near the back. After ordering, they gazed outside.

"Look at all the carp swimming past," Mariko said, her face close to the glass.

They hadn't talked about anything significant since she'd arrived, and he saw they were avoiding topics that if left unbroached would make their time together feel safer, less threatened by the outside world. Even now, they hadn't spoken about Nozomi, nor about a job interview in Fukui next week that he wanted to cancel, nor about Riku's departure. Although he wanted to unencumber Mariko of the deeper issues they faced, it might clear the air if they stopped being so careful with each other.

"Aren't you wondering how my meeting with Nozomi went?" he said.

She tensed at his question. "Of course. But I didn't want to bring it up in case it had upset you."

"But it concerns you, doesn't it?"

Smiling uncertainly, she looked again out the window, this time to where a small waterfall trickled down a narrow slope into the pond.

"Did your husband come back?" He was sure she would have told him if he did, but he had to ask, to introduce him into this conversation they needed to have.

"No. In the past, after an affair ended, he didn't return right away, either. I only know he and your wife aren't together anymore. Whatever else you tell me will be the first I've heard about it."

"Then I guess we're equally in the dark. I know no more than you do."

He wondered if he had been wrong to ask Mariko what he did. But surely it wasn't unexpected.

"I gave my wife the divorce papers to sign," he said. "According to my lawyer, it shouldn't take long to approve them. And she gave back some of the money she took. Hopefully she'll return the rest later, though I'm not holding my breath."

Despite saying before that she was hungry, Mariko took no notice of the food when it came. She continued to gaze out the window. "The money . . . was it enough?" she said.

He snapped apart the disposable chopsticks from his tray. She flinched at the sound. "It will be for some things," he said. "And it's more than I've had since she left."

"How much was it?"

Her wanting to know the specific amount surprised him. "Almost eight hundred thousand yen. Her family loaned her the money."

"You're finally free to do anything you want."

Again her comment took him aback. He didn't know how to reply.

"I would understand if you decided not to live with us anymore. Especially after what Riku did."

"The only reason I'd leave is if you feel I'm an imposition."

She looked at her lunch as if seeing it for the first time. They ate in silence. When they finished, she thanked him for introducing her to Miyoshi-an. "I'm afraid I ruined the mood," she said. "You shared good news with me, after all. You must wonder what's going through my mind. I'm wondering myself, actually."

"Let's just try to enjoy Kanazawa together."

She smiled faintly. "I'll try not to let myself worry."

The sun poured down as they made their way around the landscape garden. Now that they had eaten, Mariko wanted to see where Sedge had helped the injured heron back in March.

That evening they dined at Huni, an *izakaya* near their apartment where Mariko found herself interested in, for Riku's sake, the sophisticated Buddhist and Shinto carvings the owner had made. Afterward she stopped Sedge on the riverside and said, "I'd like to see where you used to live. Is it too far to walk to?"

"Nowhere's too far to walk to in Kanazawa. But we've walked a lot today."

"When I'm with you I'm not tired."

He took her hand. "Why do you want to see it?"

"I'm curious about where your life was before we met. But if it makes you uncomfortable, let's not go."

"No," he said quickly, "it's fine."

They walked through the Kazuemachi geisha district. The long path there ended at the Kobashi bridge, where a loud croaking across the river stopped them. There was just enough light to see a large tree in the concrete river wall. Sleeping in the middle and lower branches were a dozen herons. Two perched close together opened their wings to each other and more deafening croaks filled the air. Sedge and Mariko watched them until the mosquitoes that gathered over the river during the summer buzzed in their ears.

Mariko suggested the herons were a good omen for them. "Good things always happen after we see herons together."

When they reached Korinbō, Sedge showed her the hotel where he and Nozomi had met. He pointed across the street to the apartment Mariko wanted to see. "We lived on the fifth floor, in the corner unit overlooking the street."

Watching her gaze lift to the apartment window, Sedge didn't expect to feel so composed after all that had happened to him here, both yesterday and in the more distant past.

"Someone lives there now," she said. "It has curtains in the windows and the lights are on."

"I would imagine so. It's been a long time since I moved away."

He recalled the day he moved out. Even then he had felt the absence of his life between its walls, the sadness of a ghost wandering through its former existence. He was struck now by that sadness. Standing beside Mariko, he wondered if she, too, were to disappear, would he feel the same dark void as when Nozomi had left him? The thought left him newly shaken.

"Why did they leave us?" Mariko said.

He scanned the other windows to see which apartments had no one living in them. He couldn't tell in the dim light, and in any case it didn't matter.

She pulled at his arm until he faced her. "Did she explain anything at all?"

"Not in any way I could understand," he said in frustration.

He suggested going back. They cut through the Daiwa department store and followed the path around the grassy area skirting Kanazawa Castle Park. As they turned at Imori Moat, Sedge glanced back at the way they'd come. Beyond the open space they'd walked through, Korinbō, rising in the distance, threw the bright lights of its buildings across the far half of the sky.

He had lived in Kanazawa for nearly six years. But already home had become someplace very far and different from here.

They saw and did things in Kanazawa that they'd never seen and done together before. Sedge didn't push again for them to discuss any serious subjects. After what he'd told her about meeting Nozomi, dealing with their lives beyond these moments didn't seem urgent.

They drove back on Sunday after eating a *kaiseki* lunch in a hundred-year-old restaurant on Mt. Utatsu. When they returned to her car he told her, "I've never been so happy to spend money at an expensive restaurant."

"It helped," she reminded him, "that we stayed for free at Shinji's apartment. But you have to promise not to squander the money Nozomi returned."

"You must think I've been terrible not to ask about Riku," he said on their way back to Yamanaka Onsen. "He's been on my mind, but I didn't want him to hang over us this weekend."

"He's been on my mind, too."

"Have you told him about his father?"

"Before he left for Echizen I told him we may see him again soon. All he did was shrug. I'm sure it bothers him, though."

"When does Riku come back?"

"Tonight. I'll pick him up at Kaga Onsen Station between eight and nine."

The road they were on would soon merge with a highway connecting Ishikawa to Fukui. But here it was a curving, rolling road that alternated between one and two lanes, surrounded by rice fields and offering occasional views of Hakusan, which rose jaggedly almost nine thousand feet to the east. When they reached the highway, he couldn't keep his thoughts about Riku to himself any longer.

"What do you think the solution is for Riku?"

"The solution?"

"Is there a psychologist he could see?"

She shook her head. "I wouldn't know who to trust with him. Anyway, there aren't many psychologists he could see around here."

Sedge suspected that if they were in a larger city like Tokyo or Osaka, it would be different. But he'd often heard that the need outstripped demand. "I realize he's only sixteen, but he can't live with you forever. It was me he went after last week, but who's to say he won't attack you one day, too? If he does to you what he tried to do to me, he'll kill you."

"But he hasn't hurt me before. I don't think he'd ever lift a finger against me."

"That's a dangerous attitude to have—possibly a fatal one if he doesn't learn to control himself. Frankly, I'm not sure he can."

"He's not used to you. You have to give him a chance to trust you. You may not believe it, but he's much calmer now than when Kōichi was around."

"He threatened to kill me. Did you believe him when he said that?"

"Until you came to live with us, he made the same threats to other people."

"I knew about the fights," Sedge said, "but not the threats to kill anyone."

"Don't you think he does it out of fear?"

"Of course. Which is why he has to learn to control his feelings. Who else has he threatened to kill?"

She began to name them: the students and teachers who bullied him; local craftsmen who he thought unfairly disciplined him; the men in town he caught flirting with her; anyone who, either as a joke or to show their dominance, tried to humiliate him somehow. His father. And now Sedge.

"It's true he's hurt people," she said. "But he knows when to pull back. And I'm sure he won't be like that forever."

"But if he is, he'll ruin your life and the life of whoever tries to get close to you. How are you supposed to have a life if he's circling around it all the time?"

"He's my stepson! I have a mother's responsibility to him. What kind of life do you think he has knowing his father left him and his mother refuses to see him? I'm all he has. And you . . ."

He didn't ask her to finish what she started to say.

"I don't know," he said. "But I worry you'll find out at the expense of your life."

They were silent until they approached the turnoff that would bring them back to Yamanaka Onsen.

21

Riku fell back in the rear seat of Mariko's car and spoke slowly, his fingers drumming each word on the suitcase beside him. "Father. Is. In. Prison."

Mariko nearly lost control of the car as she pulled out of Kaga Onsen Station, where she and Sedge had picked up Riku. She turned to him in the back seat. "How do you know that?"

"The police called Grandma and Grandpa and told them."

"But why? What did he do?"

"I'm sure the police will contact you soon. They said they came to the house already but saw you were away."

"If you know, tell me, Riku. This isn't a game."

"I know it's not a game." He yanked his backpack off his lap and it ricocheted off the door. Sedge looked back at him with a warning in his eyes, but the boy only glared at him.

"Was it a fight?" Sedge said.

"A kind of fight. But I guess it got out of control."

"Please tell me he didn't kill anyone," Mariko said, swerving slightly again even though there were no other cars in the road.

"Do you go to prison for that?" The exaggerated confusion in Riku's voice showed he was still having fun with this.

Sedge leaned toward Mariko and whispered, "Just ignore him."

"He killed an old man," Riku said, his voice sounding almost triumphant.

This time it was Sedge who spun around to face him.

He made Mariko pull to the side of the road and flip on her hazards. They both turned toward Riku and he went on without them asking him to.

"Father says he didn't do it. The story the police told was that he wouldn't admit to killing the man because he couldn't remember doing it. He was drunk when they brought him in, his clothes all splattered with blood. I'm surprised the police didn't call you."

"My god, what am I going to do?" she said.

"Who was the man?" Sedge asked.

"A bar owner somewhere. In Nagoya, I think."

Sedge shuddered. He was relieved Nozomi had left him when she did.

"I guess he'll get what he deserves," Riku said. "I feel sorry for the old man, though. My grandparents said he was stabbed a half-dozen times."

Mariko was shaking all over. Sedge pulled her close and held her. He didn't know what to do or say.

After a few minutes Riku said, "Who's going to drive us home now? I have school tomorrow morning, you know."

The violence Mariko's husband perpetrated left Sedge shocked for several days. Because Kōichi was already notorious for his behavior around Yamanaka Onsen, and because people knew he had left his wife and son multiple times, there was more empathy than scorn shown Mariko. Where there was scorn, however, Sedge sensed that it was part of a general disappointment in her having taken up with another man and started living with him in her own home.

As for Riku, he admitted to Sedge that his classmates targeted him more. In and out of class, they told him they knew all the horrible things his father had done. School had always been a place where he suffered for being different, but his father's imprisonment, and the frequent reportage on his crime, tested

Riku like never before. Every day he got into skirmishes, though he swore he never started them. The increase of teacher complaints about him talking back, he also contended, was because they, too, brought attention to what his father had done.

In the evenings when Riku should have been working on his homework instead of watching TV inside the house, Mariko and Sedge counseled him to be patient and asked him to tell them whenever someone at school treated him unfairly.

Sedge was alone at home one day when a car pulled up to the house. The doorbell rang, and when he slid the door open he wasn't sure who was more astonished, the high school administrator, who clearly wasn't expecting a foreigner to greet him, or Sedge, who couldn't imagine why this man had driven Riku home in the middle of the day.

"I'm sorry, I'm not sure I have the right house. Riku said he lived here, but . . ."

"This is the right place. Is something wrong?"

"Is his mother here?"

"She's my stepmother," Riku corrected him.

The man glanced at Riku irritably.

"She's at work," Sedge said. "What's going on?"

The man looked again at Riku. "He got in a fight, not just with students, but with the vice-principal, too. He was lucky we didn't call the police."

It was only upon hearing this that Sedge noticed the scratches on Riku's hands and the swollen lower lip and point of his chin. He saw now, too, the stretched school uniform collar and scuff marks on his sides.

"What happened to the boys who started it?" Sedge said.

"Who says they started anything? We're investigating what happened and why. We think it's better if Riku doesn't come to school again for some time." From his shirt pocket he removed a small, lacquered case and handed Sedge a business card from inside it. "Please have Riku's stepmother call me as soon as she can. The school considers the matter urgent."

Sedge remembered Mariko telling him that Riku's summer vacation would begin in three weeks. "He'll be able to finish the semester, won't he?"

"That's something we need to decide. Again, please tell his stepmother to contact me as soon as possible."

When the man left, Riku pushed past Sedge to enter the house. Sedge found him standing in front of the bathroom mirror, inspecting his face.

"I'll be at the dining table if you want to talk." Sedge walked away and sat down where he'd been before the school administrator brought Riku home.

"There's no need to talk because my side of the story doesn't matter," Riku called from the bathroom door. "They're discussing among themselves what story to agree on. I've said it before, but this time I mean it. I'm done with school. There's no reason for me to go back."

"What are you going to do, then?"

"I'll figure something out."

Sedge walked back to him before he could disappear inside the kura. "Why was it necessary to fight those people?"

"They started pushing me around. They wanted to fight because they thought the three of them would demolish me. Plus, there were other people egging them on. Tell me, what would you have done?"

"Walked away."

He laughed. "They would never have let me."

"And you beat them all up? Even the vice-principal?"

"It takes more than three students to take me down. The addition of an adult makes it a fairer fight. But I'd already taken care of them before the vice-principal showed up and started yell-ing at me."

"You're going to have to learn a different way to deal with people."

"Tell that to the bullies at school. You know I only get into fights there."

Sedge couldn't believe that Riku had forgotten attacking him just over two weeks ago. Or did he not consider that a fight since he didn't actually win?

"That's untrue. You've gotten into fights with people in this neighborhood—and with me."

Riku's face clouded over. "Anyway, I've chosen a different way. I'm quitting school for good."

He headed again for the front door. For someone who claimed that his violence was always provoked, his slamming the door and stomping to the kura suggested differently.

22

Several craftsmen in town said Riku was too young to apprentice with them full-time, but the woodturning studios where he'd
again been working a handful of hours agreed to let him come
more often. By mid-July he had secured part-time jobs at three
separate studios and would put in a total of thirty hours a week at
them. Mariko, to Sedge's surprise, had consented to this arrangement. From what he could tell, she didn't know what else to do.

Riku entered the house late one night and sat at the dining
table where Sedge and Mariko were talking. Leaning forward on
the table, Riku rested his head in his hands and turned to look at
Sedge.

"I have a little problem," he said.

"What is it?"

Although Sedge had asked this, Riku turned to Mariko when
replying. "You know how I interviewed at the different studios
where I'll be working? Even though I quit school they all still want
me to study English. And since they know an American lives
here, they said he should teach me. With all the foreign tourists
around these days, they think I'm in a position to help them."

"Ask Sedge properly," Mariko said. "You shouldn't assume
he'll do whatever you say."

Riku turned to Sedge impatiently.

"After what happened upstairs between us several weeks ago,
I have doubts about us working together. I'd like to help you eventually, but right now you'd do better learning on your own."

Mariko sat back and crossed her arms, making no effort to
mediate between them. He knew she would have liked him to

help Riku—she'd remarked before that teaching him English might provide them a way to warm up to each other again—but she could hardly blame him for putting his foot down. If Riku was interested in English, wouldn't he have asked before that he teach him? To Sedge, Riku was only doing what he'd been told to do, but he had no real interest in learning. It would be a waste of time and energy for them both.

"There are a few English classes around town," Sedge said. "You should contact them and see what they offer."

"Maybe we can talk about it later," Riku said, not bothering to mask his disappointment. "It's almost midnight. I'm going to bed."

When he was gone, Sedge explained himself to Mariko, once more referring to the fight in her bedroom and the threat Riku continued to pose to her, but she stopped him before he could go further.

"I respect your reasons. But he lives here, too. I'm not going to get rid of him."

"You'll have to eventually."

She glared at him. "He was here before you were. And despite what he's done, he has just as much right to my love as you. I'm his stepmother, after all."

"I'm sorry if I was being selfish," he said. "I don't want to tell you what to do. But it's uncomfortable when I'm caught in the middle."

She calmed down at his apology. "I know that even in turning him down you have his best interests at heart. You don't have to defend yourself to me." She smiled tiredly. "It's late, like Riku said. Let's get ready for bed."

❧ ❧ ❧

The next evening, in the waiting room of Yūyūkan, Mariko stood near a far window, talking on the phone with her hand cupped over the receiver and bowing to whoever was on the other end. The police and various reporters hadn't called her in some time, but she looked like she always did when talking to them.

She had either exited the women's baths early, or he had been in the men's baths for longer than he realized. After she had bought Riku a membership to Yūyūkan, Riku came here every evening, and on the weekends he sometimes came two or three times a day. In addition to the baths, the facility had a small restaurant, a gym and indoor swimming pool, outdoor tennis courts, and a croquet field. There was even a retired train car on site and a farmers' market, too. Sedge and Mariko had started coming here each week on her day off.

He watched a baseball game on TV as Mariko pushed through a door outside to continue her conversation. Two innings later she returned, her cheeks still flushed from the hot bath she'd left probably half an hour ago.

"Another call about Kōichi?" he said as she dropped into the seat beside him.

She shook her head. "It was Kōichi's parents. The last time we spoke, we talked about Riku for a long time. They had suggested asking around Echizen about potters and woodturners who might let someone his age apprentice with them. They found a potter willing to on a trial basis. If it works out, he'd keep Riku there for several years."

"What's the difference between an apprenticeship and the part-time work he's doing?"

"Apprenticeships train people in skills that will support them later. His part-time work, though he's learning, is nothing of the sort."

"Where would he live? And what about his schooling?"

"In the beginning he'd live with his grandparents. Eventually he'd move into a room above the pottery studio. I don't know about his schooling, but I'm sure he wouldn't want to be with students when he's two or three years older than them. He could finish high school online if he was willing to. I'm thinking of telling him that if he won't do this, he can't live with me anymore."

"If he doesn't agree to it, what choice do you have?"

She breathed out forcefully, and he saw he'd tested her patience again.

"You put pressure on me when you say things like that. I wish you'd think about what's best for Riku more."

"I know he's still only a boy," Sedge said, "but this opportunity could make his future. And remove him from his present—which might save you in the end."

She leaned back and closed her eyes. "Maybe he just needs more time to figure out what to do. If he goes to Echizen and things don't work out, he'll end up back here but with fewer options. I wonder if I shouldn't push him to make a decision yet."

"If you don't, he'll only take longer to understand that every decision he makes has consequences. And he'll learn he can get away with anything. There's been no serious fallout for him after attacking me, fighting with students and teachers, and now quitting school."

She turned to him. There was no anger in her eyes, only tiredness. "I can't help feeling he needs protecting a little longer. Not all those incidents were his fault, you know."

Sedge could barely hide his disappointment at hearing her back off from the best solution yet to the problem Riku continued to pose—for Riku himself even more than for Mariko.

"Come on," he said. "Let's walk home."

❧ ❧ ❧

They found Riku lying on the tatami floor before the Buddhist altar. On the room's low table was a small plastic bag of half-eaten rice crackers, a vase of dried larkspur, and a *manga* he'd been reading. He was talking on a cordless phone he sometimes used, since Mariko wouldn't let him have his own cell phone, and Sedge realized the conversation was with his grandparents.

Mariko sat with her laptop at the dining table while Sedge stood in the kitchen, both pretending not to eavesdrop. Riku didn't say much, but instead listened to whatever his grandparents were telling him. Occasionally he made a noise to show he was listening, and sometimes he asked a question: "How old is he?" "How many people are in his family?" "Would I have any days off?" "What would I do about money?"

Sedge thought: If the boy agrees to go, and it's necessary to keep him there, I may be able to help support him with the money I have again.

Riku released a long sigh and told his grandparents he had to go. He abruptly hung up and dropped the phone on the floor.

"Your grandparents?" Mariko said, turning to him. Riku nodded. "They called me at the baths," she went on. "I didn't realize they were going to call you immediately afterward."

"It's funny how excited they sounded."

"It's better that way, isn't it?"

"I guess."

She pulled out a chair from the table for him to sit in and talk, but he stayed where he was. "Does apprenticing in Echizen appeal to you?" she said.

He smiled at the ceiling; his voice sounded dreamy when he replied. "Maybe it would be good living on my own. I could always come back here if it didn't work out."

"There's no reason for it not to work out. It's an ideal situation for you. And apprenticeships often lead to careers in the craft you've mastered."

"But if it doesn't?"

"Why wouldn't it?" Sedge said from the doorway between the kitchen and veranda.

Riku looked at him as if the answer was obvious. "I might not get along with anyone."

"I'm sure there's no reason for that to happen. They'll be invested in you as much as you'll be in them. It won't be like it was at school."

"But it always happens to me, wherever I am. The only people I've never fought with are Okaasan and my grandmother."

"You fought with your grandfather?" Sedge said.

"One time. I was younger and smaller back then. And he was stronger compared to now."

"You'll be fine," Mariko assured him. "Your grandparents want this to happen for you. And the sensei is keen to have you learn with him, under his care."

"But if it doesn't work out, I can come back, can't I?"

Mariko slowly shook her head. "If it doesn't work out, Riku, you'll have to live with your grandparents. They're old and could use someone to look after them."

"But they're farmers. What would I do there?"

"It won't be an issue if you persevere in the apprenticeship."

"But why can't I come back here?"

"I'm not opposed to you coming back eventually," she said. "But you need to be on your own for a while first. You need to find a way to change."

To Sedge's astonishment, Riku agreed with her. "I'd like to change. I just don't know if I can. I've never been any other way. Maybe Grandpa was right and I need a fresh start in Echizen.

Grandma said she wouldn't let me become like my father. I guess I remind her of him." His chest rose and fell like someone was prodding him from under the floor, and Sedge realized Riku was laughing.

"They said you can visit anytime to meet the sensei and see what the apprenticing conditions would be," Mariko said.

Riku turned pensive again. "I have to think about it. After all, I don't want to give up what I have here without being sure about things first. You've always said I'm too rash."

"I don't want to argue about it. Take your time if you need to."

Sedge couldn't tell if she really wanted him to, or if she thought this would make him trust her more and commit to what she said he needed to do.

Saying he wanted to be alone for a while, Riku announced he was going to the baths that Sedge and Mariko had just returned from.

"I know it's late, but I'm going to make a quick trip to the shrine," Mariko called from the *genkan* as Sedge washed and dried their dishes. "I'll be back in a little while."

"You're going now? Can't you wait until morning?"

"I want to make a prayer for Riku's success. I won't feel comfortable until I do it."

Sedge turned off the water in the sink. "I can come with you if you'll wait five minutes."

"It's okay. I'll be back soon."

The front door slid open and shut and then he heard her hurried footsteps on the street. When he finished the dishes, he filled a small beer glass with sake and took it outside to the bench beside the house.

Mariko had agreed to let Sedge sell all of Kōichi's Kutani-ware, though she doubted Japanese buyers would want it now. Sedge imagined that foreigners would be easier to sell to, and he had privately mulled over asking Nozomi to help him reorganize the ceramics he had hastily stored away after closing their store. They weren't his alone to sell and profit from, but he was wary about reaching out to her in case it was only an unconscious yearning to see her again.

Twenty minutes later Mariko's footsteps grew louder as she came back down the street. Seeing her pass by the carport, Sedge called to her. "I'm over here. Join me for a minute."

Mariko stopped and looked for him in the darkness. "What are you doing out here?"

He handed her his sake and she sipped from it.

"I take it you were the only one at the shrine?"

"Yes. But something was happening at the community center next door. The building was lit up and made it easier for me to see the shrine steps."

He moved over for her to sit beside him. They gazed at the sky until she said something he never expected and didn't fully understand at first.

"I think you should try to forgive Riku. And not just for the time he attacked you, though I'm sure that's foremost on your mind. It would be good if you could also forgive him for the things he's never done."

Sedge looked at her inquiringly. "How am I supposed to do that?"

"By accepting him. As long as he doesn't try to hurt you again, please try to let go of your distrust of him. Wouldn't it be better to start over?"

It was a lot to ask of him. He had already forgiven Riku more than he thought he should. Was it possible to forgive him more?

"Forgiving him everything," Mariko went on, "will help the three of us overcome some big obstacles we face. And it will get Riku faster to his destination."

As she handed back his glass he thought about this, then drank what was left in it. "Where do you think that is?"

"Wherever he can be loved and accepted. And have a life where his pain is in the past. You should forgive him so he can reach that place. He could if more people gave him a chance."

"But if he thought he could always avoid repercussions for what he did, wouldn't it encourage him to do bad things? Things that ultimately hurt himself?"

"It would do the very opposite."

He had been receptive to her until then. Forgiving Riku for everything he might yet do seemed too dangerous.

"I'll do my best to forgive him," he told her. "But it won't stop me from worrying about you."

"Thank you. I guess I trust him more than you do. Which is natural, isn't it? He knows I want what's best for him. And that I'm trying to be a good mother."

Sedge was going to reply, but she spoke over him.

"Don't confuse Riku for what Kōichi did. If you're better to him, he'll be better to you, too. Whether you intended to or not, you've taken over the place his father occupied. But you haven't done it in a way Riku needs. And please understand—I need it, too. Not for me, but for him."

"You need me to be more of a father to him?"

She shook her head almost violently. "No, no. But can't you be more compassionate? If you can, you'll fit the role he needs. As a sympathetic man in his life. If I can be like that with him, can't you, too?"

Her words echoed uncomfortably what Nozomi had told him. "You sound like Nozomi."

She glared at him. "Why would you say such a thing?"

"Don't be angry. Nozomi really did say something similar. I've been thinking about it ever since."

She looked at him dubiously. "What did she say?"

"That I didn't understand the suffering of other people. Do you think she's right?"

The anger in her face fell away. She lay a hand on his arm and didn't answer.

"I'll try to be better," Sedge said, though he wasn't sure he could. "I may need your help and reminding along the way."

She tried to lead him inside, but he wanted to sit under the night sky longer. She carried his empty glass inside. A minute later she returned it to him, newly filled. From behind her back she pulled out a second glass and the remainder of the sake he'd left in the kitchen. They drank together as the clouds floated past and in the distance the wind rustled the trees on the mountain.

23

Sedge and Riku descended into Sugatani-machi on what appeared to be a hunter's trail or road to maintain electricity pylons, several of which they'd seen while looping back from the woods at the end of Mariko's street. Though it was late afternoon and relatively cool for mid-July, the wooded area they'd gone birding in had the humidity of a rainforest, and they were sweaty and itchy where mosquitoes had feasted on them. The winds that had arisen out of nowhere were so strong he and Riku would soon dry off, unless it started raining, which looked increasingly likely.

"Normally I see more birds on the mountain," Sedge said. It had been Riku's idea to return to the village rather than hike to another clearing.

"If we go back in the morning we'll probably see more. The crows and sparrows we saw didn't do much for you, did they?"

He'd said this lightly, hoping to draw Riku out. As usual, when the boy fell silent Sedge couldn't guess what he was thinking. Perhaps he was disappointed he hadn't seen the birds Sedge tried to point out—brown-eared bulbuls, Oriental turtledoves, and azure-winged magpies—though they were common enough Riku at least knew what they were. His disappointment had been so intense, kicking at the vegetation around them to see what he might scare up, Sedge half-expected the boy to accuse him of making a fool of him. More than anything, birding required patience; he'd thought wrongly that Riku understood that.

They continued down the dirt path beside the village's Hachiman shrine, from which the clay-tiled roofs of many houses in the village were visible. From her bedroom window Mariko could point to the tops of the shrine's two-thousand-year-old ōsugi, and she and Sedge came here most evenings on their strolls.

Riku led him down to the torii at the shrine's entrance.

"I thought you wanted to go home," Sedge said. "Are we coming here now?"

Riku looked at the sky. "Do you think it's a waste of time?"

The weather had changed since they'd set out for the woods on the mountain. With the wind gusting and the sky darkening with storm clouds, the birds would be seeking shelter. Already, crows were flying high into the trees around the shrine. But because Riku didn't want to give up yet, Sedge said, "We won't know unless we try."

Before walking beneath the torii they bowed to the shrine atop the hill, which they'd passed on the way down from the woods. Sedge headed to a covered ablutions basin to wash his hands and mouth. Riku only did so after Sedge told him to.

Opposite the ablutions basin stood an iron horse on a stone plinth, one foreleg pawing at the air. Before it was a short, fenced enclosure, inside of which sat seven round rocks of varying sizes. Sedge stopped to read the sign behind them, but the cursive script was indecipherable.

"Do you know what those are?" Riku said, running up from behind.

"I can't read the explanation."

"They're banmochi-ishi. People here used to compete to lift the heaviest stone. Whenever I see them I want to try, but my stepmom won't let me. She says they belong to the shrine."

Traces of moss covered the rocks. The smallest one resembled a volleyball, the largest a giant tortoise. Sedge couldn't imagine rolling the largest rock over, much less lifting it off the ground.

"One time I snuck into the enclosure late at night. I wanted to test my strength."

"How many were you able to lift?" Sedge asked.

"The four smallest ones. I couldn't budge the largest three."

The fourth-largest rock must have weighed well over one hundred pounds. It looked impossible to get a good grip on. If Riku had lifted it, that would surely make him stronger than most men in the village.

The shrine path climbed two sets of steps. The first passed the ōsugi, which were marked by shimenawa ropes to signify their sacredness. They dwarfed a nearby camellia tree, whose fallen flowers lay scattered on the ground, brown and rotting.

"Someone left their cane by the handrail," Sedge said, pointing to it. "What a strange thing to forget if you have trouble walking."

Riku grabbed it and swiped at the air like samurais in movies do with swords, then returned it to where he'd found it. "Old people leave things here all the time."

"Where do you think we'll find any birds?"

Riku looked around them again, then at the tops of the trees. "Birds usually flit around between these steps and the shrine. We should have come here first."

They waited for something to move in the treetops or dart across the sky.

A few minutes later they climbed further. The first drops of rain started falling, and within seconds it became a torrent. Their tree-cover was insufficient protection, and as the rain strengthened they ran to find shelter. Together they charged up the second series of steps, arriving at the shrine at the same time. They sat deep under its rooftop, inspecting their rain-splotched clothes.

"Mariko told me the shrine was moved to this height almost fifty years ago," Sedge said. "It's the second time they've elevated it. Eventually they'll do it again."

Riku muttered, "I won't be here when they do."

Sedge didn't say anything for a moment. "Where will you be?"

"I want to make a new life far away from here. If both my parents could do it, so can I. But I won't do it the way they did. Especially my dad."

"There's no reason you can't be better than them."

Riku looked away and said, "When I was in school, my teacher said Bashō died thinking he was spiritually a 'tattered beggar.' I learned that on our final lesson about him."

Sedge remembered Riku's answer to his question about why Bashō had journeyed so often. "It's disappointing to think that through his journeys he couldn't escape the pain of living."

"I once asked our teacher if he thought Bashō would be happier today. He just made fun of the question, asking our class how he was supposed to know."

"He sounds unenlightened."

Riku shrugged.

"For someone who hated school, you clearly got something out of reading Bashō."

"That was the only time."

The rain sheeted down. It had collected in a groove between the eaves overhead and started dripping between them. Beyond the *torii* below, the village was gray with water and mist. The mountains encircling the valley had been completely erased.

Riku tried to peer inside the shrine where its front doors came together. His movement stirred the humid air and Sedge smelled the wet concrete of the path and the dusty wood of the seldom-opened shrine. He was about to call Riku back when the boy sat down again.

Raising his voice above the water flowing from the eaves Riku said, "Bashō lived in huts much smaller than this shrine. They had names, too. 'The Unreal Hut.' And 'The House of Fallen Persimmons.' I'm going to name the kura one of these days."

"Name the kura?" Sedge said.

"The name I want to give it comes from when Bashō found an abandoned three-year-old boy on the roadside."

"'I never heard that story."

"We studied his haiku about it. It has nineteen syllables, two more than normal. My teacher said Bashō was overwhelmed with sorrow at the boy's fate and seventeen syllables couldn't contain his emotions." He pulled a notebook from his pocket and, protecting it from the rain, flipped to a middle page. "I copied the haiku. It refers to a Chinese story about a monkey who grieved so deeply when her baby was stolen that she killed herself." He handed the notebook to Sedge. "Can you read it?"

Sedge could just make out Riku's hurried writing.

> Poets who despair at a monkey's keening,
> How would they feel hearing an abandoned child
> Crying in the autumn wind?

"What became of the little boy?" Sedge asked, handing the notebook back.

Riku shrugged. "I just know that Bashō felt bad for him, but he also thought his suffering was Heaven's will. Before he walked away, he tossed the child some food he was carrying and grieved for his sad fate."

"That seems too cruel."

"My teacher said that if we judge Bashō's actions by today's standards he seems cruel, but he acted how the times he lived in said he should."

Sedge couldn't help but think that for someone journeying to escape the pain and sorrow of the world, what Bashō had done in this instance was to deepen and perpetuate it.

"The haiku makes me want to call the kura 'The Monkey Hut,'" Riku said.

"Isn't that story too sad to name the kura after?"

Riku held out his hand until he caught the water dripping between them. After collecting a palmful, he rubbed his face with it. "Not to me," he said.

Sedge couldn't rid his mind of the story about the three-year-old left to die alone on the roadside. How could something like that happen to a child, and why did Bashō not do more to help? Was his journey so important that he couldn't delay moving on? Surprised by his strong reaction to the story, he was grateful when Riku changed the subject.

"Did my stepmom tell you that a woodturning apprentice across the street gave me a block of wood this morning? He was planning to throw it away because the grain was warped. He didn't want to give it to me, but when she explained why I wanted it, he agreed. I'm going to make it into a *kuhi* and carve a haiku on it. Then pound it into the ground in front of the kura."

Sedge smiled. "What haiku did you choose?" He hoped it wouldn't be the one Bashō wrote about the monkey.

"I'm going to write my own. I'll need time to make a good one."

"I'd like to read it when you're done."

They looked toward the village again, their eyes veering to Mariko's home. The roofs of the house and kura were only just visible through the rain.

"Are you going to marry my stepmom?"

Sedge let out a deep breath. "We haven't known each other very long. And how can I? She's still married to your dad."

"But he's in jail. There's no way they'll stay married now."

Sedge didn't reply. He watched Riku catch the rain falling from the eaves again.

"I heard you met him."

Sedge nodded. "He came to our shop once with Mariko. He refused to talk to me."

"Why did he come to your shop if he wouldn't talk to you?"

"My wife was there. He came to talk to her."

Riku poured the water in his hands onto the step between his knees. "Why did my dad run off with your wife?"

"How should I know?"

Riku frowned. "People say I look like him. I hate hearing that, especially after what he did. Do you think I do, too?"

"Yes."

"A lot?"

"Yes. Especially when I first met you. But I don't see your father in you the way I used to."

"I don't want to look like my parents. I hate them."

"Maybe so," Sedge said. "But that's no reason to hate yourself."

A long silence followed. The rain bounced off the path at their feet.

"You've been nice to me today," Riku said. "Why?"

The directness of the question surprised Sedge. He didn't know how to answer.

After another long silence, Riku stretched out his legs, letting his shoes and the bottom of his pants get wet. After the rain had darkened them he pulled them back. Sedge laughed to himself.

Riku's mood had soured and he wouldn't look at Sedge now, not even when he spoke to him. "Don't you think my stepmom's pretty?"

"Yes," Sedge replied.

Riku turned to him but still didn't meet his eyes. "I'm going back before the weather gets worse. We'll never see birds in a storm like this."

He tore down the steps in the rain. The bottom of the shrine path had become a pond. He splashed through it, bowing again to the shrine at the top of the steps before turning and hurrying home.

24

Several days later, the bird reserve's veterinarian contacted Sedge. The heron he'd brought in eight weeks ago had suffered a setback midway through its recovery. He had worried it would prove fatal, but a specialist in Hokkaido helped him adjust his treatment and the heron's condition had markedly improved. Perhaps sensing Sedge's confusion about why he was sharing this, he got to the point of his call. "The heron's injuries have healed and we intend to release it this weekend. I'm calling to invite you to watch."

"Of course I'll go," he said happily.

"Please come to the reserve early on Sunday morning. There's a resident population of herons already here. It can try to join their group, or maybe it will return to where you found it since it's not far away. Herons don't always welcome unfamiliar birds into their group, but we've seen it happen before, so we're hopeful."

Mariko was excited by the news and agreed to go with Sedge. Riku was scheduled to work from Sunday morning until late in the afternoon. He struggled to contain his disappointment when Mariko told him that night at dinner about their plans.

"Why couldn't they do it when I don't have work?"

Mariko brushed away some sawdust she was always finding on his work uniform. He pulled away when she touched him.

"The veterinarian isn't there every day," she explained. "And I'm sure his schedule is fuller than yours. Aren't you happy the bird will regain its freedom after so long? You used to worry it would never fly again."

"It's not fair how every time an important event comes up,

something gets in the way or I'm told I can't do it. I've never seen a heron released into the wild."

"You've seen me release other birds. We released one a few months ago after it flew into our window and lost consciousness."

"That's not the same thing!"

Sedge tried to calm him down. "The release itself probably won't be anything special. I'm sure it's no different from watching a heron fly up out of a field."

"If that's all it was, no one would care. You're celebrating its return to freedom."

"You have responsibilities now," Mariko reminded him. "You have to get used to that. And learn to make sacrifices. This one's hardly worth getting upset about."

Under his breath Riku said, "Why do I even have to work when I'll soon move to Echizen? Maybe I'll ask Inoue-sensei to give me the day off."

Sedge discouraged this. "Your mother is right that you have to learn to make sacrifices. And not take these kinds of disappointments personally."

"She's not my mother. And you're not my father."

"If that's how you feel," Sedge said, "why are you living here?" As soon as he said it, he wondered where his own anger came from—his lack of compassion.

Mariko touched his leg beneath the table. It wasn't the gentle squeeze he was used to.

"She's forcing me out at the end of this month," Riku said, his voice rising. "I'm only stating the truth."

"That's not at all what I'm doing, Riku."

"And after I made it a cage and spent all night by its side . . ."

He rose from the table and marched toward the *genkan*. Jamming his feet into his shoes he turned and said to Sedge, "On the way to the baths, have you seen the herons in the rice fields? On the right side of the road, four or five often stand in them."

At the intersection down the street, the road leading out of the village ran downhill if one continued straight, and sloped more steeply turning left. Mariko's house was higher up, closer to the mountains, while below it the ground leveled out in a valley where for centuries villagers had cultivated rice.

"I haven't, no."

"I can see them from Inoue-sensei's studio. Sometimes they come so close I could run outside and grab them."

"I wouldn't advise it," Sedge said.

Riku slid the front door open. "It's so unfair," he muttered toward them as he went back outside and returned to the kura.

Sedge tried to put Riku's disappointment out of his mind, but it kept returning. Until now, the heron was the strongest connection Sedge had made with Riku. Saving it had been important to them both. It wouldn't take much to bring him along Sunday morning, and if it made him happy to see the heron fully healed and given its freedom, wouldn't that be an appropriate reward for the care he gave the bird? All their talk about sacrifice was right, but they'd made their point clearly, and he didn't doubt Riku had taken it to heart.

A few minutes later, to break the silence that had fallen over the room, Sedge said, "Maybe we could call Mr. Inoue and ask him to give Riku Sunday morning off. Couldn't he make up the hours later?"

Mariko's eyes widened. "No, you were right that he can't take these disappointments personally. He needs to learn that the world isn't out to get him. And that he has to take a different view to life. I'm sure there are bird releases at that reserve fairly often."

"But he has a connection to that heron. It's obvious he felt betrayed by us. This would be a simple way to reverse that. There's no harm in it, is there? What does he do at the studio, anyway, besides keep the place tidy?"

She closed her laptop and turned to him. "Of course I'd like to bring him with us. I'm sure it would make him happy—and give us a bargaining chip with him if we needed it. But he has an obligation to Mr. Inoue. He went out of his way to give Riku a job, and Riku's only been there a few weeks. There's nothing to be done about it."

"Then maybe we shouldn't go, either."

She smiled appreciatively at his suggestion. "To show our solidarity with Riku? No, we were right to tell him what we did. He quit school and is working now. If he doesn't learn to behave like everyone else he'll never get anywhere."

"Couldn't we at least try?"

She shook her head. "We can always make it up to him later."

He drew back slightly as tears pooled in her eyes. She was an excellent mother to Riku but being an authority figure wasn't in her nature.

"Let's drop it, then. It's just one of those 'it can't be helped' moments, right?"

"*Shō ga nai*," she murmured, nodding gently. "*Shō ga nai*."

Mariko rolled off of Sedge and onto her futon. Turning to her in the dark, he traced the contours of her, lithe and hilly. Beneath his fingers, wherever he touched, she was perfectly pliable, entirely receptive to him.

She drew away when the bathroom door downstairs opened and shut. Sedge hadn't heard the back door open, which normally squeaked in its sliding frame. They remained silent, facing each other, listening for a telltale creak of the staircase or the floor in front of the room.

They had stopped pretending to sleep in different rooms after the incident with Riku one month ago. Believing he would never repeat what he'd done, Mariko refused to let Sedge install a lock. But as a precaution, when privacy was a concern, she asked him to move a small set of wooden drawers before the door.

"Do you think he was inside all this time?" Mariko said. "The light outside didn't turn on. Or did you see it?"

"No, I didn't," Sedge said. "He knows he's not to sleep in the house anymore."

Sedge moved to the edge of the back window and peered outside. He knew that the motion-detecting light, after it came on, was set to turn off again quickly. He might simply not have been paying attention to it.

A minute later the bathroom door opened and shut again, and then the back door slid across its tracks.

"Do you want me to send him away?" she said.

He didn't think she really meant to let him decide, and he didn't answer. He was listening to Riku tramp back to the kura. This time the motion detector flashed on, and Sedge leaned back from where the light angled over the jutting rooftop into the room. Riku's figure curled like a wave across the bedroom wall and shot across the curtain. Sedge moved further away from it instinctively.

Riku's shadow had crashed into the room for only an instant, but it made Mariko gasp and set Sedge's heart beating faster.

"It's a shame he's had to start life with so many setbacks," Mariko said. "They never seem to stop."

"It makes it hard to know what to do for him."

"The apprenticeship in Echizen," she murmured. "I guess all three of us know it's his best chance to be happy."

The frogs had fallen silent with Riku's intrusion into the night, but a moment later, as the outside light shut off again, they resumed all at once the chorus of their croaking.

🐦 🐦 🐦

Riku didn't speak to them Sunday morning, and though they didn't see much of him before leaving for the bird reserve, he refused to respond to their greetings or attempted conversation. His behavior upset Mariko.

On the way to Katano Kamoike she apologized to Sedge for crying. "It's true he doesn't get to see and do the things he wants, not like other kids he knows. I should have let him come with us. I could have at least tried to arrange it with Mr. Inoue."

He shared her regret, but it was too late now. "Are you going to feel the same way when it's time for him to move to Echizen?"

"I hope not. But since he's leaving soon, this was one of the last nice things I could have done for him. In another week and a half, he'll be gone."

Sedge tried to sound cheerful but his tone came out strained. "You'll have every chance to see him again. He won't even be an hour away."

When they arrived at the bird reserve, they found a half-dozen people on the observation deck, viewing through the mounted telescopes the birds on the pond and in the marsh and trees. Gathered on the outside patio below were a handful of guests like themselves. The heron stood in a better designed cage than what Riku had built, though he had made his with the bird's injury in mind, not its recovery or release. The heron's head was hunched into its shoulders, and it stared at the outside world it would soon return to.

"Do you want to film the release with your phone?" Sedge said as they descended the stairs. "Or do you think Riku would only be resentful?"

She pointed to someone at the edge of the patio with a camera on a tripod. "It looks like the reserve plans to film it. If he wants to see it, maybe we can take him here to watch it before he leaves."

The veterinarian waved and approached them. He thanked them for coming and introduced them as "the heron catchers."

After the reserve's director confirmed where he wanted the bird cage carried, the small group walked outside. Two volunteers lifted the cage by its hinged handles and walked past the patio into the grass. Their rubber boots sank into the wet ground, and the difficulty they had walking caused the heron to struggle to keep its balance. They were soon within a few meters of the pond, and, following the director's orders, set the cage down there. One of them unlatched the front door.

The heron didn't move. It simply stared out the opened cage toward the water, where in the distance dozens of waterbirds swam across the pond's surface and flew between the trees. To the left and right, gray and white herons tiptoed through the watery grass and shallows, focused on whatever creatures they could find underfoot.

One of the volunteers tilted the cage forward and the other tapped on its bars to startle the bird back into the wild. The heron fell forward, stretching its left leg before itself while its right leg stepped outside the cage. It stood in the marsh-grass, still staring toward the pond. The volunteers hurried back to the observation building and, upon reaching it, waited with the others for the heron to decide where to go.

Only when a heron to the left squawked did it seem to recognize where it was and what its choices had come to be. It raised its wings in the ungainly way herons do when starting to fly, but once it lifted off it described a beautiful arc fifteen feet overhead as it circled over them, continuing toward more herons across the pond. It returned the squawk and received a reply from somewhere. Rising higher over the dark water, it flapped slowly above the treetops before veering in the opposite direction Sedge had found it. Behind it, to everyone's surprise, was a duller colored gray heron, following the same path through the sky. It squawked, too, and in the distance the heron they'd released fell in line with it.

When Sedge and Mariko returned to the observation deck, they sat behind two telescopes, observing the birds gathered in the distance. Sedge hadn't expected the heron's release to be memorable, but it had been. It had overcome a lot to regain its freedom, and the memory of the bird's graceful flight over the trees moved him again.

He regretted once more that he had been stricter with Riku than the boy deserved. Even though Riku had attacked him, he would be leaving them soon, possibly forever. Perhaps Sedge should have trusted him more—now, ten days before he was to move away.

25

"What are those people doing?" Sedge said as Mariko drove up within sight of her house. A group of neighborhood children and older neighbors had gathered in the street before Mariko's door. Even Mr. Inoue was there, standing to one side by himself.

Mariko pulled into the carport while the people in the street stared at her in horror.

"What happened?" she called out even before she had closed her car door. Approaching Mr. Inoue she said, "Where's Riku? Why isn't he with you?"

"He was at first. That is to say, he came to my studio at eight o'clock like we arranged. For the first hour he swept and washed my studio floor, but then he disappeared. Eventually I found him outside, gazing down at the rice fields. But when I called to him he ran away. I took a few steps to check where he was going and saw him running toward some herons in the distance. I didn't notice it at first, but when he raised his arm I saw he was holding a large pole with a baggy net behind it. It was bigger and stronger than a butterfly net and not the kind of thing one uses to fish with, either. It looked like he was planning to catch one of those herons with it—they're protected, you know—so I started running after him myself, only I'm old and can't move fast. I shouted toward my studio, and a few workers came out to see what was going on. When I looked back to the rice fields, the herons were lifting up around Riku and flying off over the fields. Before I knew it, he'd caught a straggler in his net. Worried about what he was going to do next, we watched him hurry off a different way, back to your house, with the heron slung over his shoulder. I called everyone back who'd come to help me, and we've been trying to figure out what to do ever since."

"Where is he now?"

"You've got an adult gray heron in your house. All the kids had their noses pressed against the windows of your veranda, but Riku chased them away."

Mariko fell to her knees. She bowed to him and to the neighbors in the street watching her. She apologized to them repeatedly until someone interrupted and demanded that she do something.

She ran to the front door. Sedge barely caught up to her before she threw it open and flung herself inside. He called Mr. Inoue over and suggested the two of them approach Riku.

They could see Riku sitting at the back of the far tatami room, hugging his knees to his chest and staring at them. The sun shone through the veranda windows, illuminating the transom overhead, where winged bodhisattvas carved in wood hovered above him, and the Buddhist altar's gold interior reflected light onto Riku's head and shoulders.

Standing at the back of the veranda was a gray heron like the one they had seen released that morning. It appeared extraordinarily large inside the house—and miraculously unhurt—and its talons clacked loudly as it stepped gingerly back and forth on the wooden floor. Feathers and bird excrement were visible around the front rooms, and the dried larkspur Sedge had once brought over was spread across the tatami like blue paint flung from a brush. On the top step leading into the house was the net Mr. Inoue had described.

"Why?" Sedge called out to Riku. He said it twice more; it was the only word that would leave his mouth.

"Maybe it was injured," Riku finally mumbled back. "Like the one you found and brought home."

"Mr. Inoue told me what happened. If it's injured, it's because of what you did."

"It's here now. What do you want me to do about it?"

The door behind Sedge slid open and Mr. Inoue slipped back outside. A minute later he was at the rear door, trying to pull it open. But it was locked.

Mariko stood just behind Sedge. She peered at Riku, where the light from outside was much brighter than where they stood.

"What should we do?" she asked Sedge. "Is he dangerous?"

"I would imagine so," he said, knowing Riku could hear them. "He just asked what I want him to do about the heron over there."

She turned to observe the bird, which was peering through the windows. "Are either of them injured?"

Sedge looked toward Riku for an answer.

"I've never felt better," Riku said. "The heron is fine, too. Why wouldn't it be? I was maybe a little rough when I caught it, and it banged into a lot of things when it started flying around the house, but it's all right. If it's hurt, it's nowhere near as bad as the heron Sedge brought home."

"Why did you do this?" Mariko said.

This time Riku told them what sounded like the truth. "I thought if I brought home another heron, I could stage my own release."

"You're lucky it didn't hurt you," Sedge said.

The bird had walked to the back window of the veranda, but it came back now and was staring at Riku, who sat perhaps two meters away.

"I would have hurt it worse. Because I've decided that nothing will ever hurt me again."

"Riku . . ." Mariko said.

Riku slowly stood up and turned to the bird. The bird took a half-step toward him but stopped when Riku swiped at it like he might when playing with a dog or cat. The bird yanked its head back.

"I wouldn't do that," Sedge said.

"What's he doing?" Mariko said. "Why did he get up?"

"I was tired of sitting," Riku said. He took another playful swipe at the heron, and this time the bird jumped a few inches off the ground, lifting its wings threateningly.

"Don't antagonize it, I'm telling you," Sedge said, walking forward and leaving Mariko in the *genkan*.

Before he could pull Riku away, the boy reached forward once more and patted the heron on the beak. He reached for it again only to stop midway as he realized Sedge was coming toward him.

The heron struck so quickly Sedge mistook its movement at first for a flicker of light.

Riku never saw the bird lunge. He jerked his hand back, his face confused. A strange silence ensued and Riku held up his hand in the sharply angled sunlight. Blood started dripping from where two of his fingers used to be. The heron had severed Riku's fourth and fifth fingers.

Sedge stared in shock at them lying on the floor. Behind him Mariko screamed.

Horrified, Sedge was unable to move to Riku, who had fallen to the floor, writhing on his side and clutching his bloody hand. He let out a choked yell. Outside the veranda window, where the neighborhood children had regathered, shrieks pierced the air.

Mariko ran to Riku and shook him, trying to make him reveal his hand. She pulled at him to stand up but he wouldn't move from the floor. Sedge hurried over. He lifted Riku to his feet and Mariko swiped his severed fingers and stumbled outside with him tucked into her shoulder. As people on the street erupted in panicked noise, Sedge found himself inside with the heron.

There was a commotion around the carport. As Sedge rushed outside he saw a neighbor behind the steering wheel of Mariko's car, while Mariko and Riku huddled together in the back seat. Just before the car drove off, Mariko glanced out the window at Sedge. In her eyes was a sadness so compacted within her embrace of Riku, that, like a dark room shutting out light, no one could possibly enter that feeling or see what it consisted of.

He stood numbly in front of Mariko's house with the neighbors. They began to ask him questions—about what was wrong with the boy, about the father and husband convicted of murder, about the lives they lived under their roof and behind their walls.

The heron squawked, and everyone turned toward the front door. Perhaps it had seen the opening and remembered it had been rushed through it while struggling in the net Riku had carried it home in. It passed through the doorway, its head bobbing with each careful step. Raising its wings as it had before striking Riku's hand, it squawked once more. Then it lowered its wings and moved its head with a smooth sort of jerkiness, looking past the people in the street. It took another step and, with its body bending forward, flapped its wings and flew up over the houses.

Sedge watched it rise into the sky and curl back in the direction of the rice fields it had come from. Where it would have descended to return to its feeding ground, it continued flying, heading toward the center of town. When it was barely more than a gray-white speck in the blue sky, it veered right again, over the forested hills of Kakusenkei gorge—the immortal valley of cranes—and disappeared.

26

Three days later, Mariko drove Riku from the hospital to Echizen, where his grandparents had readied a room for him at their home a week earlier than planned. They lived in a large farmhouse that also had a kura, but if Riku ever wanted to move into it he would have far more to repair than in the one at Mariko's house.

Riku's accident, and the way he precipitated it, was all the neighbors wanted to talk about when Sedge ran into them. They were afraid of the boy and, knowing he planned to move to Echizen, looked forward to the village becoming more peaceful. Most people expressed sympathy for Mariko, but some grumbled that she was to blame. "She tried hard to be a good stepmother, but with the boy corrupted by his father's blood, she should have known something like this would happen one day."

Yamanaka Onsen's summer festival, Furusato, which drew several thousand spectators every year, was slated to start in two more days. With Riku's hospitalization and impending move, and with the ryokan preparing to take part in the festivities, Mariko was busier than ever.

He blamed himself for Mariko's sadness—hadn't he forced her into a decision before she was ready? Perhaps this was why he didn't oppose her letting Riku stay a final night at the house, to finish packing for Echizen and see the festival one last time.

Sedge didn't visit Riku in the hospital. The boy only wanted to see Mariko, and when Mr. Inoue and his wife dropped by, Riku insisted that the nurses not let them in his room. When Mariko asked if he minded Sedge coming to see him, he shook his head, rejecting the idea. She took off from work all three days Riku was in the hospital, staying with him from morning until dinnertime, when she drove back home.

On Riku's last night in the hospital, she told Sedge, "Sometimes I feel like a mother waiting for her son to go off to war. But tomorrow I hope he'll go off and find peace."

The doctors had been unable to reattach Riku's fingers. Mariko said his hand remained heavily bandaged and he was on a heavy dosage of pain medication and antibiotics. Whenever the medical staff cleaned his wounds, she left the room. It was too gruesome and heart-wrenching for her to watch. Not once had he cried out in pain, however, she was told.

When she drove him to Echizen his grandparents were thrilled to see him. She could tell they would make a special effort to accommodate his needs, and the thick bandage around his hand made them even more solicitous toward him. Riku immediately asked them about his living arrangements, and also about his apprenticeship. When they told him it hadn't been canceled, and that the sensei and his family hoped he would recover soon, he broke down in tears.

Mariko returned from Echizen and assured Sedge that everything would be fine when Riku visited. Sedge was inclined to believe this, if only because the boy's injury would constrain him.

"Where do you plan for him to sleep?" he said.

She looked at him imploringly. "Downstairs, if you don't mind. It's only one night and he may need help with his hand."

"I'll choose a clean futon and sheets for him," Sedge said, "and put them in the room beneath the stairs."

Sedge had held back from saying this for a long time, but he couldn't any longer. "This never would have happened if I hadn't moved in with you. If it would help to have me leave, I can go at any time."

Her face drained of color and she looked at him with worry.

"Why are you saying that? It's not true! Maybe he wouldn't have lost his fingers, but something else would have happened. Something possibly worse. I don't want you to leave, Sedge. Please never say that again."

On the morning she left for Echizen, they inspected the room a final time. When Sedge set on the windowsill a vase of flowers he'd collected from outside, Mariko turned to him in surprise and thanked him.

❧ ❧ ❧

Yamanaka Onsen had been gearing up for its summer festival for more than a month. Groups around town had long been practicing their *taiko* routines, and in other areas he passed through, the Yamanaka Bushi song floated through the air as people rehearsed their traditional dances—Mariko included. The plaza before Yamanaka-za, too, grew busier as festival organizers strung lights overhead and arranged booths around its perimeter and the narrow streets nearby.

On the morning of the festival, Mariko woke early to drive to Echizen. She returned with Riku at one o'clock; she had met the craftsman he would apprentice with, then ate an early lunch with Riku and his grandparents. Although she and Sedge scarcely had time to talk after she came home, she summarized her morning for him and said, "I'm happy with the people Riku will have in his life. I feel better about things already."

Rather than enter the house upon arriving, Riku went immediately into the kura, carrying cardboard boxes and masking tape for the packing he had to do.

Mariko left shortly after she got home, because her festival duties would soon begin; Yuki and Takahashi had assigned her

responsibilities as a representative of their ryokan. Unable to prepare for them as much as she normally would have, she was eager
to get there early. She intended to work harder than ever to help
smooth over any lingering resentments, though Sedge's leaving
had seemingly resolved them.

"Riku will probably be in the kura most of the day," she said,
grabbing a bag she had prepared for herself yesterday. "After he's
done packing, it would be nice if you spent some time with him.
Maybe you can help if he's having trouble getting things done."

"What time should I come into town?"

"Whenever you feel like it. I've asked Riku to be at my booth
at five o'clock. It's better to leave after he does, so he's not here
alone."

"You don't trust him?"

"I don't know why I feel that way . . ."

Sedge agreed not to leave Riku unaccompanied in the house.

He watched her walk down the street. As he came back inside,
he realized Riku would be here for three hours before heading
to the festival. He wondered if the boy could get done what he
needed to do in so short a time, especially with only one hand at
his disposal.

He climbed upstairs to Mariko's bedroom. Beside her futon
lay Riku's old school notebook, which she had found downstairs
last night and intended to return to Riku today. She had shown it
to Sedge, reading to him old notes he'd made for school and on
his own about Bashō's journeys and haiku.

Sitting on the futon, Sedge opened it again. On the notebook's last page were Riku's own attempts at haiku. Only two
survived without having been heavily scratched out. The first he
recognized immediately from *Milky Way Railroad*, the Miyazawa
Kenji story he and Riku had discussed two months ago.

Spring night lit with stars
The tired hunter bent over
A sack of herons

The next one referred to a heron Riku had seen in a small pond near his school. He had told Sedge once of how he watched it spear a small fish, then turn its head to the sky and swallow it.

A heron's sharp beak
Thrusts into the clear shallows
A pond loach speared through

The poems expressed a seriousness of purpose he didn't often associate with Riku. And though Sedge was no haiku expert, Riku's two poems struck him as showing promise for a boy not yet seventeen. He tucked the notebook under his arm and stood up.

From the bedroom window he saw the kura's entrance was open, and behind it cardboard boxes were heaped on the floor. The four birdhouses that had hung in front had been taken down and presumably packed away.

He lifted his eyes to the kura's rooftop. Behind it the mountain curved gracefully, and the tops of the ancient ōsugi trees on the grounds of the village shrine trembled in the breeze. When Riku and Sedge last visited those places, Riku had been enamored with Sedge's ability to identify any bird he saw or heard. Sedge had enjoyed their birding excursion despite the unexpected rainstorm that trapped them at the shrine. For some reason Riku had not wanted to go back. Something had come between them again, just as something had once made the boy want to kill him—Mariko. Riku had never accepted the intimate place Sedge assumed in her life. And Sedge, though he had tried to be more sympathetic to him, had grown tired of the boy's temperament.

He wanted to help Riku grow and to learn to accept the harder things in life, both now and in the future. But he knew that such an effort would fall into the blackness of their rivalrous feelings toward each other.

Something passed by the kura entrance. As Riku dragged a cardboard box inside, he glanced up and met Sedge's eyes.

"He'll be gone tomorrow morning," Sedge reminded himself. He waited a few minutes to go downstairs and greet Riku.

The sun had come out since Mariko left, and as he walked behind the house the oppressive heat made his clothes stick to his skin. Climbing the steps to the kura, he saw that the second door, separating the inside of the kura from its entryway, had also been pulled open. A small radio played Japanese rock music through tinny speakers, and he could hear objects being thrown around—not angrily, but carelessly, as Riku filled the boxes with his belongings.

Sedge knocked on the open door. The kura's interior was much cooler than outdoors, and he took a step inside. "Mariko found one of your notebooks last night," he said. "I have it here if you want it."

"Leave it on the floor," Riku muttered, not looking at Sedge.

Bending down to do as Riku said, Sedge spotted a massive pile of ashes on a strip of aluminum siding in a corner. Seeing this, he recognized in the air the faint smell of something burnt. "What's all that ash from?" he said.

Without even glancing at what Sedge pointed to, Riku said: "My *senbazuru* collection."

Sedge stared at what had been perhaps several thousand paper cranes. How many hours of work had he thrown away? How many chances to make peace later if he needed to?

"When did you burn them?"

"On the night before the heron release."

With his feet Riku pushed his things into a tighter pile on the floor. He stopped momentarily to survey the mess around him. He had more boxes than he needed, and he began to throw whatever he could reach into whatever box that would hold it. He didn't bother to label them. And if something stuck out, he forced it down with a foot.

Inside one box were his birdhouses, their roofs all broken off.

"Give me a roll of tape and I'll seal the boxes you've filled," Sedge offered.

"I'm waiting until the end to do that."

Sedge wanted to ask about his hand, but he suspected Riku would resent it. Knowing he might even consider it a provocation, Sedge stood there mutely, unable to find anything they could communicate about. Finally he said, "Are you looking forward to the festival?"

"Not really."

Sedge paused again. "You don't have to do everything now, you know. You can always finish in the morning."

"I leave in the morning. Thanks to you, my stepmom's making me go to Echizen."

Sedge had to swallow more than once to make the pain of the boy's remark disappear. He didn't want Riku to blame him for what had happened to his hand, nor did he want him to view his apprenticeship as a punishment Sedge had pushed for. "You don't think the move will benefit you?"

Riku didn't answer. He still hadn't looked at Sedge since he'd entered the kura.

Sedge decided to leave him in peace.

As he turned, Riku said: "The move will benefit you most of all. If my father could see you now, having gotten rid of his son and planning to live alone with his wife, he'd . . ."

The unsaid words hung between them. Sedge made no reply, knowing that whatever he said would be misconstrued, used to fuel Riku's anger.

"I'll be inside if you need anything," he said gently and left. Before he was out of earshot, he heard what sounded like Riku kicking a box into the air and all its contents raining to the floor.

🌑 🌑 🌑

Sedge returned to Mariko's room and, not knowing what else to do, lay down. Without intending to, he fell into a borderland of sleep. And in this strangely vivid, half-lucid state he dreamed.

He found himself trailing behind a man wearing the long black robe of a Zen monk and a bamboo hat that was old and bleached by the sun. Although simple woven sandals clad his feet, he walked briskly, using a bamboo cane. Sedge had difficulty keeping up with him.

Along the path were *kuhi* engraved with Bashō's haikus. For some reason, he was sure the monk ahead of him was an acolyte of Bashō. Afraid he would lose sight of him, Sedge picked up his pace, determined to catch up.

Running along the path, he soon grew out of breath. He stopped to rest where a *kuhi* lay on its side. Similar to those in Yamanaka Onsen, it was dust-blown from countless gales over the years and draped in moss. He stepped closer to read the poem on it.

> In the old kura
> *Senbazuru* burned to ash
> The boy's cold fury

The haiku startled him. Only Riku could have written it. What was it doing on a *kuhi*? He hurried even faster to catch the man ahead of him, assuming he would know.

Soon he came across another *kuhi*, this one lying before a tree. With fresh mud clinging to its base, someone had newly uprooted it. The haiku on it read:

> Broken birdhouses
> Dumped into cardboard boxes
> Banished to Echizen

The path extended straight into the distance. Before it turned again he could see the monk progressing quickly. Sedge called out, but the monk didn't stop. Sedge ran forward again for some time, only to see another *kuhi*, this time fallen in the middle of the path. Its three visible sides had no writing on them, but when with all his strength he rolled it over he found another haiku.

> Through the high window
> Resplendent in summer moonlight
> Her heron-scarred flesh

Finally he caught up to the monk. Sedge wanted to ask what the purpose of his journey was. But, out of breath, his voice wouldn't come. The monk was leaning into another *kuhi* Sedge hadn't seen, and soon toppled it over. Apparently he had knocked down all the ones Sedge had seen along the path. Looking down at it, Sedge read its haiku.

> A foreigner came
> Mother loved him more than me
> Two missing fingers

Sedge raised his eyes to the monk. "I've followed you all this way," he said, finally able to speak. "Would you allow me to ask a question?"

The monk jumped forward and swung at Sedge with his cane. Sedge parried the blows as best he could before dashing for safety into the nearby woods. When he returned to the path, the monk was gone.

He felt he had no choice but to keep going. However, he was soon stopped again, not by a *kuhi* in the middle of the path but by the sight of a young man sunk to his waist in the dirt. As if the path were quicksand, he was twisting back and forth, unable to pull himself out. It was Riku.

Where the boy was trapped, the lower half of his body had sunk straight into the earth. Responding to Riku's calls for help, Sedge approached him carefully, not wanting to suffer the same fate.

He dropped to the ground and with both hands began digging a circle around Riku, deep enough for him eventually to escape. But with every inch he cleared away, Riku sank further. Sedge couldn't afford to stop digging, because if he did Riku would disappear completely. Already he had sunk into the path to his chest. From all the digging Sedge had done, his fingers were raw and starting to bleed.

He didn't want to fail Riku, or abandon him. He knew that if the path swallowed him completely, he would never make it out again. And while for some reason Sedge understood that the boy wouldn't die even if he became packed into the hard earth, he would be stuck there forever, for all the seasons of his life, surrounded by cold and darkness, tortured by his unfair fate.

Sedge dug and dug, until he awoke in a sweat. Riku had opened the back door and was walking across the floor, which shook beneath his steps.

"Riku," Sedge called out.

Without answering, Riku entered the bathroom at the bottom of the stairs and slammed the door.

27

The kura entrance had been pulled shut and behind the high windowpane in its door it was dark. Sedge wasn't bothered that Riku had left for town without telling him.

He sat at the dining table, drinking the last quarter of a bottle of sake. He had been drinking slowly, trying to read *Milky Way Railroad* in Japanese, with a second cup sitting across from him. On the off-chance Riku came inside again, he would fill the cup and, despite the boy's age, invite him for a single drink. But Riku hadn't come back, and after ninety minutes of waiting Sedge poured out the last drops for himself.

At six-thirty he changed into a *yukata* and slipped on a pair of *geta* Mariko had bought him. He set off into town and quickly found himself walking behind other villagers in their *samue* outfits and *yukata* who were going into town as well.

He walked the back way, close to the mountain, until the road ended and veered sharply left. Soon he crossed Cricket Bridge, with its old Bashō *kuhi* on one side of it and a small shrine to the gods of the gorge on the other. Beneath it roared the Daishōji River. The path on the other side rose steeply to meet Yugekai Road, and the festival music that had been but a murmur before grew louder here.

He didn't expect to see Riku on the way to Yamanaka-za, but he looked for him nevertheless. From halfway down the street he could see the Kikunoyū baths and, all around it, white tents in which the owners and employees of local businesses ate and drank together while waiting for the evening's traditional dancing to begin.

When he reached Yamanaka-za, a woman's voice called his name. He turned toward where the voice had come from but didn't see anyone he recognized. He jumped when the voice came again from his side. Yuki stood next to him, her face red and shining in the summer heat.

"This must be the hottest night this summer," Sedge said by way of greeting.

"I've been outside all day preparing for the festival. I'm exhausted."

Sedge hadn't seen or spoken with her other than for a few pleasantries since moving out of the ryokan. He was glad to see her, and yet seeing her reminded him that Nozomi might still stay there sometimes. He asked if she was here tonight.

"She nearly came back from her mother's house for the festival, but she didn't want to make things awkward for you. She talks to me about you sometimes."

"She invited me to stay with her for a few days in Kanazawa. I turned her down."

"Did you tell Mariko?"

"It would have only upset her."

"I see." She looked around the bustling crowd, then turned back to him. "Nozomi seems to have had a delayed reaction getting over you."

"I really don't care."

"It's probably better that way. Takahashi thinks so, too."

Sedge hadn't expected Takahashi to side with him, but after Kōichi's arrest it was hard to do otherwise. "He's not worried I'll go to the police now?"

She shook her head. "You're the least of his problems these days."

"You mean Kōichi . . ."

"He's relieved, at least, that Nozomi came back unharmed."

She glanced at the clock tower and said, "It's nearly seven o'clock and I have things left to do. It was nice seeing you."

He bowed to her as she disappeared into the crowd.

When he arrived at the first tents, he couldn't find the one for Takahashi and Yuki's ryokan, and he had to thread the barely walkable space between rows of food and entertainment booths before looping around to the opposite side of the plaza. He found Mariko's tent only because he spotted Riku in front of it, watching the top of the clock tower open and turn, and the figurines inside perform Yamanaka Bushi. Festivalgoers' voices drowned out its song, but Sedge had heard it so many times he knew it by heart:

> Haaa—
> Don't forget the road to Yamanaka
> To the east, Pine Mountain
> To the west, the temple of the Healing Buddha
> In the valley, the sound of water flowing
> On the peak, a rainstorm
> In between hovers the fragrance of Yamanaka's hot
> waters.

He looked back at Riku. His bandage, which Sedge had only partially seen from inside the kura, ran nearly to his elbow, and he was holding his injured hand close to his body. As he turned and saw Sedge, he stepped to the side of the tent and disappeared.

Mariko stood inside with a dozen of her coworkers. Takahashi sat at a folding table, drinking sake from a paper cup with his employees. When he saw Sedge, he loudly called him over. On his way to the table, Sedge touched Mariko's arm.

She smiled brightly at him. Like everyone else in the tent,

her face was red from a combination of the afternoon's lingering heat and drinking. "Have you seen Riku?" she asked. "He said you were pestering him in the kura."

"I offered him my help and some company, but I guess he didn't see it that way."

"Consider all he's been through. Please try to be patient with him."

Takahashi called him again, and Sedge joined him at the table with the others.

"I want to thank you and your mother for helping Nozomi return some of my money," Sedge said out of earshot of those around them.

In his drunkenness, Takahashi struggled to make a proper reply. "I guess you'll both find a way forward somehow."

"Yes, but not together."

"She regrets what she did. I hope she can return the rest of the money to you soon." He slapped Sedge's back and smiled. "Come on, let's drink tonight and not talk about the past."

Whatever awkwardness had recently existed between them had no traction here, though he knew it might only be due to the alcohol Takahashi was drinking. What Yuki had told him, however, made him hopeful.

Sedge exchanged greetings and small talk with everyone while Takahashi jumped from his chair to get more sake. The ryokan staff gathered around Sedge with smiles and jokes, and he was the focus of toasts for the next half-hour. By the time he escaped, he could hardly walk without swerving into other people. Mariko handed him a plate of *yakisoba* outside the tent; putting food in his stomach settled him a bit.

"Has Riku eaten?" Sedge asked after finishing his food. "Maybe I'll buy him a plate of this. Or invite him for some ramen up the street."

"He said he wasn't hungry. I think his medicine has been hard on his stomach. Doesn't he look thinner to you?"

Riku had always been wiry with muscle, but perhaps she was right that he had returned looking thinner.

"Takahashi told me to make sure Riku didn't enter the tent."

Sedge was floored. What worry did Takahashi have about the boy in his condition? "Why? Because of his hand?"

"He said if Riku loses his temper inside, he'll be responsible for whatever happens. I reminded him that he'd just lost two fingers and he's not about to start trouble. But he was adamant. I was proud of Riku for not getting angry."

All around them people were moving about, and a small group in another tent had broken into a traditional dance, though there wasn't any music yet.

"I'm going to get a beer from a stall and walk around," Sedge said. "Can I get you anything?"

She shook her head. "Our dance will start soon, so don't wander too far away."

He stepped outside. As he made his way forward, someone began walking at the same pace from behind the tents to his left. In the spaces between them, the figure moved with him, like his own shadow projected twenty feet away. At the separation of the next two tents, he peered closely toward the figure. He imagined it was Riku, though he couldn't see him clearly. But even if it were him, what did it matter?

The beer line was long, and by the time Sedge had bought one an announcer bellowed out for all the dancers to assemble. Dozens of people began hurrying toward the plaza. When Sedge walked away with his beer, the area where he stood had visibly thinned of people.

He turned back to the tent, thinking he'd make sure that Mariko had left, and was startled to see Riku back in front of it, watching Sedge from the corner of his eye. Sedge turned in the opposite direction, though it was slightly longer that way to Yamanaka-za.

When he reached it, he found it completely transformed from how it looked during the day. A red *yagura* stage with paper lanterns hanging from it had been erected in the center of the plaza; two elaborately dressed women were singing Yamanaka Bushi beneath a roofed enclosure, while beneath them, on a low open stage, three women accompanied them with their *shamisen*. Dancers in summer kimono held up signs with the names of the local businesses they represented, half-walking, half-dancing in the slow traditional manner one associated with Japanese festivals.

Mariko floated into his vision. At the far edge of her group as they danced, her smile never left her face. He wondered what she was thinking, looking as happy as he'd seen her in several days.

As her group continued to dance in a slow circle around the plaza, Sedge glanced around him again. Casually taking in all the spectators, he turned behind him, to where a large weeping willow hung over part of the crowd. His eyes fell again on Riku, standing a few rows behind him.

Sedge laughed at the unlikelihood of seeing him for the second or third time like this, and he nodded at him. But Riku neither smiled nor nodded back. His eyes drifted back to where Mariko joyously flicked her hands to the song.

What had she told him last night as they lay on her futon? That all she had ever wanted was to be a wife and mother, to support her husband and help a child of her own grow up and become someone better than she herself had managed to be. She said she still could, if Sedge were willing to help her. She would always want to do the best she could for Riku, but her best so far hadn't been nearly enough for him, or for any of them. Sedge had tried to assure her that none of the bad things that had happened to Riku had been because of her. But she stopped him from saying more, because she was certain that what she'd said was true.

That night Sedge hadn't slept well. From night until morning her words turned inside him, and he decided that even if the boy hated him, he would try to do his best for him like Mariko wanted to do. If he could manage this, he'd be helping Mariko achieve all the modest things she wanted out of life.

Walking into empty spaces in the constantly shifting crowd, Sedge followed Mariko around the plaza. Two or three times he caught her eye as she twisted in her dance, and she winked at him before returning her attention to her group. When he'd circled back to the men's baths, he looked around to see if Riku was where he'd just been. But with the large group of dancers and the *yagura* in the middle of the plaza, it was impossible to see clearly the people on the other side.

Hot and sweaty, he backed away from the crowd and found a box in which to recycle his cup. Small statues of white herons stood near the entrance to the baths, and he walked to the hot water in a shallow pool at their feet, scooping some into his hands and rubbing his face with it. He wiped his face dry on his *yukata*, and when he opened his eyes again Riku was before him, clutching his bandaged hand to his chest.

"Are you following me?" Sedge said, hoping his smile might dispel Riku's hostility. "I waited for you to come inside the house before you came here."

"Why?"

"I thought we might have a cup of sake together."

"I'm only sixteen. You know I'm not old enough to drink."

"It was a gesture. I thought you might like it."

"I just told you no."

A family with young children walked past them, the children

pointing at the herons across from the entrance and laughing. The parents stopped and took the childrens' photos before continuing on. Sedge was glad the interruption hadn't made Riku walk away before they'd finished talking. He had something on his mind he needed to tell the boy.

"What can I do to make up for what happened to you?" Sedge said. With the festival noise increasing, he nearly had to shout for Riku to hear him. "I wish I could go back and fix things so you could attend the release at the bird reserve. But it's in the past. And you've suffered for it. But I'm asking you again now to help me. How can I make things better?"

"Better is in the past."

"What do you mean? In the past when?"

"In the past before I was born. My parents never planned to have me."

Sedge recoiled as if he'd taken a blow. "How do you know that?"

Riku smirked. "They told me. There's no way for you to make anything better now. Only I can."

"How?"

Riku didn't answer.

Trying to lower the tension between them a notch Sedge said, "Come with me. I'm going to buy a small bottle at the convenience store. We can find a seat away from everyone and watch the dancing and singing. Do me the honor of sharing it together. It won't make you drunk."

"I'm taking medication."

"Then I'll buy you something else. Whatever you'd like."

When Riku gave no more indication of what he wanted to do, Sedge walked past him, toward the brightly lit store.

"You intentionally led me to the statues of the cranes," Riku said, coming up behind him.

"Don't be absurd," Sedge said, and tried to laugh. "Besides, you were following me, not being led." The convenience store's automatic doors opened and Sedge walked inside. Considering there was a festival one hundred feet away, surprisingly few people were in its aisles. He turned around. Riku was there. Irritated with him and feeling warm from the sake and beer he'd drunk, he attempted a smile and said, "And those were herons, not cranes."

Riku closed the distance between them at the back of the store, where Sedge stopped to consider the small sake bottles lined on a refrigerator shelf. "Is there a brand you're willing to try? Some of them are dry, others sweet. Sweet might be better if you're not used to it. What do you say?" The glass display showed his and Riku's reflections, but the condensation on it clouded their faces.

As Sedge reached for the refrigerator door, Riku shoved him into the glass and pinned him there, his shoulder in his back. Sedge could have easily escaped since Riku only had one hand at his use, but he didn't move. A strange calmness pervaded him—a surety that harmony would prevail between them and in the end they would finally set aside their differences.

"I'd still have my fingers if you'd let me go with you to the bird reserve!" Riku shouted into his ear. "Whenever I see where my fingers used to be, I hear you telling me again I can't go!"

Sedge winced at Riku's accusation. "I know I haven't been as good to you as I should have been. But I had nothing to do with what happened to your fingers."

Riku leaned into Sedge harder. "I blame you for everything."

Sedge never saw the rock Riku had been hiding crash down on his head—though right after it struck him he realized it had always been coming toward him.

He fell again into the refrigerator door, slumping to the ground with his hands covering his head. Blood oozed over his fingers, but there was little pain to speak of. He foresaw that coming next, and it did as Riku began kicking him wherever he had room to in the narrow aisle Sedge was sprawled in.

Customers began screaming, Sedge couldn't tell how many or from where in the store, and mixed with those awful sounds was that of Riku half-shrieking with each kick he landed on Sedge's body.

Sedge grabbed the foot Riku wasn't kicking with, and when he pulled with all the strength he still had, Riku fell.

He landed on his injured hand. As he rolled around in pain, a store clerk dove on him. The man wrenched Riku's bandaged hand behind his back to immobilize him, and Riku screamed.

The pain in Riku's voice was the last thing Sedge remembered.

28

After the cherry blossoms had fallen and scattered the road to Yūyūkan, cosmos, irises, and fawn lilies bloomed in Mariko's garden. From the carport to the mossy stone wall separating the house from the kura, she had divided the long flowerbed into two: the half closer to the street for flowers, and the half closer to the mountain for vegetables. Despite the limited area, she hoped to get as much of a yield from it as possible.

Though Mariko was often at the ryokan, tending both had become part of their daily routine. So was keeping the crows away, not only from their vegetables but also from the birdhouses Riku had left behind, which Sedge had fixed and placed around the yard. Birds occupied three of the four, but the one nearest the kura entrance remained empty. Sedge and Mariko planned to return them to Riku eventually, but it would be more difficult now that birds had made homes in them. Since it was spring, they could sit in the veranda or on the wooden bench beside the house and, if they stayed still, watch the birds. Sedge kept a list of them. Mariko wrote their names in Japanese, and beside these Sedge wrote their equivalents in English.

In May they discovered termites in the kura. One day they were inspecting the inside with the idea of renting it out as an artist studio or turning it into a guesthouse. A few days later, however, when they went back inside, they found the first floor covered with termite wings. They were thickest where the *senbazuru* ash had been heaped.

Months ago, Sedge had covered Riku's boxes with a plastic tarp, but after the termite infestation he peeled it back and reorganized them. He wrote their contents on labels, affixed them to each box, then sealed the boxes with tape. Afterward, he hauled them to the second floor and stacked them in a corner. Whenever Riku needed them, Sedge and Mariko would transport them to Echizen. She didn't want to transfer them before he asked her to.

Sedge also carried to the second floor the wooden post Riku had been given to make a *kuhi* inscribed with his own haiku.

When he came back to the first floor, Mariko sighed and looked around. "We'll need an exterminator," she said.

The next day two men from a neighboring village came, prying up the floorboards and poking around the dirt below. "With a stone foundation like this," the older of the two said, "humidity gets trapped under the floor. Now that you've had an infestation, you could use a pesticide to repel them, but they'd come back every year. Pesticide might work in town, but here in the mountains I recommend bamboo charcoal." What he suggested cost two hundred thousand yen.

"It's more we'll have to spend on renovations," Mariko said after they left.

"Luckily," Sedge said, "we're both making enough money that it's not the problem it would have been last year."

"But your online store still hasn't matched your sales in Kanazawa."

"Every week it does a little better. And the renovations will be worth it." He would only resume his search for an English-teaching job if the store he'd started failed.

She seemed to have forgotten that he'd recently received the remainder of the money Nozomi had taken from him. It had come through Takahashi, who'd invited Sedge to the ryokan twice in the last month, both times to share a bottle of sake and make what Sedge thought were attempts to reconcile their differences. On Sedge's last visit, Takahashi told him that Nozomi was going away to Shikoku to walk all one thousand two hundred kilometers and visit all eighty-eight temples on the Shikoku Henro Pilgrimage. Takahashi wasn't happy about her leaving again, but this time, at least, she promised to stay in touch.

A few days later Sedge took a stroll on the paved path along the Daishōji River. Near the end of it, with the Bashō Hut in view, he stopped. A woman in a sunhat and sunglasses stood before it, gazing at the large *torii* beside it and the path extending from there up the small mountain. For a moment, her outfit made her look much like Nozomi had at the hotel in Kanazawa where they'd last met.

The woman turned and began walking toward Sedge. Immediately he realized it wasn't Nozomi. The hat and sunglasses had fooled him, but their bodies and gaits were nothing alike. Now that he could see her closely, it was almost laughable how different they looked. And according to Takahashi, Nozomi had moved last fall to Tokyo and was living temporarily with a relative.

The woman nodded hello as she passed him. If the river hadn't been so loud here, he imagined she'd have heard his heart thumping.

And yet there was a sense of déjà vu in what had passed. He had seen Nozomi here, too, a month after Riku had attacked him at the festival. He had come across her at the same place, facing the Bashō Hut and not seeming to recognize that he stood nearby watching her.

At the time, not wanting to speak with her, he had nearly returned the way he'd come. Instead, he had kept walking toward Kurotani Bridge, one hundred feet past her, which would take him back to town. Walking by Nozomi he'd nearly spoken her name, but continued on.

Nozomi hadn't looked at him when he passed by, and if she'd recognized him from behind she hadn't called to him, either.

Halfway to the bridge, however, he'd stopped and turned around. She'd passed beneath the *torii* and was standing on the sloping path, as if trying to judge the difficulty of climbing it.

She had nearly slipped as she began climbing the path, but regained her balance and continued her ascent. A recent storm had dropped branches and leaves on the path, but she'd stepped over them nimbly, unbothered by the obstacles they posed.

The path turned and she'd followed it. A moment later she'd disappeared behind the trees.

Continuing along the path, Sedge wondered again how he could have mistaken the woman for Nozomi. Eight months had passed since he'd last seen her, and now they were divorced. He thought he'd like to meet her again in a few months when she returned from Shikoku. Would it be possible to tell her then that he forgave her?

☙ ☙ ☙

Sedge wanted to arrange for the exterminators to come soon so he and Mariko could start renovating the kura before summer made this an uncomfortable prospect. According to Mariko the renovations they wanted to make were nearly the same as Riku had wanted to do if he'd had the resources. She wanted to lay protective boarding over the mud walls and afterward cover them with white stucco that would brighten the interior, finishing what Riku had started. He and Mariko had already agreed on a hidden lighting system as well. And they still needed to install a shower and toilet.

A week later, the exterminators came. After Mariko showed them to the kura, she told Sedge, "I didn't know the company was located in Echizen. Isn't it weird that it's in the same town where Riku will be moving? I wonder how he's doing."

"Do you suppose his grandparents in Echizen have heard from him?" Sedge said.

She checked her watch. "Maybe I'll call them now. I haven't talked to them since New Year's."

Sedge and Mariko had visited them in Echizen in early January. Mariko had driven in a light snow through the Fukui countryside until reaching the old farmhouse where Kōichi had grown up and where Riku planned to live after leaving Mariko's house last summer.

Sedge hadn't met her in-laws before, and though she had told him they were kind and friendly, he half-expected there would be trouble. Although their son was in jail, and Riku was in a juvenile detention center, they didn't blame Mariko for the bad things that had happened. If anything, they found in her someone uncommonly good with whom they could commiserate.

One of their first questions was if she would agree to let them adopt Riku, because they had started to research what this would involve and worked out how they could manage it. They felt he needed to know he had a family who would always love and support him. Mariko broke down in tears and thanked them. When they asked if Sedge was the new man in her life, she said he was. This opened the floodgates to more questions, including when Mariko's divorce would be finalized. She said it would be official by the end of January, and they congratulated her. Mariko's father-in-law brought out a bottle of local sake to share with Sedge, along with small plates of pickled vegetables from their farm. Half an hour later and carrying it off too perfectly for Sedge to believe it had been unplanned, Mariko's in-laws made a big lunch that consisted of buckwheat noodles and mixed tempura, yellowtail sashimi, and simple dishes of tofu and burdock root marinated in sesame oil. It wasn't typical for New Year's, except for the volume of food.

Before leaving, Mariko spoke with them about Riku's future. He would be released when he turned eighteen. Sedge was surprised he was studying *zazen* in a class the facility offered. It was meant to aid his rehabilitation.

Sedge shared not only their concern for Riku, but also their hopes for his happiness in the future. After everything that had transpired between him and Riku, they had every reason to put their past behind them. Sedge wanted to be better for Mariko's sake, but also for Riku's to the extent he remained in their lives.

Mariko and Sedge left in the late afternoon. The snow was falling harder, and the TV where they were eating and talking had forecast a lightning storm by evening. They thanked her in-laws for their hospitality and wished them the best for the coming year. As they stood in the doorway, Mariko's mother-in-law disappeared briefly only to return with two Kutani teacups. Each had a fitted top with the kanji for the new era, though it had begun last year: Reiwa, which meant "resplendent peace." Mariko had taken one and asked them to save the other for Riku.

Fifteen minutes later Mariko returned to the back of the house where Sedge stood watching the exterminators come and go.

"Did you get hold of Riku's grandparents?" Sedge asked.

She nodded. "They invited us back to visit."

"And Riku?"

"They said they're looking forward to his release." After a long silence she said, "The last time they spoke with him, he nearly convinced them to buy ducks to keep in their fields. At the last moment, they decided to wait until next year, when he was living with them again and could help keep them. They said he was excited by it."

After an early dinner, they took their evening walk in the village. They passed the priest of the temple two doors down, who in the fading light was planting hydrangeas around the perimeter of the parking lot across the street. He pointed to the rice fields in the valley below, whose rice shoots were submerged in water, and commented on how beautiful the village was in spring. They turned and walked down the sloping path beside the lot.

Above a rice field a few hundred meters away, a gray heron descended from the dusky sky. A moment later it landed in the shallow water. When it slowly stepped forward, it gave the illusion, where the water mirrored the sky, that it was walking through the clouds.

They continued in its direction. At the edge of the field, Sedge stopped.

"What are you doing?" Mariko said.

He pulled her beside him and wrapped his arms around her. They stood opposite the heron, which continued its slow progress through the water.

"I wonder if it considers this home," she said.

"I'm sure it does. Its ancestors have for hundreds of years."

They continued their stroll through the village. In the near-twilight, the road they were on, which skirted Kakusenkei gorge, appeared in the distance to have no end.

"Should we turn back?" Mariko asked.

"Let's go a little farther. Maybe it will lead us someplace we've never been."

She looked at him strangely and ran ahead, her arms outstretched like she was flying.

ABOUT THE AUTHOR

David Joiner made his first trip to Japan in 1991—a five-month study program in Hokkaido—and three years later moved for the first of seven times to Vietnam. In Japan, where he has also moved numerous times, he has called Sapporo, Akita, Fukui, Tokyo, and most recently the western Japanese city of Kanazawa home.

Joiner's writing has appeared in literary journals and elsewhere, including *Echoes: Writers in Kyoto 2017*, *The Brooklyn Rail*, *Phoebe Journal*, *The Ontario Review*, and *The Madison Review*. His first novel, *Lotusland*, set in contemporary Vietnam, was published in 2015 by Guernica Editions. His second novel, *Kanazawa*, was published by Stone Bridge Press in 2022 and was named as a Foreword Reviews Indie Finalist for multicultural novels.